INTRODUCTION

Where Angels Camp by Dia~~r~~
When Graf Christian von ~~...~~ ~~...~~hl to
hire a well-known armorer, ~~...~~ ght-
ful meeting with the old ma~~...~~ ~~...~~ty Years
War with the Swedes is raging, and taking the armorer and his
daughter to Christian's castle to work could put the rest of the
armorer's family in danger. Will God work a miracle so love
has a chance to bloom?

The Nuremberg Angel by Irene B. Brand
Trenton, New Jersey, of 1776 is overrun by Hessian soldiers
who were brought to the Colonies to aid the British. Comfort
Foster and her family have no choice but to house one of these
feared soldiers in their small home. Can their family survive
the tension when her brother fights for American freedom and
her father doctors sick American soldiers?

Dearest Enemy by Pamela Griffin
Brigetta Linder is tired of war and uses the crumbling castle in
the Black Forest for her retreat from pain and hunger. But one
day she discovers a wounded American soldier in her hideaway.
What should she do with him and how would her family react
if she decides to help him?

Once a Stranger by Gail Gaymer Martin
When Madeline Stewart questions a fellow American about a
unique children's festival they are witnessing in Dinkelsbuhl, a
friendship is forged. Jacob works in Germany as a carpenter, and
Maddy is there on vacation to celebrate the completion of her
master's degree. When Maddy adopts a crazy idea to restore a
castle in the Black Forest, could she be alienating her new friend?

German Enchantment

*A Legacy of Customs and Devotion
in Four Romantic Novellas*

Irene B. Brand
Dianne Christner
Pamela Griffin
Gail Gaymer Martin

BARBOUR BOOKS
An Imprint of Barbour Publishing, Inc.

Where Angels Camp ©2002 by Dianne Christner
The Nuremberg Angel ©2002 by Irene B. Brand
Dearest Enemy ©2002 by Pamela Griffin
Once a Stranger ©2002 by Gail Gaymer Martin

Cover photo: ©PhotoDisc, Inc.

ISBN 1-58660-396-5

All Scripture quotations, unless otherwise noted, are taken from the King James Version of the Bible.

Published by Barbour Books, an imprint of Barbour Publishing, Inc., P.O. Box 719, Uhrichsville, Ohio 44683, www.barbourbooks.com

Member of the
Evangelical Christian
Publishers Association

Printed in the United States of America.

German Enchantment

Where Angels Camp

by Dianne Christner

Dedication

Dedicated to my brother Bruce,
who traipsed through Germany with me.
What fun it was to explore Dinkelsbühl together!
To my sister-in-law, Teri, for her support,
and my loving husband, Jim, for making the trip possible.
Your love and encouragement inspire me above all else.
To those who made this writing project such a pleasure—
my coauthors and editors.
To Dinkelsbühl, such a sweet city!
And to my Lord, Creator of all the above.

*The angel of the LORD encampeth round about them
that fear him, and delivereth them.*

PSALM 34:7

Chapter 1

Dinkelsbühl, Germany, 1632

The hinges on the large, plank door creaked as *Graf* Christian von Engel peered into the armory. An elbow-cop, hung in an amusing manner, hailed him. Inside, the tang of metal and smoke instantly filled his nostrils. The unattended shop contained many things to interest a man, even if the idea of going to war did not.

He caressed the smooth surface of a breastplate, then stepped up to examine an odd-shaped helm. An army wearing such a headpiece would frighten the enemy to death. He turned it this way and that, then slipped it over his head.

The rusty visor snapped closed. Christian gave it a jerk. Stuck tight. Sucking in a breath of hot moist air, he fumbled with the lock, but the visor would not budge. He tried to shove off the infuriating chunk of metal. The helm clamped itself around his throat. In his shuffling about, his feet bumped something, and he nearly lost his balance.

"Be still. You'll hurt yourself."

Every muscle in his body tensed at the soft musical voice. Hot coals of embarrassment burned the pit of his stomach.

"Stand still, now. Let me help," the female voice insisted.

"I need no help." The helm's ventail, with only narrow slits for breathing, muffled his words. He felt a light touch on his shoulder and stilled. The working of the visor's spring pin pressed the helm against his cheek.

"There. Now it should open."

Christian jerked the visor. Fresh air cooled the top segment of his face. A pair of soft blue eyes gazed up at him. Surrounding her face was hair the color of golden grain. The eyes twinkled, and the woman's lips curved. She averted her gaze to the arming-nail, glancing up at him once or twice while she unfastened a clasp by his neck. Christian did not stir.

"You may remove it now," she said and stepped back.

Slowly, he lifted. It slipped off.

"The helm is a relic." She cocked her head and studied him. "Perhaps you should consider keeping a squire."

"The land is too dangerous for a squire's travel," Christian grumbled as he replaced the helm in its proper place.

"*Ja*, it is that," a deep masculine voice boomed. Christian jerked his gaze away from his lovely rescuer-tormenter and spun around to get his first look at the German craftsman. The stocky armorer had bushy, light curly hair, wrinkles, and a stern face.

Christian exhaled deeply, like one who had discovered a rare treasure. "I have traveled a long distance to meet the armorer over whom the entire kingdom raves."

Gerrard Trittenbach's expression softened, and they exchanged introductions. "If you heard that I am a man who takes pride in his craftsmanship, then you have heard no falsehood."

From the corner of his eye, Christian noticed the lovely fräulein slip away. "I need a new suit of armor. My entire armory is in disrepair." The man did not reply, only leveled a penetrating gaze. Unsure of how to persuade him, Christian foolishly rambled, "Cleaning, buckling, leathering. . ."

"Oh? Are you preparing to go to war?"

"Nein." Christian shook his head. "Only to defend my land. The Swedes are ravaging nearby estates. It is only a matter of time until—"

Gerrard's eyes lit. "So your loyalties are with the emperor?"

"I would prefer to remain neutral." He shrugged. "The Swedes and French who invade our German lands disregard such a stand. In their eyes, if you do not join up with them, you are considered their enemy. I suppose it is the same with the emperor."

"Ja. No middle ground." The armorer's expression darkened. "Let me show you a few pieces."

Christian followed Gerrard about the workshop as they discussed details.

"We must fit you," Gerrard said. "Come. Stand here and remove your outer clothing."

Christian did as the older man bade and dispensed with his doublet. The armorer took measurements. A small boy peeked out from an open doorway that led to a rear shop door. But what really bothered Christian was that the fräulein remained in the room in a far corner, sewing. Although she paid him no attention, her presence unsettled him. With his arms suspended over his head and the armorer poking about his body, he wondered what one was supposed to do with his gaze in such a circumstance. More to the point, how could he keep it off the fräulein? He glanced at Gerrard. A scowl darkened the older man's face.

Finally, with a grunt, Gerrard dismissed him. Christian instantly lowered his arms and snatched his clothing.

"Where are you staying tonight?" Gerrard asked.

Christian tugged at his doublet. "My men and I intend to camp outside Dinkelsbühl."

"As you implied, the countryside is not safe. We will find you beds inside the city wall. How many men?"

"*Sechs.*"

Gerrard glanced over his shoulder and softened his voice. "Amelia, Daughter, can you come here a moment?" So the fräulein was his daughter.

She crossed the room and stood before the armorer. *"Ja?"*

"Would you run to Watchman Hurtin's house and see if we can find lodging for *Graf* von Engel and his six men?"

Amelia gave Christian a brief saucy glance, then nodded respectfully at her father and departed.

"Thank you for your kindness, Herr Trittenbach. I'll see to my men and return." As Christian left the shop, he heard the clatter of small feet. A boy's voice could be heard through the open window.

"Who was that, Papa?"

"Why, that was *Graf* Christian von Engel of Engelturm."

"Where is that, Papa?"

Christian couldn't help but smile. So what if he had made a fool of himself? He had met the respected armorer and had taken care of a necessary task. He had secured safe lodging for his men. Best of all was the armorer's daughter. He strode down the narrow, cobbled street. As he passed by the colorful shops— each topped with an orange-tiled, steeply pitched roof—he thought, *Dinkelsbühl. A sweet city.*

Hours later, Amelia fiddled with the black velvet lining, irritated with her crooked stitches. Father, her only living parent, valued her work as an integral part of their armor merchandise. But ever since *Graf* von Engel had entered their workshop, she had torn out rows of uneven stitches. When the count had opened his visor and gazed into her eyes, weakness and desire swept over her in one warm rush. Her face felt hot even now in remembrance.

Many men frequented her father's workshop. But none had ever interested her nor earned her father's approval. She had even traveled with her father to other villages and castles. But never had she recalled meeting anyone who stirred her like this.

The familiar sound of the shop's creaky door hinges drew her gaze. There stood the object of her thoughts. The count shifted his stance and scrutinized her with sky-colored eyes.

She pushed aside her work and squirmed to her feet. "Good news. We found you lodging."

A smile softened his lean, angular face. "You are too kind. Is it far?"

Amelia gestured toward the watchman's home. *"Nein.* Just beyond the *Tor."*

The count nodded. His center-parted, brown mane brushed against the shoulders of his doublet; its full curls cascaded down his upper back. He glanced out the shuttered window to the gate. "Could you take me there?" His eyes teased. "Otherwise, I might take a wrong turn. The countryside is very dangerous."

With her father occupied in the back room, she pretended to consider. "Since you paid Father such splendid praise, *Ja.* I will go with you."

Christian swept open the door. She brushed by him, and they stepped out onto the cobblestones. They had not walked far before the count spoke. "You are quite charming."

"How can you say so? I took advantage of your moment of weakness."

"Indeed you did. But if you had not come to my rescue, I might still be stumbling in circles."

Amelia's laughter bubbled forth. "Where is Engelturm?"

"On the edge of the Black Forest. West, not far from the River Rhine."

"Oh, I have seen the Rhine. How lovely it is."

"I am glad you liked it. You travel often?"

"*Ja.* But look, here we are." A round-faced woman stuck her head out an opened window of a house built into the city's wall.

Graf von Engel hung back and frowned. "So soon. I am disappointed."

"Come," Amelia urged. "I will introduce you."

Amelia left the count and returned to the workshop, humming. When she entered, her father was seated at a workbench.

"Where have you been, Amelia?"

"Why, the count returned. I took him to the watchman's house."

His eyes darkened. "I wish you wouldn't associate with him."

Amelia was shocked at her father's blunt remark. Was he not the one who had suggested they find the count and his men lodging? "Why would you wish such a thing?"

"Our kingdom is at war. It is not a good time to fall in love."

"Love?" Amelia gasped, even more shocked. "Don't be absurd. We just met."

"I saw the way you looked at each other. For all we know, he could be a spy."

Amelia just gaped at him.

Her father sighed heavily and stretched forth his stocky arm. "Come." She crossed the room to him. "If he hurts you, my own heart will break."

Amelia's eyes stung, and she nodded. It was her greatest pleasure to serve her family. Although she did not understand why her father was concerned about the count, she certainly could not deny her attraction, nor was there any reason not to trust her father's judgment and abide by his request.

The next morning Christian entered the armory and watched in amusement as the armorer's little son galloped about the room. In his make-believe, his hands grasped an air bellows—the reins and neck of his horse—which he brought to a halt before a standing suit of armor. "You! Draw your sword and defend yourself!" He laid the bellows aside. "Wait here, Beauty," he commanded, then turned back to the faceless helm. "You, Sir, are a coward!"

"Gut! Sehr Gut!" Christian clapped. "Good! Very good!"

The boy ran up to Christian, his eyes bright. "Are you a knight?"

"My *opa* was," Christian spoke fondly of his grandfather. "Are you?"

"I hope to be. But Father says that the knights are fading out." He pointed to the empty suit of armor. "My papa made him."

Christian knelt down beside the lad and held back a chuckle. He touched the boy's shoulder. "What is your name, Son?"

"Nicolaus."

"How old are you?"

"I'm five!"

"Hello, *Graf* von Engel," Gerrard greeted.

Christian straightened. "I was just getting acquainted with Nicolaus."

"I hope he has been minding his manners."

Christian glanced into Nicolaus's pleading eyes. "Indeed, he has."

The boy beamed and turned back to his father. "May I play?"

"*Ja.* Run along."

"A fine lad." Christian's gaze swept across the room in search of the armorer's daughter. "I wanted to thank you for all your kindness."

"*Ach,* think nothing of it."

"Will you come to Engelturm and set my armory in order?"

"I have not decided. I shall have an answer upon your return."

"Do consider it," Christian said before he opened the door and strode out.

"Humph!" Christian whooshed—the breath being knocked from his chest. When he could breathe again, he muttered, "Of all the clumsy—"

"Me? Clumsy?" Amelia fumed from the ground.

"*Nein.* Me. I am the clumsy one. Here, let me help." She eyed him warily and rejected his outstretched hand. He apologized as she stood and brushed off her long skirt. "Truly, I am sorry."

Amelia nodded. "We are even now. You have seen me in an embarrassing situation, and I have seen you—"

"Stop!" He held up his hands in defense. "Enough." They looked at each other and burst into laughter. The count shook his head. "You are a delight."

Her brows arched. "Am I?"

He softened his voice. "I wish I didn't have to go. But my men await."

A glimmer of alarm passed over Amelia's face. "May I pray for your safety?"

Christian's heart swelled. "I would welcome it above any other thing." He boldly stated, "Upon my return, may I see you?" Her face paled. Christian frowned. "You are not spoken for?"

"*Nein*. But, of course we shall meet again. You have dealings with Father. Godspeed."

"Farewell," he tried to say, but she was already gone. Pondering her abrupt behavior, he strode away in search of his men.

Chapter 2

The silk lining was flawless, a labor of devotion. Someday *Graf* von Engel would wear it over his heart. As Amelia stitched, she also prayed for his protection.

"Finished?" Gerrard asked.

"Ja. I think I need a stretch."

"Go. You work too hard."

"No more than you." Amelia rose from the heart-shaped, wooden chair and left the stifling shop, smoky from the fire needed to work the metal. She had not walked far alongside the street named *Unterer Mauerweg* when two small bodies darted from behind a cart.

"Nicolaus! Heidi!" Amelia shouted for them. *"Anschlag!"*

The two little bodies jerked, and their feet stopped churning. Their faces slowly turned toward Amelia. She crooked her finger, beckoning them. Their tiny shoulders instantly sagged, and their hands stole behind them. Amelia smelled mischief as the two dawdled forward.

"What is behind your backs?"

Heidi thrust forward her arm. "Buttercups for you!"

Nicolaus joined in the false tale. *"Ja.* We know how you like them."

Amelia stifled her amusement and accepted the bouquet. "And aren't they a lovely gift?" The hills beyond the city were clad in brilliant yellow. She cast a dreamy gaze toward the wall. Somewhere out there was the count.

"Can we go play now?" Nicolaus tugged on Amelia's sleeve.

The children were forbidden to go outside the city wall since Swedes had been reported to be in the vicinity. The sad restriction was for their safety. "Where did you find these? From someone's window box?"

Heidi's face paled. Nicolaus's mouth formed a pout. Amelia accusingly arched a brow. Nicolaus set his hands on his hips. Heidi pointed toward the wall.

With a sigh, Amelia knelt down. "You did a very dangerous thing. The enemy's army would like nothing better than to catch *kinder*, to whisk children up onto their horse and carry you off to their camp. Then they would barter you *kinder* to capture the entire city. You would not want that to happen, would you?"

"Oh, *nein*. There was nobody out there." Heidi's braids whipped from side to side as she shook her head.

"There was not even one horse." Nicolaus clearly did not display any signs of regret.

"They could be hiding and gallop out in an eye blink to snatch you up before you could run to safety." Amelia watched Heidi's eyes widen as the child scratched her arms. Hopeful she had instilled a measure of caution into the children, Amelia gentled. "Let's take half of the flowers to Heidi's mother so she can share the beauty. Shall we?"

Amelia touched their shoulders and urged them forward. "And you know, *kinder*, buttercups are poisonous. We'll have to scrub."

Nicolaus straightened his arms toward the cobblestones

and clenched his hands into fists. "Ugh!"

Amelia stifled a giggle.

Frau Hurtin had a houseful of daughters. The oldest, Lore, looked up from her weaving as Amelia paraded the children through the room and deposited them with Frau Hurtin. In this warm household, it was easy to see why Nicolaus loved to come and play. Lore, who had listened to the children's chatter, left her work to cross the room to Amelia.

"Are there really enemy soldiers beyond the wall?"

"Don't worry, Dear. Our walls are thick and strong."

Lore nodded, but her expression remained doubtful.

Nicolaus reappeared, his face scrubbed red. "Frau Hurtin says that Heidi cannot play anymore today."

Amelia gave Lore a parting smile and drew Nicolaus away. "Nor can you. Let's go home." He shrugged away from her touch but obeyed.

At bedtime Amelia listened to Nicolaus's rote prayers. He hugged her neck as she leaned over him to adjust his feather coverlet. She kissed his cheek and smiled.

"Can we pray for Count von Engel?"

Amelia blinked. "You met him?"

Ja. He was nice to me. He's very tall and brave."

"Brave? How do you know?" She fastened her gaze on Nicolaus's carved headboard, hoping that her cheeks would not give away her emotions.

"Because he's out beyond the wall. And he's getting fitted for war."

"Oh. *Ja*. Let's pray for him."

Nicolaus scooted out from his feather coverlet and knelt on the floor. "God. Keep Count von Engel safe so I can see him again."

These were the very words she had been praying every day this past week.

Christian paused outside a brass-studded door, selecting a key from a large metal ring. The lock needed working, but it released. Inside Engelturm's armory, a gray blur scurried across the floor, through a leg greave, and disappeared beneath a knee-cop. As Christian's gaze meandered over the room laden with sword and rivet, its neglect embarrassed him. The servant, who had lagged behind, now drew up alongside and followed his master's stare.

"Set this place in order." Christian ignored the servant's dour expression and crossed the room, swiping a cobweb from his pathway. He opened an arched window. Sunlight caught the dancing dust particles he had just roused.

The servant sneezed hard, twice.

"Ja. Bring the maids to dust. And ask the steward to take inventory."

Since his journey to Dinkelsbühl, Christian had brimmed with plans for the armory. He had witnessed, firsthand, the remains of ruined castles and burned villages. Cousin Leopold was a gifted scout. Otherwise, they surely would have skirmished with the small clusters of soldiers that roamed the countryside.

Christian was not a coward. He was trained at arms, but his heart was not in warring. How could God condone such a thing? Nor did Christian fear death. When his own father died, there was peace in the aged eyes. During his father's long illness, many matters at Engelturm had fallen into neglect. Now it was Christian's responsibility to protect the people within his castle and those who lived in the nearby village of Engelheim.

Beautiful Engelturm stood like a sentry atop a magnificent cliff that seemed to reach up to heaven itself. Below, the River Wurm meandered through a lush green valley. Christian gazed out across the bailey, reminiscing his childhood.

Suddenly Nicolaus came to mind. The child had wormed his way right into Christian's heart. As had Amelia. He must persuade Herr Trittenbach to put Engelturm's armory in order. Not only would he make ready his defense, but also he would see the lovely fräulein again.

He turned from the window to his servant, who now held a small cloth over his long bulbous nose. "Let's go see how the upper chambers fare."

Weeks passed. Amelia combed through her wet, waist-long tresses. Water from the moat powered her father's grindstone and glazing wheel. Reluctantly, she left the refreshing stream's edge, proceeding past their home and into the back entrance of the shop.

"Count von Engel!"

"Fräulein Trittenbach." His face shone with pleasure. "What good fortune that we should meet."

His gaze roved over her hair. Amelia tossed it behind her back and felt an uncustomary warmth creep up her neck. "I assume you had safe travel?"

Ja. Danke schön for your prayers."

"Father has been expecting you. I am sorry, but he is running errands."

He looked pleased. "I am in no hurry."

"Would ye care for a drink?"

Christian smiled at her. "*Ja*. If it's not too much trouble."

Moments later Amelia leaned against the closed door of her living quarters and fanned her face with her hand. Next, she hurriedly knotted her hair at the back of her neck, and then she crossed the room to a jug and poured water into a flowered cup. Some sloshed over the side onto her puffed sleeve. She snatched a cloth. After drawing several deep breaths, she returned to the shop. The count's back was toward her. He was inspecting his finished armor.

"Perhaps you should try on the helm."

He flinched, but when he turned, his eyes twinkled. "Once caught, but not twice."

She handed him the drink and nodded. "Wise, indeed." Amelia watched him empty the cup. He handed it back to her, and she withdrew a few steps. "I will go find Father."

"Please, stay." His voice was gentle. "My arrival is no secret. With my men at large in the city, your father should come bounding through that door any moment. And I had hoped—"

"Ah, *Graf* von Engel. I see you have found your suit." Her father's voice sent a rush of relief through Amelia.

Christian arched a brow at her, then shifted his gaze onto the approaching armorer. "Herr Trittenbach. It is ready then?"

"*Ja*. Try it on."

"First I would discuss Engelturm with you."

"Come and sit." Gerrard motioned toward two brightly painted benches. Grateful, Amelia slipped away.

"Herr Trittenbach. I see no hope for my armory unless you

agree to come to Engelturm." Gerrard crossed his fingers in front of his belly as if he had not fully discarded the idea, so Christian continued to persuade him. "I brought a dozen men. Enough for a safe journey."

Gerrard tapped his chin. "I have no other pressing commitments. Truth is, I am only a short while from having to make candlesticks. I loathe the idea. But one day soon it will be the fate of every armorer." Gerrard brightened and brushed away the topic with a sweep of his hand. "But that is not your problem. Should I agree, I would need to take a wagon full of supplies, perhaps two." Gerrard drummed his fingers on the table. "Seems I have no choice but to agree."

Chapter 3

Amelia looked up from her dusting and frowned at Valdemar, the mercer. She always dreaded his visits to their shop, especially his forward behavior.

"You are not happy to see me?" Valdemar strode forward.

"What can I do for you, Herr Valdemar?" her father asked.

As soon as Valdemar turned to acknowledge him, Amelia tactfully removed herself from that part of the room, but not before hearing Valdemar's next remark. "You have to tell her sometime." Curious now, she paused—just out of sight—to listen.

"Keep your voice down," Father warned. "What do you want now?"

"Your name rests upon the lips of the band of strangers roaming our city's streets."

"The matter is my affair."

"Ever since I discovered that you supplied the French with armor, everything about you concerns me. Next you will be aiding the Swedes. I have every right to keep a sharp lookout over your affairs. And if you are not cooperative, I may let my tongue slip. It would be a shame for the city council to learn about the French."

"*Graf* von Engel's hired me to put his armory in order."

"And you remember our agreement?"

"*Ja,* I remember."

"Then leave the boy."

Amelia heard her father sigh, then soon after that the clatter of Valdemar's boots as he departed. What kind of agreement did they have? And how was Nicolaus involved? Hurrying across the shop, she saw her father's flushed face. "Father? What is it? Are you ill?"

"*Nein.* Sit and let's talk. We are going to Engelturm."

"But I thought you did not want us to associate with the count."

"I understand your surprise. My feelings on the matter have not changed. *Graf* von Engel has a large armory. The job will give us needed income." While Amelia digested this news, he added, "We will leave Nicolaus with Frau Hurtin."

"But why? What agreement was Valdemar talking about?"

She saw a flicker of surprise in Father's eyes, but he waved his hand. "Just business. About Nicolaus, I heard him coughing this morning."

Amelia nodded. "*Ja.* I did too, but I hate to leave him."

"We prepare today and tomorrow. The next day we shall leave. First, you must speak with Frau Hurtin. I will start making arrangements for supplies."

Amelia stood. "Are you sure you are feeling all right, Father?"

"*Ja.* Run along now. There is much to do."

Seeing it would do no good to argue, Amelia hurried from the shop and gazed up and down *Unterer Mauerweg,* hoping to catch sight of her little brother. The boy was not in view, but she noticed several strangers. Most likely the count's men from

Engelturm. This made her errand seem all the more urgent. She hurried toward Frau Hurtin's cottage. Perhaps Nicolaus was playing with Heidi.

"May I join you?" The count's familiar voice jolted her. It was as though he appeared from nowhere. Before she could reply, he had swept off his large plumed hat and fallen into step beside her.

Do not associate with the count. Picking up her pace, she replied, "I am not out for a pleasure walk. I have errands to run. If you will pardon me." She caught a blur of his swinging arm and hat from the corner of her eye. If she looked straight ahead, perhaps he would catch the hint and leave.

The count was not that easily dissuaded. "Would these errands have anything to do with a journey you will be taking?"

Clearly, this was a man used to having his way. She gestured with her hand. "There are several men about this city who seem to be under your command. Surely, you have more important matters to consider."

"I presumed your errands were on my account; therefore, I hoped I could—"

"Please. I do not wish to be rude, but I must go." She brushed past him. Pride forbade her to look back until she reached the Hurtins'. By then, the count was gone.

Two days later, a small group of people gathered at the *Wörnitz Tor* to bid farewell to Amelia and her father. Nicolaus begged to go along.

Father squatted down to address him. "We discussed all of this already. The journey will be hard. We cannot risk your health."

"And who would play with Heidi if you go?" Amelia asked. Nicolaus's mouth drooped; he shrugged his thin shoulders. "You are young. There will be many other castles." His father opened his arms.

A choking clutched Amelia's throat as she watched them embrace. She could cry after they had left the city, not now. Her father's knees creaked as he rose. She forced a smile and hugged Nicolaus tight. "You be good for Frau Hurtin."

He ignored her cursory remark. "I want to hear all about the count's castle. I. . ." He covered his mouth to muffle a spasm of coughing. Amelia gently set Nicolaus at arm's length and cast a glance over at the count. Nicolaus followed her gaze and pulled loose. "Godspeed, Sister." He tossed the flippant farewell over his shoulder and hurried off to where the count stood next to his tall brown steed.

Without releasing the reins, Christian knelt down, his expression tender. "If you do all that your father and sister have asked, when I return, I shall take you for a ride on Champion. Would you like that?"

Nicolaus nodded. "Ja. And will you have on your new armor?" His eyes lit up as he glanced at the gleaming blade strapped to Christian's side. "And can I hold your sword?"

Christian appeared to consider the request. "Many brave men fight in battles. But the sword should be one's last recourse." Nicolaus screwed up his face in confusion. The count ever so lightly patted the boy's shoulder and rose.

Nicolaus shrugged and ran off to join Heidi, whose fist bunched up a wad of her mother's skirt. With her other hand, the little girl reached out and clasped Nicolaus's hand. Frau Hurtin smiled reassuringly at Amelia and her father.

Amelia felt a touch and turned with a start. "Herr Valdemar."

"Have a good journey. I will be anxious for your return."

Pulling away, she frowned. *"Danke schön.* I do not know when we shall return."

Father cleared his throat. "Ready?" Amelia let him hoist her up onto the first of two wagons. The wagon sagged beneath her father's weight. The count's men mounted their horses. Watchman Hurtin opened the *Wörnitz Tor,* and the traveling party proceeded out of Dinkelsbühl, wheels clattering across the moat's bridge.

The wagon fell into a rhythmic sway. Amelia clasped the seat beside her. Ahead, the count's brown steed trotted through the tall grass and buttercups. They crossed the River Wörnitz and entered the open countryside. Amelia cast a final backward glance. The gates of Dinkelsbühl were already closed tight.

Shortly before dark, Christian gave orders to prepare camp in the shelter of a wooded area while he and Leopold rode ahead to do a routine scout. They had not ridden far when Christian reined in Champion. "Didn't we pass by here on our way to Dinkelsbühl?"

"Ja." Leopold nodded. "The road is just beyond. Why?"

Christian pointed through a thick copse of trees to a small meadow. "Look, there." The tall grass was tramped down. They dismounted to examine the area. Cold ashes indicated the source of three separate campfires. Christian removed his wide, feathered hat and mopped his brow.

"Looks like they camped here while we were in Dinkelsbühl."

"I pray we don't run into them," Christian replied, replacing his hat. "Let's turn back before it gets dark."

At camp, Christian saw Herr Trittenbach preparing a bedroll beneath the wagon. Amelia was headed toward the stream. Christian dismounted. "Herr Trittenbach. All is well I hope?"

"I was about to ask you the same."

"No sign of trouble," Christian said, believing he spoke the truth. "Do you have everything you need?"

Gerrard chuckled. "My only needs are a meal and a bed. Both seem to be shortly forthcoming."

"*Gut.*"

Christian led Champion to the stream to tether alongside the other horses while his gaze searched the predusk area for intruders or anything that might harm Amelia. She had not sought a private place, so he observed her from a distance. Her hand dipped into the water, then patted her face. Next she seated herself on a rock in the midst of a bed of cuckoo flowers with clusters of funnel-shaped white blossoms.

Thoughts of her had been swirling in his mind for days, like a corralled horse circling the same territory. Why was she avoiding him when flames of desire leapt forth from her eyes? He often caught her watching him. If he approached her now, would she rebuff him? Or would her eyes reveal interest? Finding out was worth the risk of another rejection. He strode toward her. "It's beautiful, isn't it?"

Her chin was propped in her palms, and her face turned toward the pink and gold horizon. "*Ja.* This is a peaceful spot."

"The sunsets are spectacular at Engelturm." He studied her a moment. "Is there anything I can do to make this journey more comfortable for you?"

She straightened and gave him a half smile. "I am a bit hungry."

"And I'm starved. Come, let's go get something to eat." He

extended his hand to help her off the rock. "Careful."

At the camp's entrance, the armorer called out, "Over here, Amelia."

"I hope you weren't worried, Father. I couldn't take my gaze off the sunset."

Christian was so stricken at the fierce look the armorer leveled at him that he continued to worry over it until they had finished their meal. He could only assume that it concerned Amelia. His opportunity to clear up the matter came when the armorer drew away from the campfire.

"Herr Trittenbach. May I have a word with you?" Christian asked.

The armorer hesitated, then followed Christian to a private spot. *"Ja?"*

"I felt your displeasure when Amelia and I returned from the stream. I assure you that it is my utmost concern to make sure that no harm comes to your daughter."

"I do not fear for her personal safety as much as I fear for her heart." The armorer's tone contained a dagger's warning and certainly cut straight to the core of the matter.

"I understand your concern, but. . ." Christian suddenly wondered if Amelia's behavior was linked to her father's attitude. "Have you warned her away from me?"

Ja. And now I am warning you away from her. I trust you will take heed."

"I intend to do all in my power to make your stay at Engelturm comfortable and enjoyable. But most of all, I shall prove to you that I am honorable and trustworthy."

The armorer gave a gruff "Humph" and strode back to his place by the fire.

Things were more complicated than Christian had expected.

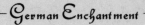

First, the father must be won. He was proving to be a pig-headed man, but surely with time he could be persuaded to think differently.

Chapter 4

The next day a wall of clouds shut off the sun. Everything that was not tied down or close-fitting flapped and billowed. Huddled against her father, Amelia pushed away strands of hair that whipped her eyes to tears.

"This makes me glad we did not bring Nicolaus along," Father said.

Amelia spit the corner of her square collar out of her mouth and secured the fluttering cloth with her hand. "I suppose we did the right thing."

The traveling party entered a more sheltered stretch of road skirted at both sides with tall trees. Amelia shivered from the deepened shade and cast an apprehensive glance at the slit of menacing sky.

The count rode up alongside their wagon, his long hair streaming away from his lean face. One hand secured his hat. "I'm taking Leopold to scout ahead and see what the weather holds," he shouted.

Father nodded. *Graf* von Engel hugged his horse's flanks with his cuffed, high-topped boots, yelled orders to one of his men, then rode off with his cousin.

The incident made Amelia wonder. Had the count finally lost

interest in her? Breaking camp that morning, there had been a perfect opportunity for him to speak with her in private. Instead, he had gone to help her father secure the canvas on the supply wagons. All day he had been courteous, but not the persistent, charming pursuer she had come to expect. Was it the result of her efforts to discourage him? Or was it her father's doing?

"Warm enough?" Father asked, giving her a quick hug.

"*Ja*, Father. I am fine."

"It looks like we'll stay dry as long as we keep moving," Christian shouted to Leopold.

"*Ja*. But once we make camp, the rain will surely catch up with us."

"We'll need shelter." Christian considered the landscape beyond.

"Isn't there a rock outcropping this side of the River Neckar?" Leopold asked.

Christian nodded with enthusiasm. "East of Stuttgart. *Ja*. That will be perfect."

With that settled, Leopold remarked, "This stretch of road would make a good place for an ambush."

"*Ja*. I was thinking the same thing. Let's scout the area."

Christian and Leopold left the trail and entered the thick, dark green forest, not going far until Leopold gestured. Christian also saw it. Four tethered horses. Off to the right were two soldiers with their backs turned toward them. Another leaned up against a tree, and one soldier stretched out on a fallen log, his eyes closed. The yellow-edged blue bands around their hats identified them as Swedes.

Communicating with hand gestures, Christian and

Leopold eased their mounts slowly forward until, with swords and pistols drawn, they were close enough to charge.

"Drop your weapons!" Christian shouted as they broke into the camp.

The soldier by the tree jerked rigid, his gaze darting back and forth. The one on the log jumped up into a half crouch. The other two Swedes had wheeled about, their arms spread.

"Now!" Christian demanded. But the soldiers remained frozen and did not drop their weapons.

"Perhaps they don't understand German," Leopold suggested.

"Dismount and collect their arms," Christian said while keeping his pistol leveled at the Swedes.

Leopold slid from the saddle and went to the nearest soldier. He nudged him with the tip of his sword. One of the other soldiers uttered a string of foreign words. Instantly all their weapons thudded to the ground.

The foreigner glared at Christian and, to Christian's great surprise, said in stilted German, "As you wish."

"Move in closer to each other," Christian said. The Swede's eyes darkened with resentment, but he interpreted the command for his comrades. Soon Leopold had them penned in like cattle. Their expressions were cold and full of hatred, and the gleam of fear in their eyes indicated they expected to be slaughtered like livestock too.

It would be a senseless killing. But Christian couldn't take them as prisoners either. That would endanger Amelia and her father. Anyway, stashing them in his dungeon would only incite the enemy into a full-scale battle at Engelturm, where he had the villagers to protect.

Christian kept a steely edge to his voice. "I apologize for this intrusion. We are scouts with a group of travelers who wish you no harm. I do not care to kill a man for no good reason. If you agree to a peaceable parting, we will unhand you."

The German-speaking Swede looked surprised, even relieved. He quickly replied, "I give you my word." When he passed the information along to his soldiers, they seemed just as amazed and confused.

"Mount up," Christian told Leopold, then added quietly for his cousin's ears only, "We'll test them. Turn slowly and retreat. But be prepared for action. Better they challenge us now than later with their many reinforcements against our few men."

If matters had not been so dire, Christian would have chuckled at Leopold's expression, which clearly indicated that although he would obey the command, he thought Christian had lost his mind.

"Guten Tag!" Christian shouted and wheeled his mount around, Leopold following suit. They slowly retreated in a deliberate act of trust, their ears in tune for the slightest sounds of resistance. Christian's heart galloped, and time seemed to suspend until, at last, he felt confident that the Swedes did not intend to attack. He reined Champion back around to face the enemies.

The Swedes had retrieved their weapons and stood in a defensive position. The German-speaking soldier saluted.

Christian smiled and returned the gesture. When he turned back to Leopold, he said, "We can go. They mean no harm." They urged their horses onward through the heavy woods until they reached the road. When the danger was far past and they were riding abreast, Christian warned Leopold, "Let's keep this matter to ourselves."

That evening, Amelia busied herself stirring a pot of the cook's thick beef stew. They had camped beneath a protruding rock ledge. Beyond her, Father waited to speak with the count, who was busily instructing his men. When *Graf* von Engel had finished, he gave the armorer his attention.

"This is an excellent encampment," Father said.

"*Ja*. It will protect us from the wind and rain."

"If you run your castle as efficiently as you do this troop, I will enjoy my work at Engelturm."

"I only hope my armory doesn't reflect badly on Engelturm."

"There is no fault in a man who sees a need and fixes it."

"And I, for one, am most happy with our arrangement. With my own father deceased, I can hope to learn from you, Herr Trittenbach."

Amelia bit back a smile. Had the count changed tactics? He was certainly lavishing his charm on Father. Dare she hope that in time her father would relinquish his admonitions against the count? It was still a puzzle. Father liked the count. So why forbid her to associate with him? War seemed like a flimsy excuse. The German lands had been at war since she was a child.

"I'm going to check on my supplies before it gets dark," Father said.

Amelia watched his retreating back. The count caught her gaze. The intensity in his blue eyes deepened. He started toward her.

She stared into the pot of beef stew and gave it several good rounds with the spoon.

"Smells good. Was your day *Gut?*"

Her stirring paused as she looked up. "*Ja*, but it feels good to be out of the wind. I couldn't help but overhear, and I agree with Father. This is a good encampment."

"Engelturm is built into rock much like this ledge."

"You often speak of Engelturm. You must love it very much."

"*Ja,* I do." He gave her a warm smile. "I hope you do too."

"Oh? Well. . ." She gave a hesitant glance toward their wagons.

"Your father has asked me not to pursue you."

So she had not imagined the count's reformed behavior. Now he seemed to be waiting for her to express her intentions. "*Graf* von Engel. I do not like to do anything against my father's wishes. I love him very much."

"Please. Call me Christian."

Amelia frowned. "Why? Don't you understand what I just said? We cannot be friends."

Christian gave a confident smile. "But we already are. And I intend to become much more than mere friends. May I call you Amelia?"

"But you just said you spoke with Father."

"I did not agree to his terms. Do you think I can win him over, Amelia?"

"I shall have no part in your scheme. I fear you are on your own, Christian." Amelia saw his face light up at the familiar form of his name. She chided herself. Why had she done that?

"It is enough for now." He leaned close to her. "I have enjoyed our conversation. But I must go lest I bring you trouble and defeat my purpose. It has been a pleasure, Amelia."

She cocked a brow at him and fought the urge to smile.

"Better not let the cook come back and find you burned our meal. By the way, did I tell you that I like the way that fire lights up your hair?"

"Oh!" She gasped, turning quickly back to the bubbling kettle. She was glad he could not see her broad smile.

Chapter 5

The sandstone castle that crowned the top of a craggy height above the River Wurm came into view, pink and glowing. "Oh, my." Amelia tugged on her father's arm, then pointed. "Look!"

"Ja. It looks aflame."

Together they watched the magical spectacle, straining for fleeting glimpses along the climbing, winding forest road. After the sun dropped off behind the cliffs, Engelturm lost its shine. But even weary as Amelia was from another full day of travel, this first encounter with the castle deeply stirred her.

Soon a wall and moat appeared. Christian had ridden ahead with Leopold, so the drawbridge was already lowered. Torches lit their way. The wagon rattled across, and Amelia bent over the side to peer down. It was too dark to see, and she could only imagine the depth of the moat and ravine. Inside the bailey, servants swarmed to welcome them.

Christian appeared at her father's side with a lighted torch in his hand. "We will wait until daylight to unload the wagon except for any personal things you want removed tonight."

Father pointed out the vicinity of one small trunk that would suffice, then helped Amelia down. Her father's hand at her elbow, they followed Christian and a servant through the bailey. A stone arch provided entrance to the castle. Christian explained, "A private *sittingraum* separates your bedchambers, which are located directly above the armory. My own chambers are in the same tower on yet an upper level."

"Perfect," Father replied.

"I know you are fatigued. You have only to tell the servants your wishes. A bath? A meal? My staff will gladly serve you. In the morning, someone will bring you to *Frühstück,* and we will plan our day while we eat this meal."

"Thank you for your kindness," Father said.

"Engelturm is lovely. I see why you adore it," Amelia added, ignoring her father's frown.

Two servants preceded them through the south wing corridor to their tower bedchambers.

Amelia's chamber was comfortable with a large fireplace. She bathed, ate a meal, then fell into a large canopy bed, feeling as if she had gone to heaven.

In the morning, Amelia blinked at the unfamiliar wall paintings, wrapped a blanket around herself, and shuffled across the room to peer out an arched window. Swallows swooped to and fro. To the east, the view contained a river valley and a village of orange-tiled rooftops. There were fields and meadows, each appearing the size of a *taler*—only square instead of round like the German coin. Farther beyond was the dark green forest.

If only Nicolaus were here to see the way the moss-covered castle wall plunged eternally downward. Her heart gave a sad tug. She could only imagine how thrilled her little brother would be to explore Engelturm. Homesick as she already was for him, nothing could squelch her own excitement. Amelia hurried to a handsome, carved wardrobe and threw open its double doors. A servant had unpacked her small trunk. Amelia quickly slipped into a blue, high-waisted gown and joined her father, who was lounging in the adjoining *sittingraum*.

"I heard you stirring."

"Thank you for waiting, Father. Do you have a window in your chamber?"

Ja. Magnificent view."

They chatted amiably and followed a servant down a winding staircase, through a corridor, and into a great hall with a large, ornate table. *Frühstück*, a light morning meal consisting of *Brot, Wurst*, and *Käse* was served. Christian and Leopold instantly stood to greet them. Amelia hoped no one heard the rumble of her stomach. As she ate her portion of the bread, sausage, and cheese, she listened to the ensuing conversation.

"I can show you the armory first. Later, the wagon can be unloaded under your supervision."

Amelia beamed at Christian. He did seem—what was the word her father had used that night at the rock-ledge encampment? Efficient. *Ja*. Christian seemed very efficient and capable in any situation. The count openly returned her smile.

Father cleared his throat.

Instantly Amelia lowered her gaze.

Ja. That is a sound plan," Father said.

Elated to have such special guests at Engelturm, Christian could have skipped down the corridor as he led Herr Trittenbach and Amelia from the hall to the armory. A servant opened its great door, and a rustle could be heard as a gray rat scurried across the floor. Christian grimaced. He had told the servant to set traps and had hoped they would be rid of all their rodent tenants by now.

Gerrard seemed not to mind as he stepped into the room. "Ah." He nodded. "I see there will be plenty of room to work. The light from that window is good." The armorer examined the area with its shelves of weapons and armor. "Do you have a list of the men you will outfit?"

"*Ja*. I will get that at once. Is there anything else you need?"

Gerrard shook his head.

"See that Herr Trittenbach has everything he needs until I can come and help," Christian told a servant.

To Christian's pleasant surprise, Gerrard smiled and gestured with his hand. "Enough formality. *Bitte*. Please," he repeated, "call me Gerrard."

"I would be honored. And you will return the favor?"

Gerrard nodded again.

Christian gave Amelia a half smile, then left them alone with the servant. Time passed quickly. When the morning was half spent, Christian returned to the armory, hoping that Gerrard would not consider him a pest. Alone in the room, Amelia stood staring out the armory window.

"I hope you grow as fond of that view as I am."

She spun. "*Graf* von Engel. You startled me." Amelia studied him a moment. "Why do you hope that?"

"So that you will never want to leave."

"You intend to lock me in the dungeon?"

He shook his head. "What a delight you are."

She gave him a teasing frown. "*Ja*. You said that once before."

Christian advanced toward her—so close he could have touched her rosy cheek. "I remember. In Dinkelsbühl." He paused. "The day we met, when I caught my first glimpse of you through the slit in that rusty visor, I was spellbound. Your own gaze spoke volumes. You were witty and coy, but our souls meshed. Do not deny it. But then your manner toward me changed. I was crushed and returned to Engelturm, questioning every word I had spoken to you, every action that passed between us. I tried in vain to figure out what I had done to cause you to withdraw." She quietly listened, her face vulnerable. "Then on our journey, when your father told me he feared for your heart, I hoped that it was only his warning that had changed your mind about me. Was it?"

Amelia nodded.

"Then I ask that you give me a chance to prove to him that I would never hurt you."

Amelia hesitantly touched his arm. "I wonder why Father is so adamant about us?"

"I intend to find out." An intimate moment of silence passed between them. "What does he think of my armory? Did he say?"

"It is the perfect challenge for him. In need of work but not a total disaster."

Christian released a sigh. *"Gut.* That is good."

"It did not take Father long to begin its organization. Until this moment, he has been directing the men, coming and going with loads of leather, metal, and tools."

"Amelia." They turned their gazes to the door as Gerrard's voice preceded him into the armory. Two bolts of material were draped over his arm, and a troop of servants trailed after him, equally laden with cloth. "See what I have? Where would you like to set up your work area, by that window?"

"Oh, *Ja.*" When she blushed, Christian knew she was remembering his earlier comment about the view.

Gerrard dropped the bolts near the count's feet. "You can arrange the cloth and your supplies as you wish."

"Certainly, Father. I'd be happy to."

"Is there anything I can do?" Christian offered, while handing over the list of men he needed to outfit.

Gerrard stuffed it into his pocket. "Everyone is so helpful. I suppose you have other affairs you should be managing?"

"Well, *Ja.* But I'd be happy to assist here."

"*Nein,* Christian. See to those other things. If you have time, when you are done. . ." Gerrard's voice dwindled off, and he crossed the room to inspect a stack of metal sheets.

Christian cast a final glance around the room, pleased that all was going so well. Then reluctantly, he left.

That night Christian entertained Amelia, Gerrard, and several of his men over a meal. They dined on boiled pork and dumplings with cherry cake for dessert. It turned into a merry gathering with everyone joking and sharing stories of their recent journey from Dinkelsbühl.

Keeping with the general high spirits, Amelia remarked, "And to think we worried about running into the Swedes."

An eerie quietness befell the room until Leopold said, albeit too exuberantly, "*Ja.* To think that!"

Gerrard's eyes widened. "Christian? Did you come across some Swedes?"

Christian cleared his throat. "Why, *Ja,* Gerrard, we did. But I didn't want to frighten Amelia."

She pointed at him. "You saw the Swedes? Where?"

"*Ja,* where?" Gerrard echoed.

Waving his knife in the air and trying to keep the incident trivial, Christian replied, "Remember that second day when Leopold and I went scouting?"

"Ja. Go on."

"We scared up a few Swedes." Christian took a bite, thoroughly chewing his meat, then waved his knife again. "Disarmed them, rounded them up in a little huddle, and talked some sense into them."

"Did your sword do the speaking?" Amelia asked.

Christian toyed with another bite. "We came to a peaceable agreement. Didn't we, Leopold?"

"Indeed, we did. To my surprise."

Amelia gasped. "Did you kill them?"

"Daughter!" Gerrard scolded. "It is not in our place to—"

"Nein!" Christian hurried to dispel Amelia's worry. He softened his voice and met her gaze. "We did not kill them. We let them go."

"It seems you can accomplish most anything," Gerrard muttered, his eyes twinkling with amusement. He shook his head. "Are you sure you even need me here, Christian?"

"I most certainly do need you here. As I told you before, I hope the war never reaches Engelturm, but that's almost too much to wish for. *Ja.* I need you. Now, enough about the Swedes." Christian's mind groped for another topic. "Did I show you the chapel, Gerrard?"

"Nein. I have not seen it."

"You must. Feel free to use it whenever you wish. We do not have a priest here at Engelturm, but there is one in Engelheim."

"Danke, Christian."

He nodded, then glanced at Amelia. Her hands were primly folded in her lap, and she gazed at him with an expression close to adoration. His heart leapt.

When the meal was cleared away, Christian rose. "Would you care to see the chapel now? Or perhaps I can challenge you to a game of chess?"

"I prefer to retire to my chamber," Gerrard declined.

"We are very pleased with everything at Engelturm. I'll go with you, Father. *Guten Abend.*"

"Good night," Christian replied with the others, everyone scrambling to their feet.

Once his guests had departed, Christian gazed across his assembled men. "Which one of you wishes to challenge me to a game?"

"I will," Leopold answered.

Several plays into the chess match, Christian lingered too long over his next move.

"I believe my friend is in love," Leopold said.

Christian jerked up his head. His cousin appeared to be serious. "That is yet to be determined. But I can guarantee you it shall not interfere with my chess abilities."

Leopold chuckled. "We shall see."

Christian was wrong. He could not concentrate at all.

Chapter 6

From the armory window, Amelia and her father watched Christian and his musketeers practice. Some used flint-lock pistols. In the few weeks that had lapsed, Christian had recruited all of the physically capable men at Engelturm, as well as those from the village of Engelheim, for routine training.

She remembered Christian's advice to Nicolaus. *Many brave men have fought battles, but the sword should be one's last recourse.* Yet, Christian was arming his people. She also recalled the incident during their travel to Engelturm when Christian had released the Swedish soldiers unharmed. Most men whom her father armed were eager to greet action. Christian was, indeed, proving to be a man of honor. Surely he would not break her heart. Why then did her father distrust him?

"Watching them makes me long for a bit of practice myself. The metal I brought from Dinkelsbühl was a new batch. We shall have to proof it soon, before we progress much further. Would you care to help?"

Amelia brightened. "You know I would."

That afternoon Christian entered the tower in time to see Amelia descending. He halted at once. "What a pleasant surprise."

"How are your drills going?"

Christian shrugged. "Some of the men are skilled. But those from the village still need much practice. I detest the idea of matching them against Swedish soldiers or those of the Imperial army."

"It is commendable that you possess such a passion for your people."

Wishing to extend his time in her presence, Christian grasped at the first idea that came to mind. "Have you had a tour of the inner courtyard?" When Amelia shook her head, he gave a swooping arm gesture. "May I?"

First she cast a hesitant, backward glance, then smiled. "I am in need of exercise and fresh air. That would be nice." They passed through the gallery and to a door that led outside. "It's lovely. I often wished to come here, but I didn't want to intrude."

"It is my personal courtyard. But you are most welcome to come anytime you wish."

The square courtyard in the center of the castle was unlike the bailey and outer courtyards, where all the work of the castle took place. This one was designed purely for pleasure. They walked among plantings of plum, apple, and pear trees. The cobblestone path was edged with flowers and plants. Stone benches and statues added elegance.

"I have watched men prepare for war. You are different. Why do you care about your enemies?"

"Jesus Christ loved to the point of death. When I ponder this, I know that He would want me to love my fellowman."

"Love? I am also a Christian. But I don't *love* everyone."

"I don't always feel loving, but I try to act with compassion." He saw that her expression remained puzzled; but before he could further explain, a fish broke the surface of a small pond, and the moment was lost when Amelia giggled and started toward it.

At the pond's edge she paused and asked, "How did Engelturm get its name? Angel Tower seems such a curious name."

"You are full of questions. But I am happy to oblige you. There are times, especially at sunset, that the cliff almost glows."

"*Ja.* I saw it the first night we arrived. Father and I watched in amazement."

Christian shared her enthusiasm. "So you understand. A tale goes that angels make their camp on this mountain. So when the castle was built, it was fittingly named Angel Tower."

"That's beautiful."

"The Württemberg dukes built Engelturm to use as a hunting castle. When Frederick I knighted my *opa*, the duke also gave him Engelturm. *Opa* gave the castle a verse."

"He was a poet?"

Christian smiled. "A Bible verse, Psalm 34:7. 'The angel of the Lord encampeth round about them that fear Him, and delivereth them.' *Opa* made sure we all memorized his verse, giving God the glory. Castle walls alone do not protect those within. God is in control. Grandfather said that even angels are not to be praised for they are merely God's messengers."

"I believe that is a lovely story and a most appropriate name for your castle. As to your faith, I must add that it does not hurt if the walls are made strong."

With a chuckle, Christian said, "I agree. Strong walls and strong faith make the best defense."

They moved away from the pond. "After watching your men train this morning, I am eager to do some shooting myself."

"You want to learn to shoot?" Christian stammered, his steps faltering. "I–I don't think you understand. The muskets are much too heavy, and the pistols misfire so easily that—"

"Christian, I can shoot."

He stared, his mind churning. "Your father taught you, didn't he?"

"*Ja.* We proof our own armor. I can fire a flintlock. I have used a matchlock musket, but you are right. It is too heavy and awkward. And I can wield a sword."

"Once again, you amaze me." He shook his head. "You and your father duel?"

Amelia laughed. "I'm not very good. But I enjoy it."

"Are you bored here, Amelia?"

"*Nein.* I am enjoying myself at Engelturm."

"*Gut.*" After a moment of silence, Christian said, "Now let me show you something else that is marvelous about Engelturm."

He led her to a stone bench. "Sit. Close your eyes. And wait just a moment." He returned. "No peeking. Keep your eyes closed."

"I am."

Christian knelt, his *hosen* scraping the cobblestones as he faced her. "Open your mouth."

Amelia's lips parted, and Christian swallowed twice, wondering what it would be like to kiss her.

"Christian?"

He plopped the plump berries on her tongue before he lost control.

Amelia's eyes flew open. "Mm! Delicious!"

"I must confess, in season, I sneak in here to rob these bushes every chance I get."

"So you do have a weakness after all."

He tenderly took hold of her hand, giving her an intimate

look. "Many weaknesses."

After a moment, Amelia drew her hand away. "Which reminds me of Father. I must be getting back before he comes searching."

Once they finished the berries, Christian reluctantly returned her to the tower. But their time together left him brimming with a multitude of emotions. Feeling the urge to expel some of his nervous energy, Christian headed to the stables to fetch Champion. He spoke to the groom, then departed through the castle gates and over the drawbridge. The road hugged lush, green, sloping hills and at one point cut into thick, evergreen forest—teeming of birdcalls and rambling bush. It emerged at a solitary lookout point, where he dismounted, tethered Champion, and strode to the rock ledge that he often visited to sort out his life. He had come here when his father was ill and again after his father died. Settling in amongst a patch of bugleweed, he gazed beyond their blue flower spikes to the surrounding German countryside.

So much was on his mind these days. His loyalties and sympathies did not match. He owed his loyalties to a prince who supported the emperor. If Christian were pressed into this war, he was obligated to fight the Swedes. But he did not agree with imperial politics. His sympathies lay with the protestant princes in league with the Swedes and the French. "Lord, help me to do what I have to do," he prayed.

Next he prayed for Amelia. Gerrard was doing wonders with the armory. He could sense the man's attitude warming. Soon Christian hoped to obtain his approval to pursue Amelia. Even though Gerrard was occupied, he kept a strict watch over his daughter. There had only been a few instances since her arrival that Christian had been alone with her.

Today in the courtyard he had wondered if Amelia were a true believer. If not, perhaps he could lead her to God's truth. He hoped that wasn't the only reason that God had brought her into his life. Each moment spent with her excited him as nothing had ever done before. Such abilities. She could sew, stir a pot, and help Gerrard with his armor. He envisioned her shooting or wielding a sword—just the capable, spunky sort of countess his castle needed.

His thoughts turned to the village sprawled out below and to his father's dying words. *Be iron-fisted in protecting your lands but allow Christ's love to guide you.* Christian bowed his head to conclude his prayer before he returned to the castle.

The next afternoon, after military exercises had finished, Christian accompanied Gerrard and Amelia to the practicing field. Two servants carried several breastplates to set up against stationary targets. Gerrard wished to test the metal with the sword stroke and firearms.

Hoping to impress Amelia, Christian gave the sword stroke his best. Gerrard was pleased when their blades easily glanced off the armor. Next they backed off the appropriate distance and brought out a German flintlock pistol. Christian continued to enjoy the practice until Amelia's turn came. Then his emotions began to do strange things. A protective impulse rose so strong that he could not help but fret for her safety.

He sucked in a deep breath as she took the flintlock from Gerrard. She loaded the pistol herself. It took several maneuvers—first she brushed the pan free from the last shot, then placed a few grains of priming powder into the pan, closed the frizzen, and cocked.

Christian held his breath again when Amelia fired at the target. Her shot hit the breastplate. She brought her arms down and gave him a lopsided grin. "Your turn, Christian."

He exhaled and carefully took the gun, his chest bursting with admiration.

After the round was completed, they examined the targets and inspected the armor. Christian ran his finger over the marks, which, though visible, had barely dented the breastplate, and nodded his approval.

"The finely tempered German metal is superior over any other," Gerrard boasted.

"I noticed your work lacks ornamentation compared to others. There must be a reason that you keep the rivet plain."

"A very intelligent observation. Weapons glance off smooth surfaces easier than those that are embellished."

Christian's heart soared with hope under the other man's praise. They returned to their shooting positions. The gun was wiped down with a cloth before they started another round. The proofing was such a pleasant experience that Christian was sorely disappointed when it was time to return to the castle.

"I am pleased with what you have already accomplished, Gerrard. Now that you are settled in, perhaps you would like to take a tour of Engelturm. I have tomorrow afternoon free."

"Settled, perhaps, but my work has just begun."

"Another time then." Christian turned to Amelia. "What about you, Amelia? Would you have time for a tour?"

"I would enjoy that very much." She turned to Gerrard. "Father, could you spare me for awhile in the afternoon?"

Gerrard's mouth drooped, and his eyes saddened.

Christian quickly added, "Of course a servant will accompany us."

Amelia cast him a conspiratorial grin, then turned to Gerrard. "Father?"

"*Ja*. A short tour. There is much to do."

Christian bit back a triumphant smile.

Chapter 7

When Amelia saw the count's fine breeches and sapphire blue doublet, she was glad that she had donned her favorite, pale blue gown for their planned tour of Engelturm. With such luxuriant ringlets, Christian had no need of a wig like so many other men wore.

"Amelia. You look lovely." He offered her his arm.

Embarrassed that she had been caught admiring him, she replied, "And you look as though you are expecting the emperor."

"I hoped to make a good impression." They left Amelia's *sittingraum*, and a servant fell into step behind them at the appropriate distance. "I feared Gerrard would find some excuse to keep us apart."

"Do not be surprised if the castle comes crumbling down around us from all his pacing."

"I know that you are a prize, but I do believe he is overly protective."

"*Ja.* But it is not like him. That's why it perplexes me so."

"Might I hope it is your fondness for me that worries him?"

"A lady would never answer such a question."

Christian chuckled. They stepped into the gallery. Although Amelia had passed through this wide passageway before, she did not know the history of its many exhibits. Along one wall, windows revealed the inner courtyard. Opposite, several openings and an arched doorway displayed the great hall. Otherwise the massive walls exhibited portraits. Amelia removed her hand from the crook of Christian's arm to caress a sculpture, then studied a man in an ornate, gold-gilded portrait.

"That is Württemberg's Duke Frederick I. My ancestors are at the far end of the gallery."

In slow progression along the gallery, Amelia marveled over the noblemen and women, intrigued by their antiquated fashions and weapons. Christian respectfully gazed at a portrait of a white-haired man.

Amelia readily discerned the family resemblance. "Your father?"

"*Opa.* I am the last of the family line. There are cousins, of course. Leopold you have met."

"Your grandmother was beautiful." Amelia moved farther down and stared at a painting two spaces over. "And so was your mother." Beneath her portrait was a wooden chest, intricately carved with flowers and birds. Amelia stooped down and felt the inlaid jewels on its lid. "How lovely."

Christian knelt beside her. "There is a family of woodcarvers in the village, the Linders. Father refurbished the castle and Herr Linder did much of the ornate woodwork. He presented this gift to my mother. Father provided the jewels. I am told that she loved it. Herr Linder also fashioned my cradle, which remains in the nursery. Mother died soon after I was born."

"I'm sorry you did not get to know her. That is the way it was for Nicolaus."

Christian laid his hand upon Amelia's. "Nicolaus is fortunate that he has a sister like you. Do you miss him?"

"Very much. I was surprised Father did not bring him along. We usually do. He had a cough, but. . .I don't know." She shrugged. "Father is acting strange lately. But let's not talk about Father."

"I agree." Christian's hand still covered Amelia's, atop his mother's wooden chest. "I always intended to give this chest to my bride as a wedding present." Amelia felt a flutter of excitement in her breast. "That is why I am so glad that you like it." Christian stood, drawing her up with him. He caressed the tops of her fingers with his thumb. "Someday, I'd like to speak of this again."

Amelia glanced at the servant at the far end of the gallery and withdrew her tingling hand, placing it back beneath his arm. "Perhaps someday, Christian."

He smiled at her, and they continued their tour. The gallery extended to the northwest tower. On the ground level was the chapel. It was a room of splendor with its stained glass window and intricate altar hangings, but all Amelia could see was the count.

When they returned through the gallery, Christian stopped at one of the windows that overlooked the inner courtyard and placed his hand at the back of her waist. "I enjoyed our interlude in the courtyard the other day. We could meet there again."

She fingered her lace collar, struggling with the idea of going against her father's wishes. Her own will, however, waged stronger. "Tomorrow I could slip away about midday for just a few moments."

"Stolen moments I will treasure. But now, I must return you to Gerrard."

"*Ja.* We must return."

That night Christian had felt bolstered by the secretive smiles he and Amelia had exchanged over the evening meal. As usual, once they had finished eating, Gerrard had whisked her away to the privacy of their *sittingraum*. Since the Trittenbachs' arrival at Engelturm, Christian and Leopold had whiled away most of their evenings with chess. This evening was no different.

"She seems to have fallen under your charm at last," Leopold said.

"It is the strangest thing. As if some natural force is drawing us together, as if there is nothing we could do to stop it even if we wanted to."

"Hm." Leopold studied the chessboard. "Definitely not your charm."

"I think not. I'm hoping it is God's work."

"I do not think it is anything new. Probably just common, old-fashioned love. But since God is love, then in a way. . ." Leopold shrugged.

"Have you ever been in love?"

"*Nein!*" Leopold splayed both hands to ward off such an odious idea. "One lovesick person in this castle is enough. I have more important matters to consider."

Christian tilted his head and wrinkled his brow thoughtfully. "I don't think there is anything more important than love."

"*Ach!* You have it bad. So when are you going to approach Gerrard? He looks and acts like an angry bull every time he sees you watching Amelia."

"Did he do that again tonight?"

"*Ja.* And if you aren't careful, he's liable to sweep her up and away from Engelturm just to separate you."

Christian shook his head. "I don't think so. He enjoys working in the armory. But I do mean to have a talk with him. When the time is right." He moved his chess piece. "Checkmate! I believe, Cousin, you have missed your calling."

Leopold scowled. "How is that?"

"You are a natural counselor. You should have been a priest."

The next day Amelia stepped into the inner courtyard, and instantly Christian appeared.

"I'm so glad you came. Shall we walk or sit?"

"Let's walk. Oh look!" Amelia pointed at a flock of swallows overhead, their songs filling the courtyard. "I saw their nests outside my window. I've watched them swoop down to the river."

"And have you seen our stag? He appears near twilight to drink from the river. I think you could see it from your chambers."

"I have not, but I shall look for him."

"He has appeared for several years. I have forbidden any of my men to shoot him."

Amelia saw the awe in his expression. "Is he special?"

Christian shrugged. "Like any other deer, I suppose, only older, wiser, wild, and very protective."

"Protective? How is that?"

"At certain times of the year I see him with several doe. He lifts his antlered head to sniff for danger and stamps the ground with his front hooves. He is a fearsome sight."

"He sounds much like you."

"A frightening sight?"

Amelia's laughter tinkled throughout the garden. "You are protective of those in your charge."

"Perhaps you are right. When Father died, I thought it could not be. I did not want to take on the responsibility of the castle and the village. I had been living a very carefree life."

"I suppose there are many things we wouldn't do if there weren't others depending upon us."

"Meeting you has helped me."

Astonished, Amelia asked, "How? I have done nothing." She shook her head, "I do not understand."

"Why, you've given me a purpose, Amelia. I'll admit I've been a bit wild in my growing-up years. Father had so much patience. But now, since I've met you, I don't resent being master of Engelturm. Rather, I get the urge to see that everything runs smoothly, to improve the conditions of the castle, to protect, to settle down and live with. . ."

Amelia released a whoosh of air. "I fear you misplace the source of your inspiration. I certainly deserve no credit for your behavior, good or bad." Christian frowned, and Amelia rambled on, "Though I believe it seems to be mostly good. At least from what I have observed. . ."

His frown turned to a smile, and he gazed at her with adoration in his eyes.

Amelia returned to the armory, practicing in her mind how she would bring up the subject of Christian. Her father sat on the stone window seat, hunched over a barrel filled with sand and vinegar. He had been cleaning some of Engelturm's rusty plate armor. When he heard her enter, he looked up, his eyes bright.

"Come look, Amelia! See what I have found!"

She crossed the room and joined him on the bench. "What is it, Father?"

With a cotton cloth, he quickly hand-polished a small area and exclaimed, "See this armorer's mark?"

Amelia leaned forward to inspect the tiny mark. It was a small side view of a helm with a star at the top. She ran her finger over it. "I like it."

"It is the mark of either Desiderius or Coloman Colmon. The son and father used the same mark." His voice held awe.

"Who are they?"

"They came from a family of armorers that have been around since the thirteen-hundreds. They served many of the emperors."

"How old do you think this piece is?"

"If it is the father, it would be one hundred years old. If the son, perhaps half a century. Fascinating." Father mumbled to himself as he rose to rummage through some similar pieces of plate armor.

"Father, about Christian. Do you like him?"

He came hustling back to the bench. "I'll bet this is yet another piece of their work." He plopped it into the barrel.

Amelia sighed. It seemed that this was not going to be a good time to discuss Christian. She would let it drop for now.

Chapter 8

Christian paced beneath the pear tree—his rendezvous spot with Amelia. He was nervous because, after three weeks of meeting her like this, today he planned to confess his feelings of guilt. And he did not know how she would react to this news. But it was wrong to go behind Gerrard's back. Possibly everyone else in the castle knew what had been transpiring. At first, it had seemed like a good idea; but Christian had felt farther from the Lord each day this façade had continued.

That morning a Bible verse had struck him hard, admonishing "whatsoever is not of faith is sin." What he was doing reeked of sin. He was not trusting God but making things happen on his own. In doing so, he had dishonored God to the servants—who did not miss a lick of gossip—to Leopold, and to Amelia. And he was undermining the trust of the very man he hoped to win over.

He glanced up at the sun. What was keeping her? She was never this late. His concern and impatience grew, until in his agitated state, he resolved to find her. Although he had already asked God for forgiveness, he would not find peace unless he also asked for Amelia's.

Quickly he covered the passageways that led to the southwest tower and the armory. Amelia and Gerrard instantly looked up at him, then Amelia let out a little gasp and glanced at the window. "My, the time has slipped by this morning, has it not, Father? I was so busy I hadn't noticed."

Gerrard chuckled and said to Christian, "She has always enjoyed painting."

At that moment a servant knocked, then entered. "The additional leather has arrived Herr Trittenbach."

"Wonderful. Just on time. Will you excuse me?" Gerrard hurried from the room. The door closed.

"I missed you in the courtyard."

Amelia wiped her hands and placed the brush in a barrel. "I am sorry. I did not do it intentionally."

"I am glad it happened. Even though I cherish the time I spend with you, it has been wrong."

She frowned. "Please explain."

"I was wrong to suggest something your father forbids. Wrong not to trust God in this matter."

"Oh." Amelia looked contrite. "I confess it has bothered me too."

Christian released a breath of relief. "Can you forgive me for persuading you to go against your father's wishes?"

"Of course. I was just as much in the wrong as you."

"We must make things right. I will talk to Gerrard at once. Then. . . ," he paused and shrugged, "we will go from there."

"I will also speak with Father, though I have been trying to do so for quite some time."

"As have I." Christian gave her a crooked grin, wondering how he could have doubted her sweet-spirited reaction.

The door opened, and Gerrard directed several servants

with bundles of leather. Christian watched him for a moment, then loudly cleared his throat.

Gerrard glanced sideways at him. "Did you want something, Christian?"

"*Ja*. I would have a word with you as soon as you are available." Christian forced himself not to glance at Amelia, lest he give away his intentions without a word in his own defense.

"I suppose we could meet after supper. Is that soon enough?"

"That would be fine," Christian said, happy to have the time to form his address.

Christian faced Gerrard. "Would you care for a drink?"

"*Nein*." Gerrard yawned. "I'm a bit tired."

Whether or not the yawn was feigned, Christian chose to ignore manners and press forward. He seated himself close to Gerrard and fastened his gaze on the older man. "I would like to bring up the subject of your daughter, Amelia."

"I believe I know my daughter's name," Gerrard grumbled.

"Very well. At one time you told me you did not want her heart broken. I have no intentions of doing so."

"*Gut!*" Gerrard said, rising from his chair. "Glad that's settled. If that is all—"

"*Nein!*" Christian said, his voice rising. "It is not! Please be seated."

Gerrard raised a brow at Christian but reseated himself, clamping his teeth together.

"I would like to ask for Amelia's hand in marriage. I love her."

The older man's jaw slackened. He closed his eyes, then opened them. "It is not possible."

"Your answer is not enough for me. I need a reason."

Gerrard narrowed an angry gaze at Christian. "If you had only listened. It was never possible. Amelia is spoken for."

"What? But that cannot be. I would know if Amelia—"

"Amelia does not know yet!" Gerrard ground out as he jumped to his feet and pointed his finger at Christian's face. "And now because you would not listen and have won her heart—for I assume you have or you would not be addressing me—you will also break it. You have done the very thing I warned you against."

Christian fumbled to his feet. His face burned. Through an escalating dizziness, he repeated, "Amelia is spoken for?"

"I realize that you are the master of Engelturm, but I am your elder, and as I am Amelia's father, you should have respected my wishes."

In agony, Christian pressed his eyes shut. "The heart does not listen well."

"But it will mend. Keep away from her." Gerrard turned abruptly and strode from the room.

When silence surrounded him, Christian slumped down into a chair and stared at the hearth.

After an immeasurable period of time, he heard the whispering of his name. "What?" he croaked.

"I asked if I may come in."

His eyes still glassy, Christian gave Leopold a weak wave.

His cousin took the chair that Gerrard had abandoned. "I'm sorry. It looks as though your audience with Gerrard did not go well."

"Amelia is already spoken for."

Leopold's brows slanted. "What is the situation?"

Christian's face scrunched up in a distasteful scowl. "Gerrard did not explain anything. He only cursed my clumsy behavior. I must withdraw my attentions."

"But why would Amelia lead you on? Perhaps she does not want this arranged marriage."

"She does not know about it."

"Whew!" Leopold exclaimed. "He is selling his daughter."

Christian clenched his teeth, imagining what Amelia might have to endure. "If I am not in God's will with this, then I will only make matters harder for Amelia if I pursue her."

"I thought we had decided love is a matter of the heart."

Confused, Christian reasoned with himself. Hadn't he just this day turned the matter over to God? Might God be punishing him for going behind Gerrard's back? *Nein*. God forgave him. "I do not like it. But I have no choice right now. I must wait on God."

Leopold also scowled, and they spent the remainder of the evening staring into the hearth fire.

Amelia waited impatiently in her *sittingraum*, though it was not long until her father appeared. She noted his unusually red face but refused to let this perfect opportunity to speak with him about Christian slip away. "Father. I wish to speak with you."

"Not tonight," he grumped.

"*Ja*. Tonight. I want to speak about Christian. I have a right to know what has passed between you."

Father folded his hands in front of his stomach and rocked on his heels as if he were forming an explanation. "We will speak of this in the morning."

Amelia stood, emboldened by her desire. "I will not let you push the matter away."

He stepped forward and squeezed her shoulder. "I need

time to think. You are right. We need to discuss the matter. Only give me until tomorrow morning."

"All right, Father. Tomorrow."

He nodded, released her, and crossed the room to his chambers. Unable to fight back the emotions that overwhelmed her, Amelia hurried to the privacy of her own chamber and allowed her tears to freely fall. As she lay on her bed, she determined not to let him evade the issue tomorrow. She barely slept at all and was up early, waiting for her father in the *sittingraum*. When his bedchamber door opened, she jutted out her chin. "Father!"

He joined her on a settee. "You are up early."

"I did not want to miss you. We have something to discuss." Father gestured with his hand for her to begin, so she said, "I have tried to ask you a question for many weeks. Do you like Christian?"

"I like Christian very much."

The answer startled Amelia. Dare she hope? "You find him honorable?"

"I do."

Her heart raced faster. "Then why forbid me to see him? I find your protective behavior ill-placed."

He placed his hands in a prayerful position and tapped them against his chin. "I only wanted to spare you from hurt." He drew them down. "The truth is, I have already promised your hand in marriage to another."

At first this preposterous explanation left Amelia speechless. Of course, she had known that someday her father might bring someone around for her to look over, but to think that he had arranged such a thing behind her back absolutely infuriated her. Anger began to course through her already pulsing veins. She and Father worked so closely, shared intimate thoughts. . . . She just always assumed he would want her to be happy, that he would take into consideration her own desires. How could he do this? Christian. He would know what to do. "Did Christian ask for my hand?"

"*Ja.* But I have promised another."

"But I want to marry Christian." Amelia strove to keep her voice calm. "Father, I never thought you would do such a thing behind my back."

"I did not want to."

Once again Amelia's mouth fell open, and her calm dissolved. "But I love Christian."

"This is not about love."

She no longer cared about keeping her voice low. "Tell me. What is this about? And who is this chosen man?"

"It is the mercer."

Her arms gestured wildly, and she paced. "Herr Valdemar? *Ach!* I cannot stand him! How could you?"

Her father's voice became stern. "I want you to listen well. There are times when we must do things we do not especially want to do. This is one of those times."

She glared at him. "And why?"

"Do you remember when I took the commissions for the French?"

Amelia jerked a nod.

"Valdemar found out and has threatened to tell the city council. With the way the war has been going, I would be a traitor. Our entire family would be in serious danger. Valdemar has had his eye on you for a long time. Because he loves you, he will look aside. I believe he will treat you kindly. But if you turn him down, he will ruin us."

"Ach!" Amelia said again, only this time with even more distaste. "I am already ruined if I marry him."

Father's voice took on a harsher, authoritative tone. "You must grow up. You have until your birthday. Then you will obey your father, who has provided for you all of these years. And you will marry Valdemar."

"I shall never!" Amelia spat back at him. Father flinched. She did not care, but filled with fury, she turned her back to him and flew into her chambers.

Chapter 9

Christian fasted and prayed. But regardless of his good intentions to trust God with his heartache, he fell into bouts of self-pity. Frustrated at his lack of faith, he sought the privacy of his inner courtyard. He meandered about, sending prayers heavenward, then sat on a stone bench. He heaved a great sigh, absentmindedly plucking berries off a nearby bush and plopping them onto his tongue, remembering another time and Amelia's red, juice-stained lips. He bowed his head to the Father.

"Christian?"

His head jerked up. It was Leopold. He rose. *"Ja?"*

"I thought you would want to know that Amelia is out on the practicing field by herself with a pistol."

"Ach! Of all the insane things." He strode toward the castle, giving Leopold a nod. *"Danke."*

Amelia had spent the morning in her bedchamber. By afternoon, her grief gave way to anger until it became a mighty river of rage. She stomped into the armory and grabbed one of the flintlock pistols off the shelf.

Her father quickly asked, "What are you going to do with that?"

"Shoot it," Amelia snapped, helping herself to the ammunition that she would need.

He stepped forward. "You're not going to do anything foolish?"

"I'm not putting it to my head, if that's what you mean. Let me pass!" Amelia had never spoken in such a disrespectful manner, and she half expected him to reach out and slap her. But he did not. He looked so sad. She was glad, for she was still very angry with him for ruining her life.

Withdrawing from the armory, she marched out to the field with the large pistol, all the while trying to come up with a logical solution to her problem—like pointing the pistol at Valdemar, or perhaps a Frenchman, or a Swede. But she knew that was not an option.

Targets still remained in their places from morning exercises. Amelia stomped to the location where she had earlier helped to proof armor and tried to dismiss memories of that charming day from her mind. She prepared her firearm, and with both arms extended, she raised it up and aimed.

"Amelia!"

Her arms jerked, the gun went off, and she missed the target entirely. Trembling from head to toe, she spun around. "See what you made me do!"

"I'm sorry," Christian said. "But what are you doing here alone?"

Amelia tried to rein in her anger. "What does it look like, Christian? I'm shooting."

"You're ferocious."

Her chest heaved. "I have every right to be, aren't you? Or are you relieved that I am promised to another?"

Christian ventured closer. "You know about it then?"

"I just found out. It does not please me at all." One corner of Christian's mouth tipped up, and Amelia noticed his red-stained lips.

He stepped forward. "I wish there was something I could do. I don't want to hurt you."

"Sometimes I have dreams of what I'd like to do. But I always push them aside for Father's sake. But this time. . . ," her voice grew cold, "I do not care about disappointing him."

"What is it that you would like to do?"

She glanced over at the armory. Her father watched them from the window. It angered her anew. "I should like to do this." The pistol slipped to the ground, and she stepped forward. Christian blinked. She rose on tiptoes, wrapped her arms around his neck, and kissed him full on the mouth. At first his lips were firm and unsuspecting, but it did not take long for him to respond. Amelia felt her body melt and knew that she must pull away. Her hands splayed against his chest, she gave him a reckless smile. His features still displayed shock.

Amelia tapped his lower lip with her forefinger. "You had berries on your lips. Anyway, Father was watching from the armory window. I wanted to spite him." Christian jerked. "Do not look," she warned and stooped to pluck up the pistol. "My anger is gone now."

"I rather liked you angry," he teased.

Together, they walked back toward the castle. "I told Father I would never marry Valdemar."

Christian took hold of her hand. "I love you."

Amelia returned to the armory the next day. An unspoken

truce of sorts had been struck with her father, enough so that they could continue their work.

Once, Christian stuck his head inside the room. Amelia admired him for venturing into such hostile territory. What a mess they had gotten themselves into. She motioned to him with a black, paint-speckled hand.

"How do you fare today, Amelia?"

"Better. Work helps."

"I agree. Prayer is also good. After I quit feeling sorry for myself, I found peace."

"When did you quit feeling sorry for yourself?"

"When you kissed me yesterday."

Amelia blushed. Now that her insane anger was spent, she was embarrassed over her behavior. "I apologize for my forwardness. You must think I'm a—"

"I think you are a passionate woman. I was walking around in a daze until that kiss. But I still believe that we must give God a chance to work in this. I thought perhaps we could pray together."

"Now?"

He shrugged. "Such opportunities seldom arise." Christian tentatively reached out to touch her puffy sleeve. She gave him a nod, and Christian prayed. "Father. We have gone about things our own mindful way. Only because we love each other." He looked up from his prayer. "At least, I love you."

"I love you too," she whispered, feeling her face heat.

His face broke into a wide grin. Finally, he closed his eyes to continue. "We love each other and ask for Your forgiveness for our actions in the past. But please, Father, change Gerrard's heart. We need a miracle so that we can be married. We place our faith in You. Amen." Christian looked at her, then encircled her waist in his hands and whispered, "Have faith, Amelia."

She nodded and gave him a quick hug. *Ja.* I'll try."

Christian released her. "I must go. I love you."

"I love you," Amelia said, embarrassed at the newness of the spoken words.

She watched him go. Her mouth dropped open in horror. The door closed. She swallowed. Two black handprints splayed across the back of his doublet.

Christian left the castle and went to the practice field.

"You seem in a good mood," Leopold greeted.

"I'm at peace," Christian said.

"Faith?"

"Ja. It's hard, but God is my only hope." Christian turned away to assist in an exercise detail.

"Uh, Christian?"

He looked over his shoulder. "What?"

Leopold crooked his finger. "Come here." Christian backtracked. "I believe you have Amelia-prints on the back of your doublet. Unless you want Gerrard and every man here to know you've been embracing, I would suggest you remove your doublet."

Christian remembered Amelia's hug, and his face burned. But before he could do anything about the situation, his attention was riveted to yet another distraction. The watchman hollered, "Riders approaching!" Christian and his men hurried as one body toward the entrance gate. "It is William from the neighboring castle."

"Lower the bridge. Let them in!" Christian yelled.

Three riders crossed the bridge and entered the bailey,

reining in next to Christian. "Welcome," Christian said to his neighbors.

"We do not stay. But bring news."

Christian motioned his men away, except for his select few. "Tell us."

"We know that you keep the Dinkelsbühl armorer. He will want to know. Dinkelsbühl has been under siege by the Swedes for weeks."

Frowning under the terrible news, Christian thanked them for their trouble. As they rode away, he turned to his remaining men. "Assemble in the chapel. Leopold, come with me." They strode toward the armory. "Gerrard won't take this lightly with Nicolaus remaining in Dinkelsbühl. This may be the spark that starts the war we've been dreading."

When they reached their destination, Gerrard already stood in the open doorway, a wary expression on his face. Christian glanced at Amelia across the room. "I must speak with you in private."

"Is it about the riders?"

"*Ja*. And it concerns you."

Amelia rushed forward. "Something about the Swedes?"

"Tell us," Gerrard urged.

Giving Amelia another glance, Christian said, "Very well. The riders were from a neighboring estate. They say that Dinkelsbühl has been under siege by a very large company of Swedes for several weeks."

Amelia gasped and closed her eyes. Gerrard's face paled, and his hands formed fists at his side. "Nicolaus!"

"My men are assembling in the chapel. Will you join us?"

Gerrard huffed. "I need to leave. I must save Nicolaus."

"We need to work together." Christian usurped the right of

command. "We will pray first. Then we will draft a plan. This is how we do things at Engelturm." Instantly, Christian felt a pang of guilt. He had not handled his situation with Amelia that way. But God had forgiven him for that. Today was another day. He was thankful that God provided for new beginnings. His voice softened. "Will you join us?"

"Father?" Amelia urged.

Gerrard gave a jerky nod and strode silently after Christian and Leopold.

When they reached the chapel, Christian explained the situation to those he kept in confidence. "Let's pray. Search your own hearts and listen for counsel." He removed his hat and went to the altar to kneel down. Everyone followed suit and prayed in silence.

Time passed. With a semblance of peace about the situation, Christian stood and turned to face his men. He looked over the tiny assembly, forming his words when his gaze rested on Leopold. His cousin did not seem to be taking the matter seriously. It was not like him to act so foolish. His face was contorted, his mouth stretched to one side, and his head ticked hard against one shoulder. Next he gazed heavenward, frowned, and wagged his brow.

Christian frowned back. By now he was totally distracted. "You wish to speak?"

"Nein," Leopold replied, shaking his head.

Christian bit his lip in frustration. Then his gaze swept across the chapel, and he noticed a red-faced epidemic. He narrowed his brow in thought, then all of a sudden he comprehended the situation. With the serious nature of their problem, he had forgotten about Amelia's handprints on his doublet, which by now, every person in the room had discovered. He gave an expression that dared anyone to make a remark, removed and folded his doublet, and laid it over a stone bench. Leopold visibly relaxed. Christian did not chance a look in Amelia or Gerrard's direction. "I have a plan." Faces returned to normal hue, and a murmur spread through the chapel.

Christian continued, "We are far outnumbered. It would mean defeat to attack the Swedes, but if we could sneak into the city, we might be able to rescue Nicolaus. Once Nicolaus is safe, we will offer our services to the city's defense."

"Through the wall?" Gerrard's voice sounded rusty.

Christian nodded. *"Ja.* You have told me how you used water power."

Gerrard's face became animated. "My shop has access to the moat!" Amelia's eyes also lit with hope.

But the plan was fallible. Christian hoped for everyone's sake it did not fail. "We could sneak troops in but not horses. While some men would remain to aid the city, the rest would bring the Trittenbachs back to Engelturm for safekeeping. Reinforcements seem impossible. I cannot knock on castle doors, not knowing each man's stand. The neighbors that were kind enough to bring us the message did not even volunteer their help."

Ideas interchanged for the next hour. When they had discussed all that was necessary, Christian ordered, "Quickly, prepare for travel." His men filed out of the chapel, and Christian told Gerrard, "I am sorry this has happened. I am also sorry for the misunderstanding between us."

Gerrard dipped his head. "Everything seems hopeless."

"There is hope with God."

"Many people die in war. Faith is no guarantee."

"Ja. But I would rather face the worst with God. Without Him. . ." Christian shook his head. When Gerrard did not

reply, Christian instructed, "We'll take the armor and weapons that are ready. We ride in the morning. I must go. There is much to do."

"I will be in the armory getting things ready."

"I'll send you help."

"I'm going too," Amelia said.

"Nein!" both men wheeled about and shouted simultaneously.

"I am sorry to have become such a rebel, Father. But you cannot stop me." She turned to Christian. "If you all die, I do not want to live. I'm going."

Christian opened his mouth to speak, but Gerrard said, "I can use your help then. Let's go get started."

Christian watched them depart, Amelia's back straight as an arrow. Such courage. He wished his faith were as large as he professed it to be. In reality, their situation looked about as hopeless as jumping out of one of the castle windows that overlooked the cliffs and expecting a soft landing. But he reminded himself of *Opa's* verse, "The angel of the Lord encampeth round about them that fear him, and delivereth them."

Chapter 10

"How are you faring, Amelia?" Christian asked on the second night of their journey.

She drew her gaze away from the campfire and gave Christian a weak smile. "I give it no thought. My mind is so occupied with Nicolaus. . .and prayer."

"I admire your courage."

"Why? It is by your example I have discovered a strength in the Lord."

Christian's gaze swept across the camp: twenty-four men, thirty horses, and one supply wagon. "When this is over, I plan to tell you many things that are on my heart. But now is not the time for it. You do better to dwell on Christ. I hope you can get some sleep tonight."

"You too, Christian. *Danke.*"

Her brave, grateful attitude clutched Christian's heart and rekindled his mind to the urgency of their mission. Leaving Amelia by the fire, he searched out Gerrard and addressed him in a low, confidential tone. "Would you come with me?"

Gerrard gave a nod and followed. They rounded up Leopold and a few others and assembled on the far side of the supply wagon. "As you know, we will arrive at Dinkelsbühl tomorrow.

Let's go over our plans. Leopold, you will scout out the Swedes' camp and report back. I will take three men with me to slip into the city."

"Take me!" Gerrard said. "As your guide. We will have to find Nicolaus quickly. I know the city."

"Very well. And I will need two others." Several of the men volunteered, including Leopold. Christian shook his head at his cousin. "Not this time, my friend. You must stay back. If something happens to me, Engelturm is your responsibility. And I am placing Amelia under your protection."

Leopold reluctantly agreed. Christian chose two of his most trusted men from the other volunteers, then turned to Gerrard. "Do you have any advice for us?"

"Only that the opening in the wall is small. Are your men swimmers?"

The matter was discussed, and once all their plans were laid, Christian dismissed everyone to get some rest.

The next day they rose early and arrived at their destination in good speed. As planned, Leopold rode off to scout while everyone else occupied a wooded hill near Dinkelsbühl to wait. Finally Leopold returned, riding into the assembly, winded, and reining in his steed. The beast snorted, his muscles quivering as he settled under Leopold's control.

"The Swedes and city—over the next two rises. Something is happening. They're assembling now—at the Wörnitz Gate—to attack."

"Take charge here as we discussed," Christian grimly ordered.

Gerrard and those who would accompany Christian stepped forward. Amelia also rushed forth. She kissed her father on the cheek, and he embraced her. Next she turned to Christian. "Bring my brother back. I will pray for your safety."

"The Lord's will, we shall do it," Christian said, rallying his men. "Let's go." They mounted and galloped their horses nearly to the top of the next rise, then Christian turned one man back with their animals and they proceeded on foot.

Stealthily crouching ahead, while keeping under cover, they topped the hill and also climbed the next. On the crest, everyone lay flat and panted, peering below. The Swedish tents remained intact, but the camp was deserted. Beyond, just as Leopold had reported, mounted soldiers and foot soldiers alike were assembling outside the *Wörnitz Tor*. Christian could only imagine the carnage that would take place once the Swedes broke through the gate and into the city. He glanced at Gerrard. The armorer's face was drawn tight. With each passing moment, the chances of rescuing Nicolaus or even escaping with their own lives intact grew slimmer.

Christian pointed out the way, and everyone hunkered down to sneak past the enemy camp. At one point they had to drop to their bellies and crawl through the tall grass. They swam across the river, climbing out and over a muddy bank, then went back on their bellies to slither through the grass like snakes. When they came to the moat, they slid in quietly, keeping beneath its surface as much as possible. Gerrard led them to the arched opening behind his shop. Christian sucked in a deep breath, ducked under the water, and swam beneath the wall. His lungs felt like they might burst until he reached the other side. Gasping, he hoisted his chest up onto dry ground, wiped his eyes, and looked around. Not a person was in sight. Thankfully, he heaved himself the rest of the way out of the water and lay on his side, taking deep drafts of air while he waited for the others.

Gerrard soon drew up beside him, even more winded and

weak. "We made it," he sputtered. "Give me a little time—take you inside."

"We don't have much time," Christian reminded.

It was enough. Gerrard stood up on wobbly legs, still breathing heavily, and motioned them to follow him as he staggered toward the door that led into his personal quarters.

"Dry clothes," Christian mumbled, shivering. Gerrard hastened to a wardrobe and, with trembling hands, brought back several sets of clothing. But only he and Christian would leave the premises in search of Nicolaus.

When they stepped out into the street, Christian saw that with all the activity, no one would notice them. A loud upheaval sounded from the *Wörnitz Tor*. They fell into step with others hurrying in that direction. The city's soldiers lined the street. The council stood just inside the gate. Worming their way through the crowd, Christian and Gerrard caught bits and pieces of conversation.

"Council members now insist on surrender. . . ."

Two citizens argued loudly. "I still say we must remain true to the emperor. Surely, he'll be sending troops. . . ."

"There is not enough time. The Swedes are restless, and if we do not surrender, they will burn the city, kill the women and *kinder*, and imprison. . ."

The other man cursed. "They will do so anyway. We must fight."

"The city council has already decided, all three mayors. . . ."

A hush fell over those gathered as one of the mayors gave an order. Christian panicked. They must find Nicolaus now, for they were opening the gate! But it all happened too fast. The great *Wörnitz Tor* opened wide, and instantly, enemy troops poured inside.

Gerrard nudged Christian in the ribs and pointed frantically. "Nicolaus!" Christian saw him too. He rushed forward, but Nicolaus disappeared behind the crowd. They stopped and scanned the area. Something strange was happening. The Swedish troops had come to a halt. All eyes were riveted in one direction. On Nicolaus! And a throng of *kinder*. Singing children! Everyone watched the scene unfold, too shocked to prevent it from happening.

A Swedish officer rode to the front of the procession. He reined in and gazed over the city's elite. Squinting his eyes, he scanned the area to see who mocked them with song. But when he saw it was the children, he nearly lost his seat. A young girl led the choir of many who were not much more than infants.

"It's Lore Hurtin," Gerrard whispered and lunged forward in another desperate attempt to go after Nicolaus.

But Christian locked his arms beneath the older man's. "Wait! Not yet!" He felt Gerrard relent but continued to hold him fast. "What are they doing?" He watched in puzzlement over Gerrard's shoulder.

"Flowers," Gerrard croaked, breaking free from Christian. "They're giving the commander flowers." He placed both hands to the sides of his face, moaning. *"Ach,* Nicolaus, *Nein,* Nicolaus, *Nein."*

"Look at the colonel," Christian urged.

The colonel slowly dismounted and waited for Dinkelsbühl's tiny intercessors. They marched right up to the officer, singing, encircling him, their arms extended with fists of bouquets. Fräulein Hurtin curtsied and offered him her flowers. "Welcome. We beg your mercy." Each child filed past with his or her colorful gifts.

Gerrard gasped. Nicolaus stood straight and tall, looking up at the commander. "What is your name?" The officer asked in Swedish, but his German interpreter had taken position beside him to give aid.

"My name is Lore," the young girl replied.

"And yours?"

"My name is Nicolaus."

"I am Colonel Sperreuth, and I will do what you request." Christian heard the quick intake of gasps among the townsmen. The colonel then spoke something that only Nicolaus could hear and strode directly to his field commander. He swatted him in the chest with a bouquet of flowers. "Here. From the children." The interpreter translated the colonel's deep, gruff, "In memory of my own son, I urge you to take a gentle approach with these people."

"Yes, Sir," the flustered field commander replied.

A glad murmur spread among the German people. The town bells pealed, and the head mayor stepped forward to face the colonel. He bowed low. "May God repay your human kindness. All we can do is to thank you, to. . ."

Christian lost the rest of the mayor's address when someone from the crowd reached out and snatched one of the children to safety. Soon the little ones were all being drawn into the protective circle of their fellow Germans. "Quick, over there!" Christian tugged Gerrard's sleeve, and they made their way to the children. Nicolaus was one of the last to leave the street, but when he did, Christian clasped him tight about the waist and whisked him up into his arms. He covered the boy's mouth with his hand. "Be quiet!" he whispered and hurried back through the crowd toward Gerrard's shop.

Christian glanced down once. Nicolaus's eyes were wide

and round. He smiled and removed his hand, shifting him onto his hip. The boy's legs clasped around him, and his hands clung to Christian's clothing. When they reached the armory, the shop door swung open, and the three of them hurried through. Christian set Nicolaus down in the midst of his men.

Gerrard snatched him to his chest and hugged him so hard Christian thought the poor boy couldn't breathe. "Son. Ah, Son. Right in the midst of it you had to be." Tears washed down the father's creased face.

"When did you return, Father? Did you see me speak to the colonel?"

Christian hated to disrupt their reunion, but he knew the Swedes could come bursting through the door any moment.

"We're taking you to Engelturm, Nicolaus. Are you up to it?"

"*Ja*. But I didn't see your horse."

"He's waiting for us outside the city. Ready, Gerrard?"

The armorer nodded. "*Ja*. Of course, we must not delay." He pulled Nicolaus toward the back of the house, then stopped. "I must write a note to Frau Hurtin so she knows Nicolaus is with us."

"Hurry," Christian said impatiently.

Gerrard hastened to get paper, scribbled something, and left it on their table. "Will she find it here?"

"*Ja*, Father. Let's go," Nicolaus urged. "I want to see Christian's castle."

Christian chuckled. Pounding shook the shop door, and instantly he sobered. As it opened, creaking filled the room. "Go!" He pushed Gerrard. "I will detain them. Be off and hurry!" Christian's men quickly obeyed and swept Gerrard and Nicolaus out the back. Christian strode toward the shop.

"Halt!" a Swede ordered.

Christian froze. But when he looked closer, he recognized the face. The other man's expression also shone with recollection. "Ah! We meet again," he said in German. "Who do you have back there?"

Another Swede pushed Christian aside and started forward. An argument erupted between the two soldiers. Christian watched for a chance to flee, yet he didn't wish to lead them to the others. Would they be outside the wall yet? Finally the argument stopped, and the one soldier stomped off and left the shop entirely. "Seems you got your way," Christian said, giving the remaining soldier a lopsided smile.

"He thought you were hiding someone and wanted to take you prisoner. But I wish to repay a debt. Once you trusted me. So now I return the favor." He shrugged. "After this, I cannot promise your safekeeping."

"It is enough."

The soldier gave a stiff nod, pivoted, and strode from the shop before Christian could even thank him. And Christian fled out the back.

Amelia paced. What was taking so long? Leopold had sent out a scout, but even he had not returned. She should have managed to go with them, somehow. What if they had all been captured? She would not even entertain the thought that something worse might have occurred. She jerked her head up when she saw Leopold charge forward. *Ja!* It was a rider! She scrambled after Leopold. But it was only the scout. Still, his face was flushed with excitement.

"They come! They come!"

"Nicolaus?" Amelia asked, straining toward man and beast.

"Do they have Nicolaus?" Leopold stretched forth an arm to keep her a safe distance from the high-strung horse.

"Easy, Amelia."

Ja! The boy is along!" the scout shouted gleefully. "I'll go back with their horses!"

"Quick then!" Leopold ordered. "Everyone mount! Let's ride." He grabbed Amelia's arm, pulled her along toward the wagon, and helped her aboard. She looked back over her shoulder. "Don't worry. They'll catch up." Soon he urged the freshly harnessed team forward. Their wagon led the pace of the party's departure.

Even as Amelia rejoiced over Nicolaus's liberation, she worried about all of her friends and loved ones who still remained in Dinkelsbühl. She breathed up a prayer for them. Her world, of late, had been tipped, but she was holding steady for she had discovered a relationship with Jesus. So many things had gone wrong, but finding Jesus was right. As her thoughts ran to and fro, the whirl of passing trees, the bumpy gait—too fast for a wagon—and the deep longing for Nicolaus all blended together to encase her in a haze. She did not know how much time passed before she heard the men cheering.

Leopold slowed the wagon just enough so that Christian could deposit Nicolaus with Amelia. She leaned forward and scooped him into her arms and squeezed. "Oh, Nicolaus! I am so relieved—so happy to have you here." She did not loosen her grip until he began to squirm.

His eyes shone bright. "I got to ride Champion! And I spoke to the colonel. He was not even scary."

Amelia gave him another squeeze. "Let's get you out of your wet clothes and wrap you in this blanket. Then you can tell me all about it."

Nicolaus was still chattering about his adventure at the evening meal, where Gerrard had invited Christian to sit with them, apart from the others.

"And we had to swim under the wall. I always wanted to do that, but Father would never allow it. And Count von Engel kept his promise too. He let me ride Champion."

"*Ja.* The count kept his promise to me too," Gerrard interrupted.

"What promise is that, Father?" Amelia asked.

"More than one, actually. He promised from the beginning that he only meant to watch out for your welfare, Amelia. And that he would prove himself worthy of my respect. Now, I owe him beyond what can ever be repaid."

Christian cast a longing look at Amelia. She was all he wanted.

Gerrard arched a brow. "Matters have changed, you know. Since the city's surrender, Valdemar no longer has any hold over us. You once asked me for Amelia's hand."

"You mean we c–can. . . ?" Christian stammered.

"*Ja.* I give you my blessing. But now you must ask her."

Nicolaus's eyes narrowed. "What does Herr Valdemar have to do with anything?" Suddenly his face lit with understanding. "Are you going to marry my sister?"

"I hope so," Christian said, his gaze feasting on Amelia. "First I must ask her."

Gerrard cleared his throat. "Come, Nicolaus, let's go see how Leopold and the others fare."

"*Ja.* Let's tell him about the army, and. . ."

Once they were left alone, Christian closed the distance

to Amelia. They stood facing each other, and he enveloped her hand. "I did not plan to ask you here like this. I wanted to wait until we were at Engelturm, to take you on a stroll through the gallery, pausing by Mother's wooden chest. It seemed appropriate."

"And what would you say, Christian?"

"I would say that I love you above all others. That I want you to be my wife, to hold and cherish forever. I would ask you to be my countess."

"I remember the chest, Christian. *Ja,* perhaps we should wait until we get to Engelturm. Of course, there's always the chance that Father might take back his blessing, and. . ." Her eyes twinkled.

Christian leaned forward. "Enough! Will you marry me?"

"*Ja.* You know I will." Amelia hugged him in such wild abandonment that Christian nearly lost his balance.

He clamped his eyes closed for a moment in a heartfelt prayer of thanks. When he opened them and looked down into hers, her loveliness stirred him, just as it had at their first meeting. Only there was no rusty visor to separate their faces. He tilted his lowered head and tasted her lips.

"Amelia!" Nicolaus shouted. They drew apart. "Does this mean I'm going to live at Engelturm?"

"One thing at a time, Son," Gerrard said, appearing out of the shadows from behind Nicolaus. "And the next thing that I must do is ask your sister to forgive me. Will you, Amelia?"

She went to her father. "I already have."

Christian gently touched the child's shoulder. "And I have not yet thanked Nicolaus for saving the city." He felt Nicolaus shrug beneath his hand.

"At first I did not think Lore's idea was worth a rat's

whisker. But then Lore explained to me what you meant when you said the sword should be one's last wreck horse." Nicolaus smacked his forehead with his small hand. "But I can't believe it worked."

"Wreck horse?" Gerrard asked.

"Recourse," Christian clarified. Everyone laughed until their sides hurt. "Nicolaus, what exactly did Colonel Sperreuth say to you?" Christian asked.

"He said that I reminded him of his little boy. He just died, and the colonel is sad."

"That explains things," Gerrard said. "It was a miracle that he spared the city and did not harm its citizens. God has been good to us this day."

Christian scooped Nicolaus up into his arms. "When we return to Engelturm, I shall throw a party to celebrate Nicolaus's bravery and to announce our wedding plans. What do you think?"

Nicolaus pumped his arm into the air. *"Ja!"*

Christian chuckled and slipped his other arm around Amelia's waist so he could whisper into her ear. "And as soon as we are alone, my dear, I have many wonderful things to discuss with you."

DIANNE CHRISTNER

Dianne and her husband make their home in Scottsdale, Arizona, where Dianne enjoys the beauty of the desert. They have two grown children. Her first book, *Proper Intentions*, was published 1994, and she has three other historical novels to her credit. Visitors are welcomed at her web page: www.diannechristner.com

The Nuremberg Angel

by Irene B. Brand

Be not forgetful to entertain strangers:
for thereby some have entertained angels unawares.
HEBREWS 13:2

Chapter 1

Trenton, New Jersey, 1776–77

Hoping to avoid the German soldiers who had occupied Trenton during the night, Comfort Foster slipped quietly from the hospital and hurried across the backyard to the family home. Oliver Foster had never allowed his daughter to enter the hospital before, but he'd needed help this morning with feeding the convalescing soldiers under his care. With the approach of the enemy, the three Patriot soldiers who'd been assisting her father had returned to the Continental army.

To discourage any impropriety from the soldiers, Comfort had disguised herself as a middle-aged woman. Powdered hair, pock marks on her face made with dye, a pair of clouded spectacles, a matron's cap, an untidy dress, and a feigned rheumatic limp had fooled the patients as she'd served their gruel. Proud of her ingenuity, Dr. Foster assured her no one would suspect that beneath her outlandish costume was a petite eighteen-year-old brunette with extraordinary brown eyes full of life and a rosy mouth set in a delicate, yet strong face.

Entering the back door of their stone house, Comfort started upstairs to check on her younger sister, Erin, when a knock sounded at the front door. With the town full of enemy soldiers, Comfort was tempted to ignore the caller. When a more demanding summons followed, Comfort walked across the kitchen floor and cautiously cracked open the door.

The biggest man she'd ever seen in her life towered over her. With a gasp, she slammed the door in his face and dropped the latch. *A Hessian soldier!* With pulse racing, Comfort backed up to the door, knowing the flimsy hasp would be a feeble defense if he tried to force his way in. She needed to warn her father, but she shouldn't leave Erin alone in the house. Her chest heaved in anxiety as she remembered the things her brother, Marion, had said about the ferocity of these foreign soldiers George III had imported to crush the colonial rebellion.

He tapped again, and the sound seemed as loud as a thunderclap. The possibility of molestation flooded her mind, and Comfort started shaking.

"Go away!" she cried in an agitated voice.

"Frau Foster." His words came clearly through the wooden door. "I mean you no harm." In spite of her fear, Comfort detected sincerity in his composed voice. How strange that a German soldier spoke English with only a slight burr in his smooth voice!

"Frau Foster," he persisted, "are you still there?"

She didn't answer.

"I have a paper that explains why I'm here. Please take it."

"God, protect me," she whispered, then lifted the latch and opened the door an inch, fully expecting him to force his way into the house. Instead, a thin piece of paper was extended through the opening. She grabbed it and latched the door again. It was a document ordering the Foster family to house and feed one Hessian soldier.

"Will you wait until I bring my father?"

"*Ja,*" he answered.

Comfort ran lightly across the backyard to the log hospital, opened the door, and called her father, who was inspecting the poultice on a soldier's leg. Perhaps the tone of Comfort's voice alarmed him, for her father jumped to his feet and came to her immediately.

"There's a Hessian soldier at the house with this paper ordering us to shelter and feed him."

Father's haggard face paled, and his sensitive lips straightened as he scanned the paper. Her father was a kindhearted man, dedicated to saving lives, and it startled Comfort when a savage look overspread his face.

"I won't have this man in our house with you and Erin at his mercy. I should have sent you out of town when I heard the enemy army was approaching."

"He said he won't hurt us, and I believe he's telling the truth."

As they neared the back stoop, Father scanned Comfort's untidy appearance. "If we have to take this man in, you stay in your disguise. Erin's probably safe enough, but you might be bothered."

When Father jerked open the door to confront the Hessian, Comfort was reminded of Goliath and David. Short and slender, her father was wearing gray woolen breeches, woven stockings tucked into his heavy shoes, and a loose-fitting coat over his blouse.

The soldier must have been seven feet tall. A high, miter-shaped brass cap adorned with scrolls and heraldic emblems on the front fit snugly on his head. He wore a long, medium blue wool coat with turned-back skirts. White buttons splashed down the front of the pink-lined coat, and its collar, cuffs, and lapels were made of the same rich color. The soldier's white waistcoat was long and belted. His breeches were tight, fitted into black gaiters with brass buttons, and tucked into thick leather boots. A short-sword was strapped at his side.

The magnificence of the man overwhelmed Comfort, and she drew a quick breath. She felt like a dowdy sparrow in the presence of a bird of paradise.

The two men locked gazes for several moments, each measuring the intent of the other, until her father stepped back and motioned the visitor inside the large kitchen. The Hessian bent almost double to get through the door. He removed his pointed headgear, revealing fair skin and light hair and lowering his height by several inches.

Hearing five-year-old Erin coming down the steps, Comfort moved into the back room and held a hand to her lips. She hid Erin behind her skirts and moved into an unobtrusive corner that provided a view into the kitchen where the two men stood.

"My name is Nicolaus Trittenbach."

"We aren't equipped to take in visitors, Mr. Trittenbach," Father said in a steely voice. Comfort admired his courage.

"Nicolaus. Call me Nicolaus, please."

"I'm Doctor Foster. I'm not willing for you to stay here."

"I apologize for intruding, Doctor Foster." The soldier's voice was even, but Comfort sensed he was uneasy, for he fingered the powder pouch attached to his belt. "Colonel Johann Rall commands three Hessian infantry regiments, fourteen hundred men in all, occupying a ten-mile stretch along the Delaware. The town's barracks won't accommodate half that many soldiers, so Colonel Rall is billeting the rest of the troops in private homes. If you turn me away, your family may be evicted and your home confiscated for the army's use. I won't cause you any trouble."

Father glanced at the paper in his hand. "It seems I have no choice; but I have two daughters living in this house, and I demand that you respect them."

Was it anger or a flush of embarrassment darkening Nicolaus's face?

"I won't cause any trouble," he repeated.

Their father motioned Comfort and Erin into the room. He placed his hand on Erin's tousled hair. "This is the baby of the family, Erin." He gestured toward Comfort. "My other daughter, Comfort, is the hostess of my house and will see to your needs."

Nicolaus bowed from the waist. "I'll return this afternoon."

"We'll do our best to make you comfortable, Mr. Trittenbach," Comfort said.

Nicolaus darted a quick glance at Comfort. Had he detected that her voice was out of character with the rest of her appearance?

Comfort had estimated that the soldier was about their father's age, but he flashed a smile that revealed youthful lines in his somber face.

"Call me Nicolaus, please."

His beaming smile flustered Comfort, and she didn't know what to say, but she nodded assent.

When the door closed behind Nicolaus, Comfort and her father stared at one another in dismay.

"What are we going to do with him?" Comfort whispered. "Put him in one of the attic rooms?"

Father shook his head. "Not with you and Erin sleeping up

there. Prepare my room for him, and I'll sleep upstairs."

He peered out the room's only window. "I see soldiers everywhere. I'm not easy in my mind about this man, but what else can I do? I can't oppose the whole German army." Awkwardly, he cleared his throat. "You do understand why you must be on guard all the time, don't you?"

Comfort felt her cheeks grow hot. "I'll be cautious; but, Father, I don't believe he'll harm us. We must be kind to him." She dropped to her knees beside her sister.

"Erin, remember that we've been invaded by the enemy. You stay with me all the time."

Wide-eyed, Erin promised, "I will."

"Good advice," their father said. "For the time being, stay away from the hospital. I'll find other help. But for your own protection, keep wearing that outfit to disguise your youth." He opened the door, peered up and down Queen Street, then whispered in Comfort's ear. "Washington is gathering his army on the other side of the river, so the Hessians may not be here long."

After their father went back to work, Comfort stirred the fire, for a chill had crept into the kitchen.

"How about a piece of gingerbread, Sister?" she asked, motioning Erin to the warmth of the fire. "I haven't had time to prepare corn cakes this morning."

"I like gingerbread," Erin said, climbing up onto a stool near the fire.

"Marion bought this gingerbread from Mr. Ludwick. Just imagine, our German neighbor from Philadelphia showing up in Trenton as a baker for the Continental army."

Chewing slowly on the gingerbread, Erin asked, "Who's Mr. Ludwick?"

"Oh, I keep forgetting you were born after we moved to Trenton. Mr. Ludwick came from Germany several years ago and set up a bakery in Philadelphia. He soon became known as the Gingerbread Baker, and Mother used to buy his products."

Comfort set a bowl of porridge on the table. "You finish eating while I prepare Father's room for our visitor."

The bedroom was cold, so Comfort placed fresh logs in the fireplace and started the fire. She carried her father's clothes and other belongings upstairs. She swept the wooden floor until no trace of dust was evident. She fluffed the straw mattress, arranged fresh sheets and blankets, then covered the bed with a colorful quilt her mother had made. She pulled her father's favorite chair close to the fireplace, took a bayberry candle from the cabinet, and placed it on a table beside the chair. She arranged a pitcher of water and a bowl of soft soap on a cabinet with other personal necessities and surveyed her preparations. The room should provide a pleasant haven for Nicolaus.

As she worked, Comfort contemplated her reaction to having the soldier in their home. One of the complaints voiced against the king of England in the Declaration of Independence, passed a few months ago, was the king's importation of foreign mercenaries to complete the death and destruction already started in the Colonies by the British. According to her brother, Marion, a soldier in the Continental army, the Hessians had no mercy on their enemies, and his hints of how they mistreated women had alarmed Comfort. She should be frightened to have a Hessian living in their house, but she wasn't.

When Nicolaus had been talking to her father, Comfort had watched him closely. She'd detected a hint of loneliness, perhaps homesickness, in the steady gaze of his dark blue eyes. Considering his generous, kindly mouth and the tenderness of his voice, she didn't believe Nicolaus would be cruel to anyone.

Comfort contemplated the Colonists' efforts to gain independence from Great Britain as she mixed bread dough. Was freedom an impossible dream? The American soldiers had been defeated in almost every battle, and even now, Washington's army had retreated across the Delaware River, leaving New York and New Jersey in the hands of the British.

After she placed five loaves of bread in the oven to the left of the kitchen fireplace, Comfort hung a pot of cabbage pudding on the crane. To complete the meal, she cut the top off a small pumpkin, removed the seeds and pulp, spooned a mixture of sugar, butter, and nutmeg into the opening, placed the top back on the pumpkin, and covered it with hot ashes.

While Erin took a nap, Comfort prayed, asking God to protect her family. Jesus had said, "Love your enemies." And when He'd been teaching how His followers could be recognized, He said, "I was a stranger, and ye took me in." And she recalled another Bible verse that cautioned, "Be not forgetful to entertain strangers: for thereby some have entertained angels unawares."

If Comfort understood these Scriptures correctly, it was her Christian duty to entertain Nicolaus as she would treat Jesus if He came to her door. But by midafternoon, when his hesitant knock sounded and Comfort opened the door to admit Nicolaus, she wondered fleetingly if that was the only reason she smiled brightly and said, "Welcome to our home, Nicolaus."

He stepped inside, a hint of uncertainty in his gentle blue eyes. When his lips parted in an apologetic smile, Comfort knew that Nicolaus would never seem like an enemy to her.

Chapter 2

A large leather bag hung from Nicolaus's shoulder, and he carried a flintlock musket with a bayonet. Her father was opposed to firearms in the house, but Comfort knew she mustn't protest.

She pointed to the bedroom. "You may put your belongings in there," she said. With Erin hanging on her skirts, impeding her progress, Comfort moved to the doorway.

"I hope you'll be comfortable here," she said as he walked past her into the room.

Nicolaus's incredulous glance swept over the neat, pleasant room. *"Nein! Nein!* I didn't expect this luxury," he protested. "I'm not used to it. I won't misplace any of your family. I'll sleep on the floor somewhere."

"Father told me to prepare this room for you."

"You humble me," Nicolaus protested. "I'm an intruder, and you're treating me like a guest."

A slight smile touched Comfort's lips. "But you're under orders from Colonel Rall, just as we are. I do not blame you personally."

"Then I'll accept your hospitality, but I'm not worthy of it. *Danke schön.*"

From her association with Christopher Ludwick, Comfort recognized these words as "thanks very much."

He stood uncertainly in the center of the room. "You may join us in the kitchen whenever you wish to," Comfort said, pulling the door shut behind her.

Dumbfounded, Nicolaus lowered his long frame to the wooden chair and stretched his sturdy legs toward the warmth of the fire. He'd expected nothing more than a cubbyhole, but the Fosters had given him this comfortable room. He'd been invited to enjoy the fellowship of the family circle by sharing their meals.

"Danke, Gott," he prayed, "for providing a refuge in this foreign land." He thought of his favorite psalm and quoted softly, " 'Thou preparest a table before me in the presence of mine enemies.' "

The last two months of fighting and marching had been rough, and Nicolaus welcomed the opportunity to relax for a few minutes. Taking advantage of the first privacy he'd experienced since he'd left his homeland six months ago, Nicolaus reflected on the circumstances that had brought him to this place.

When his parents died, his oldest brother had inherited the land, so there seemed nothing he could do except become a career soldier. He'd accepted that as his destiny until he'd received a letter from a kinsman, Christopher Ludwick, who had served for years in the German army and navy. On a voyage to America, Christopher had visited Philadelphia and liked it enough to settle there. His glowing report of the advantages of living in America had started Nicolaus wondering if his own fortune lay in the American colonies.

When the British asked Hesse's ruler, Frederick II, to provide troops to fight in America, Nicolaus had volunteered. If his reception in the Foster home was indicative of the treatment he could expect in this country, he didn't want to return to Hesse.

Since he'd considered cutting ties with his homeland, before he left Germany, Nicolaus made a nostalgic pilgrimage to two ancestral sites. He'd heard all of his life about the village of Dinkelsbühl, where Nicolaus Trittenbach, for whom he'd been named, had lived as a child. It had been rewarding to walk the streets where his ancestor had played many years earlier. He'd then traveled to Engelturm, a castle in the Black Forest, where the first Nicolaus had received his training for knighthood. The castle had been partially destroyed in the Seven Years' War, twenty years earlier, but he welcomed the opportunity to ride along forest paths his ancestor might have enjoyed before he became a landowner in Hesse.

The warmth of the room eased Nicolaus's tired body, and he dozed. The face of Comfort Foster floated in his subconscious mind. How old was she? This morning, she'd walked like a tired, aged woman; but this afternoon, while her face still showed the marks of maturity, she'd moved freely without limping at all.

A slight tapping disturbed Nicolaus's slumber.

"Nicolaus," a childish voice said.

He roused and hurried to open the door. Erin spoke around the finger she held in the corner of her mouth. "Sister says come to eat."

"*Danke schön.* I'll be there shortly."

Nicolaus removed his sword and heavy coat and hung them on the rack in the corner. The Hessians had been warned to stay armed at all times, but he wouldn't abuse the Foster hospitality by wearing weapons to their table. He pushed his hair back from his forehead and unwrapped the black cloth from the foot-long thin strip of hair hanging over his back. He laid a heavy log on the dwindling fire before he entered the kitchen.

Wishing she could have entertained Nicolaus in more pleasing garments, Comfort had put on a clean overskirt and straightened the muslin cap on her camouflaged hair. She wondered how long such a mediocre disguise could fool Nicolaus.

"Father can't leave the hospital right now. Please be seated," she added, motioning to the table, where only one place was laid.

Hesitating, Nicolaus said, "Have you already had your meal?"

"No. I'll serve you. Erin and I will eat later."

"I'd be pleased if you'd share the meal with me. Or would your father object?"

"I don't know." *Be not forgetful to entertain strangers.* A biblical admonition? Should she ignore it?

Hearing Erin's approach, Comfort made a quick decision. "Come, Erin, we'll join Nicolaus at his meal." She tied a large towel over Erin's dress and helped her up on a high stool.

"Would you like a cup of cider, Nicolaus? Cider is a specialty of the region. We have lots of apple orchards in Trenton."

"Ja. Danke."

Comfort filled a mug with cider. She heaped large servings of cabbage pudding and baked pumpkin on Nicolaus's plate and passed him a wooden tray holding freshly baked bread. Erin, normally talkative, was subdued in Nicolaus's presence; but she kept eyeing him, finding him of more interest than her food.

Finally, Erin said, "That funny hat made a red streak on

your face." She leaned forward and traced the indentation on his forehead. "Why'd you wear it?"

A smile lit Nicolaus's face, and he touched Erin's little round nose with his long, delicately tapered finger. "To make me look taller and meaner than I actually am to scare saucy little girls."

Erin nodded seriously. "You scared me when you came this morning, but I'm not afraid of you now."

He tenderly touched Erin's brown hair. "You don't have to be afraid of me, but. . ." He hesitated as if he were choosing his words carefully. "There are many *soldaten* in Trenton now, and you might need to be afraid of some of them. You and your sister shouldn't go out in town unless I'm with you." He looked piercingly at Comfort. "Do you understand?"

"Yes. Maybe I shouldn't ask this, but how long will your troops stay in Trenton?"

He smiled. "That depends on your general Washington, but right now, it looks as if we'll be here all winter."

"It's obvious I can't stay in the house that long, so Erin and I will welcome your escort when we go to the market or to worship services."

"I've been assigned midnight-to-dawn sentry duty, so I can accompany you during the daytime." He turned back to Erin and said teasingly, "Now I'll tell you the real reason for our brass hats. I'm a grenadier, a member of a company that was formed a hundred years ago when soldiers tossed grenades in battle and wore soft, floppy headgear. They couldn't throw the grenades without knocking off their hats, so the heavy helmet I wear was designed to take care of that problem. We don't use grenades anymore, but brass hats are still part of our uniform."

"Marion told me that all German soldiers are seven feet

tall and have two sets of teeth."

"Erin!" Comfort reproved. "Don't repeat things Marion said."

"And who's Marion?"

"Our brother," Comfort explained.

"Erin," Nicolaus said, "a lot of reports about the Hessians are untrue, just as I imagine that some of the things our troops have been told about Americans are false."

"What, for instance?" Comfort asked, surprised.

"That Americans are savages and cannibals," Nicolaus said, a humorous glint in his blue eyes. "And that we should kill them as fast as we can if we don't want to be captured and eaten alive."

"Oooo," Erin said.

"That isn't true," Comfort protested. "Some Indians are reported to be cannibals, but I even doubt that."

"Our commanders often give the troops false or, at least, exaggerated information to get us to fight fiercely. I suspect American leaders do the same thing."

"Nicolaus, I'm surprised at your excellent command of the English language."

"My mother was English, and she taught me. Knowing English has proven beneficial on this assignment. I've been helpful to our commanders, as well as the common soldiers, who can't speak English."

"Comfort is teaching me my letters," Erin said, "but I don't know any German words."

"Then I'll teach you some."

Comfort stood, saying, "While you're having a German lesson, I'll clear away the supper dishes."

Nicolaus jumped to his feet. "I'll help. I don't want to cause you any extra work."

"You'll be helping if you keep Erin occupied," Comfort assured him.

Nicolaus sat again and pointed to the general family room behind the kitchen. "Such a room in our home is called a *scheff*."

Erin rolled her tongue around the word several times, but she couldn't get it right.

"Let's try an easier word. The German word for friend is *freund*. I would like to be your *freund*, Erin."

"*Freund!*" Erin tried the word, and she appeared disappointed when the pronunciation didn't sound the way Nicolaus said it.

"German isn't an easy language to learn," he encouraged, "but you can learn it. Since Christmas is only two weeks away, why don't we learn some Christmas words? In my homeland of Hesse, we have big celebrations at Christmastime."

"Our family has never observed Christmas," Comfort said. "We had Puritan ancestors a generation or so back, and their beliefs came down through the family. Celebrating Christmas is anti-Christian, isn't it?"

"Not to Germans. Why, it was our countryman, Martin Luther, who encouraged the children to learn the song 'Away in a Manger' for Christmas festivities. Do you know that song?"

"I've never heard it," Comfort answered, "but we do sing Luther's 'A Mighty Fortress Is Our God.'"

Drawing his chair closer to Erin, Nicolaus said, "Someday, I'll teach you to sing the song, but now I'd like to tell you about Martin Luther." He glanced toward Comfort. "That is, if your sister has no objection."

He noticed that Comfort wasn't limping now. She moved between the hearth and the table, taking care of the chores, as sprightly as a youth. The woman mystified him.

"Erin loves stories."

"Martin Luther was a great preacher, but he was also a family man, happiest when he gathered his children around him and taught them to sing. 'Away in a Manger' was a favorite of his son, Hans."

Erin listened intently to Nicolaus and clapped her hands when he finished. "Sing the song, Nicolaus, sing the song."

"Erin, you've bothered our guest enough for today. If he goes on duty at midnight, he needs to rest."

Nicolaus wondered if that was Comfort's way of telling him he'd overstayed his welcome, so he said, "Just one verse, Erin, and then I must go to my room. My mother taught me the English words, but I can't recall them at the moment. I'll sing a few lines in my native language."

He stood, somewhat awkwardly, as if embarrassed to be performing, but Comfort's hands paused at her work as she listened to his mellow baritone.

"Weg in einem manger, legte keine Krippe fü ein Bett der kleine Herr Jesus seinen süssen Kopf nieder; der Sterne im Himmel schauten unten, wo er den der kleine Herr Jesus legt, schlafend auf dem Heu."

"That was beautiful," Comfort said. "We'll look forward to learning the song. Perhaps you can sing it at our church."

"Would I be welcome at your services?"

"I really don't know," Comfort admitted. "But since you're one of the conquerors, I don't suppose anyone could stop you from entering if you wanted to."

"I'd rather not be called a conqueror. Our ruler hires his army to any country that needs us. On the battlefield, I have enemies, but I don't have hatred toward the citizens." He started toward his room. "Since there's an outside door from my room, I won't be bothering you as I come and go at night. *Danke* for the tasty meal—I haven't had any food like that since my mother died. It's good of you to make me welcome."

He paused in the doorway. *"Gute Nacht,* Erin," he said; and when the child looked mystified, he translated the words into English. "Good night."

"Good night, *freund,*" Erin answered, her face alight with happiness.

Chapter 3

Comfort put the leftover food in a cupboard and hung a pot of porridge on the crane to cook through the night. She added extra logs to the fire to keep the embers alive until morning, then she and Erin went upstairs to their bed and snuggled together under several comforters. Heat from the fireplace, filtering through the cracks in the ceiling, took the chill off the room.

Their bed was directly above the room Nicolaus occupied. After Erin slept, Comfort's thoughts dwelt on the enemy in their house. He seemed like a gentle man, so why had he taken up soldiering? She'd heard that many German rulers drafted their men and sold their services to other countries, so perhaps Nicolaus didn't have a choice.

In his words, she'd detected a warning that not all of the Hessians were as harmless as he, so there was more than one reason for her to wear a disguise. Still, she wished Nicolaus could see her as she really was.

Comfort was still awake when her father came into the house.

"Are you awake, Comfort?" Father whispered at the opening between the two attic rooms.

She eased out of bed and followed him to the cot he'd laid across the landing of the stairway.

"How'd it go?"

"All right. He has picket duty at midnight, but I don't believe he's left the house yet."

"How's his behavior?"

"He's courteous, and Erin likes him. He's going to teach her to speak German. His mother was English, so that's why he speaks our language so well."

"I've heard reports that some of the soldiers have looted Patriots' houses. And a few women have been insulted."

"That's probably true, for Nicolaus suggested that Erin and I shouldn't leave the house unless he's with us."

"Well, thank God for sending a gentleman among us." He paused, a speculative gleam in his eyes. "If Nicolaus is that friendly, perhaps you can learn British plans, and we can send them to General Washington."

"I won't spy on a guest in our household," Comfort said coldly.

"I hardly consider Nicolaus a guest. We didn't invite him to come here."

"But he's offered to protect us from his fellow soldiers, and I won't repay that courtesy by betraying his trust. I favor American independence as much as you do, but the Continental army will have to wage war without my help."

She went back to her room and got into bed beside Erin. Why had her father's suggestion made her so indignant? She didn't remember she'd ever before talked to her father in that tone of voice. Nicolaus was only a brief diversion in her life, so she shouldn't antagonize her father by treating Nicolaus as more than an unwanted visitor.

Comfort was preparing Father's breakfast the next morning when she heard Nicolaus enter his room. When her father sat at the table, she whispered, "Do you want to invite Nicolaus to eat with you?"

Father turned an angry face toward her. "No. They can make me house an enemy, but they can't force me to eat with him."

Remembering her decision of the night before, Comfort said no more. Without answering, she placed bread and preserves and a bowl of porridge on the table for her father. She brought him a cup of warm cider from the hearth. Then she prepared a similar tray for Nicolaus and carried it to his door. He had no doubt heard her father's comments, and she was embarrassed. She knocked on the door, and she heard his steps approaching.

"Here's your breakfast," she said. His eyes were weary from lack of sleep. "Would you like some coffee? We keep coffee beans on hand."

"Nein, danke. I'll drink water from the pitcher in my room."

He took the plate from her, nodded kindly, and closed the door. He probably didn't expect any better treatment, but she did wish her father hadn't voiced his opinion so loudly. Comfort sat across from her father and nibbled on a slice of bread spread with plum preserves. She poured hot water over tea leaves. Although the beverage wasn't popular in the Colonies since that ruckus over the tea tax in Boston a few years ago, Comfort still liked to start her day with a cup of tea.

Her father wouldn't meet her gaze, and she knew he was sorry for the remark he'd made, but she expected no apology either to her or to Nicolaus.

Comfort tried to work quietly so she wouldn't interrupt Nicolaus's sleep, but Erin pestered her all morning, wanting to talk to him. After their father's comment, she didn't believe Nicolaus would voluntarily come into their living quarters, and she didn't know if she should invite him. What would Father do if he came into the house and caught her and Erin eating with Nicolaus?

She took Erin into the room behind the kitchen and wrote a few sums on the slate for the child to tally. Then she read a chapter of the Bible aloud and helped Erin learn a few of the words. Their mother had taught both Marion and Comfort to read, and she was passing that meager knowledge along to Erin.

Comfort had a pot of vegetable stew simmering over the fire, and when it was almost time to eat the midafternoon meal, she hadn't heard anything from Nicolaus. She gave Erin permission to knock on his door, but he didn't answer.

Later, when she heard his steps in the other room, she called, "Nicolaus, we'll be eating in a short while."

He opened the door and stood on the threshold. "I went to the barracks. I ate something there."

Comfort didn't meet his gaze. "I'm sorry you heard what my father said."

Nicolaus shrugged his shoulders. "I understand his attitude."

Erin ran in from the back room. "Come, Nicolaus," she said, grabbing his hand. "I want to hear more stories."

Nicolaus looked pointedly at Comfort. "Perhaps she can come to my room."

"I don't want to defy my father," Comfort said, "but I think he's sorry for what he said. If you prefer to eat in your room, I'll serve you there, but Father didn't say you couldn't eat in the kitchen. Until he does, I don't see why you can't come to the table for your meals."

"C'mon," Erin said, tugging on his hand, but she couldn't budge him. "Time to eat."

"I promised not to cause you any trouble," Nicolaus said, scanning Comfort's face for signs of anxiety. He wished she would remove the clouded spectacles so he could see her eyes. But her even white teeth were evident as she smiled, a gesture that eased his loneliness.

"We'll face that trouble if and when it comes," she said. "Erin has been pestering me all morning to have you tell her a story."

Capitulating, he swooped Erin up in his arms, and she squealed as he strode into the kitchen.

"But there'll be no stories until we've eaten," Comfort said in mock severity. "I've made a pot of stew, and I expect it to be eaten."

While they ate, Comfort said, "I've never lived in a city occupied by the enemy, so what should I expect to happen?"

"Contrary to what you've heard, Hessians don't wage war on women and children. However, there are always a few self-willed soldiers; and if they get drunk, they may disregard orders."

"And you might be here all winter?"

Nicolaus squirmed uncomfortably. "I suppose there's no harm in telling you what is common knowledge."

"I'm not asking for secret information," Comfort protested.

"I don't know any secrets, but how long we stay here depends on the Continental army. War is like playing cat and mouse. If General Washington moves, we move. It's as simple as that. But it's not customary to fight in bad weather like this."

"Then I *may* have to impose on you to escort me to the market. I go on Fridays when the farmers bring in supplies."

"I can go with you as soon as I return from sentry duty." He extended his bowl for another helping. "The stew is very good, and as you see, it takes a lot of food to satisfy my appetite."

"If preparing meals for you is the worst imposition the British put upon us, I'll have gotten by very well. I like to cook for people who enjoy their food. Father and Erin are both picky eaters, but Marion makes up for that when he's home. He's a big eater."

He started to say that she seemed young to have so much responsibility, for when he listened to her youthful and vibrant voice, he often forgot her apparent age. Instead, he said, "How long have you been responsible for running the household?"

Comfort reached for Erin's hand. "Our mother died when Erin was born. I was only. . ." She flushed and stopped just short of saying that she was thirteen years old when her mother died.

"It hasn't been easy, I'm sure, but you make a wonderful hostess. I appreciate the comfort you've provided for me."

"Thank you," she said shyly.

She'd never had any thanks from anyone else before. Their father and Marion took for granted that it was her responsibility to provide for them, and she supposed it was. Still, it was pleasing to have someone notice her work. She'd had a few men court her; but if she married one of them, she'd just go from one fireplace to another. She'd never thought before about marriage being exciting; but with a man like Nicolaus, life wouldn't be humdrum. *Yes,* she mentally mocked herself, *it wouldn't be humdrum following a soldier from one battlefield to another.*

Erin had been taught to be quiet when her elders were talking, so she hadn't interrupted Comfort and Nicolaus, but she'd been fidgeting on her stool and had almost fallen off once.

Laughing, Comfort said, "All right, Erin, I'll stop talking. You can have Nicolaus to yourself while I go to the cellar to get vegetables for tomorrow."

Nicolaus turned toward Erin. "So, Fräulein, what do you want to hear today?"

"Tell me about your country. How far away do you live from Trenton?"

Nicolaus chuckled in amusement. "Far enough that it took six months for me to arrive in America."

"Six months!" Erin counted on her fingers. "That was way back at the beginning of summer."

"We were on ship only two months, but it's been a long time since I left my home in Hesse."

"Hesse?"

"Germany is made up of lots of little principalities, and Hesse is one of them."

Erin was singing "Away in a Manger" with Nicolaus when Comfort reentered the house. It was a pretty tune, and Comfort hummed along with them as she swept ashes from the hearth and filled a bowl with water from the huge pot hanging on the crane. She applauded when they finished the song.

"Do Germans do anything except sing at Christmas?" Erin demanded.

"Oh, lots more things. Have you heard of the *Belsnickel?*"

"The bell what?" Erin asked, puzzled.

Comfort picked up her sewing box and pulled a chair close to the fireplace for extra light while she knitted woolen socks for Marion.

"It's warmer near the fire," she said, pointing to a chair that their father usually occupied.

Nicolaus hesitated before he took the chair. Erin sat on a low stool near him.

"The *Belsnickel* is associated with Saint Nicolaus, so I'll tell you about him first."

"Were you named for Saint Nicolaus?" Comfort asked.

"*Nein.* My name came from an ancestor. But I consider it an honor to bear the saint's name. He was a bishop who lived in the fourth century and became the patron saint of children. When we celebrate Saint Nicolaus Day, December 6, the children fill their shoes with straw and carrots for the saint's horse. The next morning the shoes are full of toys and cookies."

Erin grinned widely, and Nicolaus tapped her lightly on the head. "That is, if they've been good children. If they haven't been, that's where the *Belsnickel* comes in."

"I've been good," Erin assured him with a serious expression in her brown eyes.

"When Saint Nicolaus makes his rounds, he's sometimes accompanied by *Belsnickel*, a boy with blackened face and a beard, who carries rattling chains and walks on his hands and knees to represent the donkey the *Christkind* rode. The Christ child is often represented by a little girl dressed in white."

"*Christkind* is the German word for the Christ child?" Erin asked, pronouncing the foreign word correctly.

"That's right," Nicolaus said, "you're learning fast."

A satisfied expression overspread Erin's face as she crowded closer to Nicolaus's knees.

"*Belsnickel* goes from house to house with the *Christkind* and gives each mother a switch to discipline her children during the coming year. When *Belsnickel* arrives, if the children kneel and say their prayers, he treats them with nuts or apples. This visiting goes on until Christmas Eve, when Saint Nicolaus arrives with the real Christmas gifts."

"Wouldn't it be nice if Saint Nicolaus comes to Trenton this year?" Erin said, her eyes gleaming with excitement. "With so many Germans here, he might."

Nicolaus stood to his full height, and Comfort gasped as she experienced a delightful tingle in the pit of her stomach. She was intensely aware of his superb masculinity. Was she attracted to him because she'd never seen such a well-built man before? It must not be more than that. Attraction to Nicolaus would lead to nothing but heartbreak.

Nicolaus must have heard her gasp, for he turned toward her, and his penetrating blue-eyed gaze traveled over her face, taking in each detail. She was keenly aware of his scrutiny, and she wondered if he suspected that she wasn't what she pretended to be. Comfort held her breath, dreading what he might say, but Nicolaus turned his attention back to Erin and patted her on the head.

"The *Belsnickel* might come," he said. "But if he does pay a surprise visit, it might be a good idea for a certain Fräulein to be sure she gets candy and nuts instead of a switch."

"I'll be good," Erin promised.

Flustered by the smoldering flame she'd seen in his eyes, Comfort lowered her head and busily plied her knitting needles. She didn't look up when she answered his *Gute Nacht*.

When Father came for his meal, the harried look on his face disturbed Comfort.

"Do you need any help?" she asked.

"Yes, but you've got enough to do. Where's Erin?"

"Already in bed. She's been asking Nicolaus questions about Germany."

"You're trusting him too far, Comfort."

"That could be true, but we may need an ally in the Hessian camp before this winter is over. So far, he's given me no reason to distrust him, and until he does, I'll take him at his word. He's offered to escort me to the market on Friday, and I accepted his offer."

"I'll just have to trust your judgment in the matter, for I'm worried about what will happen to my patients if the Hessians find them. These men fought at the Battle of White Plains in October, and the Hessians lost a lot of men there."

"So did the Americans."

"That may not make any difference." He drew a long breath and closed his eyes. "I must spend the night in the hospital, but if Nicolaus is on night duty, you should be all right."

Comfort would have felt safer if Nicolaus was in the house at night, but she didn't voice the thought. She didn't want their father to be suspicious of her interest in Nicolaus.

Chapter 4

T he frigid weather intensified during the night, and as the wind pelted sleet against the roof, Comfort fretted about Marion and the other Continental soldiers sleeping in crude shelters. She also wondered if Nicolaus had to stand outdoors all night long.

The sleet had stopped by morning, but the house was cold. After she stoked the fire in the kitchen, Comfort knocked softly on Nicolaus's door. When she received no answer, she cracked the door and saw that he wasn't in bed. She laid several logs on his fire, stirred up the coals, and took a pitcher of hot water to his room.

Their father had finished his porridge and was swigging on a hot mug of cider when Nicolaus passed the window and entered his room.

"You and Erin bundle up good if you're going to market. It's raw outside." Their father wagged his head in concern. "I don't know how Washington and the boys will manage. Too bad they let the British take Trenton, or they could have lived in the stone barracks built by the British during the last war. Instead, our enemies are quartered there."

"I'm worried about Marion."

With a sigh, her father drained his cider mug. "And I'm worried about you too. I don't like leaving you and Erin so much, but I feel I have to stay at the hospital most of the time. I'm uneasy leaving my patients if the Hessians should attack, and I don't want our enemies to get the medications Congress allotted me." He lowered his voice. "I've got a lot of bed sacks, sheets, blankets, and shirts too."

"Are they hidden?"

"I don't know where I can hide them. But," he said, dropping his voice lower, "it's reported that the Hessians haven't made any entrenchments. Colonel Rall scoffs at the Continental army and doesn't think he has anything to fear. The officers drink and play cards all night and sleep through the day, so that makes the regular soldiers lax. There's been a lot of looting, but I'm hoping they'll leave the hospital alone."

He wrapped his heavy coat around his shoulders and gestured toward the bedroom. "If our visitor starts drinking, you and Erin leave the house immediately and come to me."

Comfort agreed with a nod. She called up the stairs and told Erin to get up, then she prepared a plate for Nicolaus and knocked at his door. He and Erin arrived in the kitchen at the same time. Nicolaus ate heartily of the bread and porridge, and Comfort served him extra portions.

"Did you spend a miserable night?" she asked.

"It wasn't too bad. We've taken over a cooper's shop on the edge of town, and we alternate the patrol. It's very cold, though. Must you go to market?"

"I usually go on Friday when Mr. Stone comes to town. He brings butter, milk, and eggs for us. We have plenty of vegetables, fruits, and cured meat in the cellar, but I like to have fresh farm products. Do you want to rest before we leave for the market?"

"Not if you want to get there early."

Comfort bundled Erin into a long woolen shawl, and she put on a heavy coat and pulled a shawl low over her head. She didn't want any of her acquaintances to see her and reveal her youthful identity to Nicolaus. But she wondered if he was really fooled by her dowdy garments because she occasionally caught him watching her with a speculative gleam in his eye.

Nicolaus walked a few paces behind Comfort and Erin as they hurried northward along Queen Street and turned eastward on Fourth Street. Only a few farmers had braved the cold to bring in supplies. Thankful that Mr. Stone was one of them, Comfort approached his wagon. Shivering from the cold, he paid no attention to her until she spoke.

"I hardly recognized you, Miss Comfort. Are you ailing?"

She warned him with a shake of her head, and Stone looked quickly from Comfort to Nicolaus, his keen glance taking in the situation. "I've got your things. The colder the weather, the less milk and eggs I get, but I'm still providing for my best customers."

He placed the items in her basket, and Comfort handed him some paper notes issued by the Continental Congress that Father had received for operating the hospital.

Mr. Stone kept eyeing Nicolaus, who stood several feet away from them.

"What's he doing with you?" he growled.

"He's billeted in our home, and he offered his escort this morning. Watch what you say," Comfort cautioned. "He speaks and understands English."

"What do you hear of Washington?" the farmer whispered.

"Not much. Marion hasn't been home for a couple of

weeks, and I hope he doesn't come while the Hessians control the town."

"The Germans think Washington has sneaked away like a dog with its tail between its legs." He winked conspiratorially. "They might be in for a surprise."

If Washington was planning an attack, Nicolaus would be in danger. It had been disturbing enough to worry about Marion and the soldiers in her father's care. Now she'd added Nicolaus to her concerns.

Mr. Stone handed Erin a cookie. "Here's a sorghum cookie, Missy. Fresh baked yesterday."

Comfort thanked Mr. Stone, and Nicolaus fell into step behind them as they left the market area.

Glancing over her shoulder, Comfort asked, "Do you know where I can find the roving army baker who was in Trenton when your troops arrived? I've heard your colonel detained him before he could leave town."

A smile spread across Nicolaus's generous mouth. The rare smile always transformed his somber countenance to pleasant features and made him appear friendly and trustworthy.

Ja. His ovens are in a shack near our headquarters along King Street. Colonel Rall likes his food, and when he tasted the baker's bread, he said he hadn't eaten anything to compare with it since he left Germany. He's posted guards to keep the baker from leaving Trenton."

"If the colonel hasn't seized all of the bakery products, I'll see if Mr. Ludwick has some gingerbread. He was a neighbor of ours in Philadelphia, and we've been eating his good pastries for years."

"Ludwick, did you say? I have a cousin by that name living in Philadelphia. And he's a baker. The few messages he wrote to our family about the English colonies encouraged me to volunteer for service in America."

"Then let's find Mr. Ludwick, and I'll introduce you."

The tantalizing aroma of fresh pastries greeted them when they entered the bakeshop where two Hessians stood guard. Christopher Ludwick was a short, portly man, and when the Foster sisters entered with the Hessian, an angry look crossed the baker's round face.

German, though he was, Ludwick was an outspoken critic of George III and the foreign soldiers he'd sent to the Colonies. Christopher had prospered in Pennsylvania, but he'd donated much of his fortune to the colonial cause. And he'd volunteered to provide bread for the army, refusing to draw either pay or rations for his work.

The baker was in a bad humor, and he paid no attention to Comfort's disguise when she asked for some gingerbread. "It's an outrage," Christopher stated in broken English that was difficult to follow in spite of his many years in the Colonies, "that these foreigners have moved in on us. The Continental army is starving for my bread, and I'm forced to cook for these scoundrels."

"Hush, Mr. Ludwick," Comfort said, fearful of what else he would say that Nicolaus would understand. "I've brought you a surprise. This *gentleman,*" she emphasized the word, "is lodging in our house. He's a kinsman of yours."

Christopher cast a sharp glance at Nicolaus.

"Meet Nicolaus Trittenbach," Comfort added.

The baker scuttled closer to Nicolaus and peered upward at him. " 'Deed you could be my kinsman, but you have grown up, way up, since last I saw you." He threw his arms around Nicolaus's waist. "It is good to see one of my kindred once more."

"Your success in America made me want to come here."

126

"But I would have preferred that you didn't come to fight us," Christopher said severely.

"I'm under orders from the King of England. If I should meet you in battle, I will fight fiercely against you, but I won't attack a peaceful citizen."

Mr. Ludwick motioned to the two guards. "Not all are like that." Turning his attention to Comfort, he said, "How much gingerbread do you need?"

"Two loaves, please. Erin is very fond of it."

The baker smiled at Erin. "Then you shall have my best. I have just taken some loaves from the oven. Colonel Rall has ordered that all my products be kept for his men, but I do what I want."

Comfort wrapped the two loaves in a cloth and put them in the basket with the farm produce. She paid him with Spanish coins. Mr. Ludwick handed Erin and Comfort each a gingerbread man and one to Nicolaus also.

"Come and talk to me whenever you can," Christopher said to Nicolaus. "We have much to say to one another."

As they left the building, the guard by the door guffawed and spoke to Nicolaus. Comfort didn't understand his words, but somehow she thought they were directed toward her. Nicolaus's face darkened in anger, and his retort was harsh and surly. The incident revealed another side of Nicolaus, and Comfort realized that he could be ferocious if provoked to anger. Of course, Nicolaus wouldn't have made a good soldier if he didn't have this characteristic. How thankful she was that he hadn't vented his anger on her family.

Nicolaus stayed in his room the rest of the day, and his presence was welcome, for rowdy soldiers prowled the streets. One stopped by the house and peered into the kitchen. Comfort shrank against the wall, and he didn't see her. He pushed on the door, but the latch held and he moved on. One group of soldiers passed, their arms loaded with plunder.

By nightfall, the soldiers had banded together in a mob, and Nicolaus was called out early. Before he left, he cautioned Comfort, "Stay in the house with the doors locked. I'll try to keep an eye on your home, but I don't know where I might be stationed. A farmer brought in a load of whiskey this afternoon, and our soldiers are drinking."

Comfort sent Erin to bed early, but she stayed up to guard the house, since Father had to remain in the hospital all night. With Nicolaus and her father away from the house, Comfort took the opportunity to wash her hair. The powder that she'd used to disguise her appearance made her head itch, and if only for a short time, she wanted to freshen up.

After she washed her hair, she bathed her face with some scented soap her father had bought from a French merchant. In the darkness of the back room, she took a quick wash and put on clean clothing. She was tired of wearing the dirty dress she'd worn for the past week. She sat by the fire to dry her hair, intending to relax an hour or two before she replaced her disguise.

Comfort dozed before the fire, and she didn't know how long she'd slept before she heard the mob approaching. They bypassed the house and headed toward the hospital and built a fire in the yard. Father locked the doors at night, but this mob could easily wreck the building or burn it.

A hospital window shattered, and the drunken soldiers roared with laughter as they advanced on the building, their voices demanding and piercing. Frightened, Comfort stood in the middle of the dark room and wrung her hands, wheeling at a sound behind her. Nicolaus rushed into the house and strode purposefully toward the back door, his face hard as granite. He was in full uniform, and the brass headgear made him look like a giant. He carried his musket, fixed with the bayonet. With a mighty thrust, he swung open the door, slamming it against the side of the room.

Nicolaus fired his musket.

"Anschlag!" Shouting in German, he advanced on the mob, his bayonet threatening. He was a terrifying apparition in the glow of the fire as smoke swirled around him. He thundered at the soldiers in a coarse voice, and they turned tail and ran out of the yard with Nicolaus in full pursuit.

Throwing a shawl around her shoulders, Comfort ran toward the hospital.

"Father," she called. "Are you all right?" The door opened cautiously. "They're gone. Nicolaus chased them away." She pushed by her father and into the room.

"No damage, except the broken window," Father said in a shaking voice. "Two of the men got slight wounds from the flying glass, but nothing else. I'll put out that fire before it spreads to the buildings."

Now that the danger was past, reaction set in, and Comfort's legs trembled until she could hardly stand. She stumbled into her father's office and sat behind the desk, leaning her head on her hands. Comfort had heard of avenging angels, and when Nicolaus advanced on the mob brandishing his musket and bayonet, he could have been the archangel Michael. What if Nicolaus hadn't come when he had? Would the recuperating soldiers have been killed and the hospital destroyed?

"Be not forgetful to entertain strangers: for thereby some

have entertained angels unawares," she murmured. Had that Bible verse come true tonight? Maybe angels didn't have to wear wings and a halo like the ones she'd seen in paintings. Tonight, she believed an angel, in the guise of a Hessian soldier, had helped her family.

"Comfort," her father called, rousing her from her reverie.

"In your office," she answered and stood to greet him, thankful that her limbs were steadier now. Father rushed into the small room with the tall figure of Nicolaus towering behind him. Both men stared at her as if they'd never seen her before, and Comfort couldn't imagine what was wrong until she lifted a hand to her smooth cheek. Fingering her clean hair, her face flamed.

"Oh, Father, I forgot. My hair was so uncomfortable, I just had to get rid of that powder. With the house empty, I thought it was safe to wash my hair."

He waved his hand impatiently. "We'll talk of that later. Did you have trouble in the house?"

Comfort's gaze wandered to Nicolaus, who stared at her in astonishment. A look of wonder, admiration, and a glimmer of hope shone from his blue eyes, but he said nothing.

"No problem at all, but I must hurry back in case Erin is awake. Thank you, Nicolaus," she said. "If you hadn't come, we might have lost everything."

"Colonel Rall gave orders for the renegade soldiers to be locked up until they're sober. That should stop the rioting."

Clearing his throat awkwardly and without looking at Nicolaus, Father extended his hand. "I owe you a lot for this night's work. Thank you."

Nicolaus gripped her father's hand. "When I'm in battle, I'll fight my enemy as fiercely as any Hessian, but I won't stand by and see the wounded and innocent molested. Now that I know you're all right, I'll return to my patrol."

After Nicolaus left, Comfort helped her father nail a blanket over the broken window before she returned to the house. Father hadn't mentioned the lack of her disguise, and unless he ordered her to further conceal her true identity, Comfort didn't intend to do so. Nicolaus knew the truth now, and she would have given a great deal to know how the revelation had affected him.

Chapter 5

The grenadiers were ignobly reported to be seven feet tall, but as Nicolaus spent the next hour patrolling Queen Street, he felt as if he lived up to that reputation. He had the sensation of floating on air, his heavy boots hardly touching the ground.

For the past week he'd puzzled over Comfort's appearance, wishing he could see behind her dark spectacles, but he hadn't been prepared for the vision he'd encountered tonight when he entered the hospital. He'd thought she might be younger than she looked, but he was unprepared for her loveliness. Comfort was young, beautiful, and desirable.

Oliver Foster had shaken his hand tonight, but Nicolaus doubted that the man would look favorably upon him as Comfort's suitor. He'd been drawn to her the first day, but now that he knew she was a maiden instead of a middle-aged woman, Nicolaus realized the depth of his interest. How did one court a girl in America?

Nicolaus's father had met his mother when the British had hired Hessian soldiers during the Scots Rebellion in 1745. They were married, and she returned to Hesse with him when the rebellion ceased, apparently without any looking back. Would history repeat itself in Nicolaus's case? But he didn't want to take Comfort to Hesse—he'd be content to stay with her in America.

Comfort was amazed but relieved to find that Erin had slept through all the commotion. She couldn't believe any soldier, drunk or sober, would deliberately harm a child, but she felt the need to protect Erin anyway.

Wondering what Nicolaus had thought when he'd discovered her real identity, Comfort both anticipated and dreaded seeing him again. She checked to be sure he wasn't in the house before she entered his room and stirred the fire. She didn't intend to go to bed until she knew the Hessian soldiers had been subdued, so she left the door open between Nicolaus's room and the kitchen, hoping he'd come to talk to her when he returned.

Her mind was in turmoil, so to occupy her hands, she mended a pair of her father's breeches. Her hands stilled over the workbasket when she heard Nicolaus's steps. He paused, then turned toward the kitchen.

"Comfort," he whispered.

"Yes, come in," she said. "I couldn't go to bed until I knew we were safe."

"The riot involved only twenty men, but they did a lot of damage. Everything is quiet now."

"I'm grateful you came before they ransacked the hospital. Father doesn't own a firearm, but he wouldn't have shot at them anyway."

He came closer, and Comfort motioned to a chair. "You're probably cold, so sit near the fireplace."

Nicolaus sat down, sighed, and stretched his feet toward the fire.

"*Sehr Gut!* Very good," he repeated. "It's been a difficult night."

"Is this apt to happen again?"

"Not if Colonel Rall keeps these men confined until after Christmas. Some Germans celebrate Christmas by carousing."

The silence lengthened between them as Comfort nervously plied the needle in and out of the breeches.

"Why did you change your appearance?" Nicolaus asked.

She spoke eagerly, hoping for understanding. "With enemy soldiers in town, Father thought I'd be safer if I appeared to be middle-aged."

"A good idea," Nicolaus agreed.

"It's obvious now that the disguise wasn't necessary in your case, but we didn't know what to expect."

"You had no reason to trust me. Your father was wise to guard you."

"But he didn't tell me to resume the disguise. I'm glad to get rid of that powder in my hair, as well as those blotches on my face."

"How old are you?"

"Eighteen."

"I'm twenty-six," he said.

The room lightened as daylight approached, and Nicolaus stood. "I should go to bed."

Comfort laid aside the sewing basket. She moved close to him and laid her hand on his forearm, the first time she'd touched him. A delicious tingle moved up her arm.

"Thank you for what you did for us tonight."

His fingers were warm and strong as they wrapped around hers, and she wondered how such a large hand could convey so much gentleness.

"It's my pleasure to serve you." Smiling tenderly down at her, he continued, "You are very beautiful. I'm happy that beauty won't be concealed from me any longer."

He whispered *"Liebchen"* when he left the room. A spark of undefinable emotion gleamed in his eyes, and she feared to ask what the word meant.

A few days later, Nicolaus returned from a sortie into the country, carrying a large evergreen tree. He left the tree on the stoop.

"With your permission, Comfort, I want to set up this *immergruner Baum*—evergreen tree—for Erin. I'd like to decorate it the way we do in my homeland."

"I'll have to ask Father."

Nicolaus nodded in approval.

While he waited for Comfort to finish the midafternoon meal, for they ate only twice a day, Nicolaus told Erin the story of the Christmas tree.

"Decorating a tree was a pagan custom before Germans started it. The ancient Romans decorated with evergreens to honor one of their gods, and that's the reason early Christians refused to decorate a Christmas tree, called *Weihnachtsbaum* in our language."

Erin tried the word and, after a few tries, pronounced it correctly.

"An English missionary, Saint Boniface, brought Christianity to Germany in the eighth century, probably the first person to use an evergreen tree as a symbol of Christ. But Martin Luther is thought to be the first man to decorate a tree in his home during the Christmas season."

"What can we use for decorations?" Erin said.

"You can hang fruit on it," Nicolaus suggested.

"We have apples in the cellar," Comfort said, getting excited about the idea, hoping their father would approve it.

"We can put some of Ludwick's gingerbread men on the tree. Or take pieces of colorful fabric, put them on strings, and wind them around the branches."

"Let's put up the *Weihnachtsbaum* now, Comfort," Erin begged.

Comfort shook her head. "Not until Father gives permission. If he does, we can put it in the room behind the kitchen. It's cooler there, and the needles won't wither."

"I have something in my room we can also use," Nicolaus said. He left the kitchen and returned with a wooden angel that fit in the palm of his hand—a slender angel that stood tall and straight in a pleated-foil gown with outstretched arms, holding an evergreen wreath in each hand.

"Our word for angel is *engel*—not much different from the way you say it. This Nuremberg *Engel*," he explained, "has been in our family for generations. Before my father died, he gave it to me."

"It's beautiful," Comfort said, running her finger down the face of the fragile angel. "Is it very old?"

"More than a hundred years old. It belonged to my ancestors, who lived in Dinkelsbühl. Legend has it that the first Nuremberg angel was made by a German doll maker in memory of his daughter killed during the Thirty Years' War. Now, most every German home has a Nuremberg angel on its *Weihnachtsbaum*. It would be an honor to place my *engel* on the first tree you've had in your home."

"That's kind of you, Nicolaus. I'll talk to Father about the tree, and if he approves, we can start decorating it tomorrow."

Comfort reached for the tablet on the mantel where she tabulated the days of the month. "Today is December 18. One week from today will be Christmas."

"When you talk to your father about the tree, perhaps you can mention a Christmas feast, which is also traditional in our country."

Erin smiled broadly. "I like feasts. I'll beg Poppy to let us have one."

Comfort hadn't been in her bed long when she heard her father's footsteps on the stairs. He usually stayed until after midnight, then left an elderly Patriot to guard the hospital. She wondered why he'd left the hospital so early. She'd started to get out of bed to ask if there was any trouble when she heard him stumble at the head of the steps and fall heavily onto the cot. The cot was where it had been for a week. Why had he forgotten it?

"What's that cot doing there?" an angry voice mumbled.

Marion! Comfort's heart almost stopped beating when she realized her brother had come home—into a town controlled by the enemy. She slid out of bed and scurried into the next room.

"Be quiet!" she whispered sternly. She heard her brother disengaging himself from the comforter. "What's my cot doing over here?" he demanded.

"Hush, I tell you!" she repeated in a harsh whisper. She reached his side and took him by the arm. "What are you doing here? Don't you know this town is full of Hessian soldiers?"

"Yes, I know it. That's why I'm here. General Washington wants me to find out what they're up to."

"Do you also know there's a Hessian soldier sleeping downstairs in Father's room?"

"What!" Marion shouted. "He won't be sleeping long." With all the bravado of a seventeen year old, Marion started downstairs with Comfort at his heels.

At the foot of the stairs, she forcibly pushed him out the back door. "You're not going to bother him," she hissed. "The man protected our property last night when other Hessians were attacking the hospital, and I won't have you fighting with him. Besides, he's a huge man, a foot taller than you are. You're no match for him."

"There's not a Hessian I can't whip with one hand tied behind me!" Marion said loudly.

"Yes, just like the Americans did at Fort Washington," Comfort jeered. She grabbed his arm. Marion struggled, trying to throw off her grasp. Exerting strength she didn't know she possessed, Comfort prevented him from returning to the house. "Come to the hospital. Maybe Father can talk some sense into you. You need to get out of Trenton."

She tapped their secret signal. Her father opened the door, and Comfort quietly pushed Marion inside. Her brother was trembling, and Comfort thought it was from anger until he said, "I haven't had anything to eat for two days or you wouldn't be able to shove me around like this."

"Son, you shouldn't be here!"

"Just what I told him," Comfort said.

"I'm not here to visit my devoted family, who certainly don't seem glad to see me," Marion said angrily. "I'm on assignment from General Washington. He sent me to scout out Trenton, and I'm not leaving until I find out what he wants to know."

"That puts a new light on the situation," Father agreed.

"He can't stay at the house with Nicolaus there," Comfort said.

"Why'd you let a Hessian move into our home?" Marion demanded of his father. "I wanted to put him out, but Comfort threw a fit about it."

"Don't be foolish, Son. If you start a fight with Nicolaus, German troops will be on us in no time. You can't serve the Continental cause if you're killed or taken prisoner, so use what sense the good Lord gave you. Besides, the Foster family is indebted to Nicolaus Trittenbach."

"Make Marion stay here, and I'll go back to the house and bring some food for him."

"I'm about starved to death, Sis. In fact, the whole Continental army is hungry."

"I'll be right back," Comfort promised.

She lit a candle and moved quietly about the kitchen, filling a bowl with beans that had been left over from supper. She put a half-loaf of bread and some butter in a basket and a jar of plums she'd brought from the cellar intending to use them for a plum cake tomorrow. She filled another jar with cider and carried the provisions to the hospital.

The three Fosters moved to the office. While Marion wolfed the food, his father said, "We're in a tight situation. As a soldier, Marion has to carry out the orders of his commander. He can hide here in the hospital until I find out what Washington needs to know."

Between swallows, Marion said, "That Hessian at the house ought to know something. What's he told you, Comfort?"

"Nothing!"

"I don't want Comfort mixed up in this," their father said. "I'll send word to a few Patriots, and they'll pick up information.

Go back to the house, Comfort, and try to act normally."

"Not until Marion promises that he won't attack Nicolaus."

"Your brother isn't going to leave this building until tomorrow night. By that time, Nicolaus will be on duty, and Marion won't even know where he is."

"Nicolaus wants to help Erin decorate a tree for Christmas like they do in Germany. Will you agree to that? If so, we can keep busy with that tomorrow and divert his attention from activities at the hospital."

"That smacks of paganism to me," their father said, "but under the circumstances, it might be the best way to keep him occupied."

While she had her father in an agreeable mood, Comfort pushed for another concession. "He's mentioned a feast on Christmas Day."

"All right! All right!" Father shouted. "If you keep him in the house and away from this hospital until Marion rejoins General Washington, I don't care what you do."

Smiling, Comfort hurriedly returned to the house. The town crier, a custom Trenton had borrowed from Philadelphia, walked down Queen Street calling out the midnight hour. Comfort paused in the kitchen until she heard Nicolaus stirring, and then she went up to her bed.

Why had she forcibly prevented Marion from harming Nicolaus? She'd known this foreigner less than a month, but their association had been so intense, she felt as if she'd known him all of her life. Comfort's friends had sometimes talked of love; but among her people, love had never played a part in the decision to marry. The life cycle was set and one lived by it. You were born, lived as a child, and when you were of marriageable age, you took the most likely prospect.

Love, as she understood it, was the passionate affection of one person for another. She'd never felt about anyone like she did about Nicolaus. Was that love? Was it possible to love a person after knowing him only a few weeks? She didn't understand her feelings, but she wanted to prevent trouble between Marion and Nicolaus. Thankfully, Nicolaus had slept through all the commotion.

As Nicolaus took up picket duty beside the cooper's cabin, he reviewed the night's activities. He remembered the light touch of Comfort's fingers on his arm and her fragrance—a light rose scent that must have come from the soap she'd used to wash her hair. Thoughts of Comfort brought peace to his mind, but he was troubled about the Foster's late-night visitor.

He hadn't been asleep when Marion had stumbled over the cot. Short-sword in hand, he'd opened the door into the kitchen. He'd heard Marion's threat against his life and Comfort's efforts to get her brother out of the house.

Marion Foster was in Trenton to spy on the Hessian army. As a loyal soldier, was he guilty of betrayal by not reporting to Colonel Rall that there was a spy in their midst? He'd watched as Marion and Comfort had gone to the hospital, and he knew Marion was sequestered there. Was it his duty to arrest the boy? He knew it was, but he couldn't bring himself to make any more trouble for Comfort. Never before had he vacillated in his duty toward the country that had hired his services. At no time had he let personal bias interfere with commitment to his commander. But in a choice between distressing Comfort Foster and fulfilling his oath to serve the British, he had chosen Comfort. Why? He puzzled over the weighty question all night long.

Chapter 6

Try to keep Marion hidden? If the Hessians found out that her father was harboring a spy, the whole Foster family, as well as the convalescing soldiers, would suffer for it.

She tried to act as excited as Erin when Nicolaus nailed the evergreen tree to a board and brought it into the house. She brought a basket of red and yellow apples from the cellar. She cut stars from scraps of colorful fabric left over from dresses she'd made for Erin and herself.

She gave needles and thread to Nicolaus and Erin to string the fabric into a chain. Erin laughed at Nicolaus's clumsy efforts to thread the needle. Comfort tied strings to the apples, and Nicolaus lifted Erin to attach some of the decorations at the top of the tree. Sometimes amid their laughter, when Comfort suddenly remembered the danger hanging over the Fosters, her hands paused in their tasks and a frightened feeling overtook her.

After Nicolaus had repeatedly observed her agitation, he stepped close to her and took her hand. "Comfort, I told you when I came here that I am not a threat to you or your family. Don't you believe me?" he asked softly.

She lifted her eyes to meet his steady, tender gaze. The blue of his eyes had intensified until they were as dark and luminous as midnight. *He knows about Marion!*

"Yes, I believe you," she murmured and dropped her gaze in confusion, realizing suddenly why she'd defended Nicolaus from her own brother and why she trusted Nicolaus completely. The realization was two-edged. She was happy to at last experience this special affection for another person, but she was wretched to be so fond of a man who might be gone from her life in a short time—a man who in reality was her enemy.

Marion made it in and out of Trenton without incident, but their father and Comfort despaired of having him return to the army. The weather had turned fiercely cold, and the signs were right for a big snow. Erin and Comfort stayed in the house most of the time, and she accepted Nicolaus's offer to bring the farm products from Mr. Stone on Friday, including a plump goose— a traditional Christmas food in Germany.

Besides the goose, she intended to cook a mixture of beans and dried corn, baked squash, oyster soup, and a sweetened rice pudding that Nicolaus told her how to prepare. He had persuaded Christopher Ludwick to make a *Schnitz* pie—a layer of sour dried apples covered with cinnamon, sugar, and orange rind baked in a thick pastry crust. Christopher had also sent two loaves of rye bread and some gingerbread cookies.

The ornaments on the *Weihnachtsbaum* increased as Nicolaus and Erin thought of new items to add. By Christmas Eve, it was a heavily laden tree, and Comfort was pleased that it had provided so much enjoyment for Erin.

On Christmas Eve, Nicolaus arranged for one of his friends to appear in the role of *Belsnickel.* Nicolaus had coached Erin on what she should do if *Belsnickel* did show up. Even then, she rushed to hide behind Comfort's skirts when the back door unceremoniously opened and a huge figure, wrapped in a shaggy bearskin coat and wearing a mask, entered the room. He carried a handful of switches.

The *Belsnickel* laughed fiendishly, swung one switch, and exploded into a spate of German words. Nicolaus answered in English, "We have only one child here, and she says she's been a good girl this year."

He motioned to Erin, who somewhat reluctantly left the safety of Comfort's skirts, knelt, and clasped her hands in prayer.

Standing up, Erin stayed close to Nicolaus when the *Belsnickel* patted her on the head and gave her some gingerbread cookies that looked suspiciously like those made by Ludwick, a bag of maple sugar candy, and a wooden figurine of a woman wrapped in red cloth.

Shouting, *"Frohliche Weihnachten,"* the man exited.

Nicolaus answered, "Merry Christmas to you."

After Nicolaus went on duty, Comfort placed more coals in the oven to keep the goose roasting through the night. But listening to the wind and experiencing the chill from the window and the cold draft under the door, Comfort went to bed with a heavy heart. How could she enjoy a feast tomorrow when Marion and his fellows were camped outdoors?

Colonel Rall declared Christmas a holiday, and the streets

were empty of Hessians. Erin begged her father to eat Christmas dinner with them, and because the town was quiet, he agreed to leave his patients untended for a few hours. Comfort set the larger table in the back room for the occasion, where they could also enjoy the scent of the *immergruner Baum* that permeated the room.

For the first time, their father sat at table with Nicolaus, seemingly without animosity. Comfort blushingly accepted the praise of both men for the delicious meal. She read the Christmas story from Luke, and Nicolaus took a prayer book from his pocket and read a blessing in German. Smilingly, he translated it into English.

"God's blessing upon those who give shelter from the storm to weary travelers passing their home. May God's favor always shine upon them and bring peace to their hearts. Amen."

His gaze passed from Father to Erin and to Comfort as he softly repeated the words. "I sincerely pray that God will grant that blessing because of your kindness to me."

After the meal, they gathered around the big fireplace in the kitchen. Father stayed at the house until almost dusk, and Comfort was delighted to see the congeniality between the two men. Her father plied Nicolaus with questions about Germany and answered Nicolaus's queries concerning opportunities in America.

After he left, Nicolaus taught Erin the English words to "Away in a Manger." It took more than an hour, but soon Erin could sing the English translation. Nicolaus sang one line in German, and Erin would take the following phrase in English.

Comfort even joined them on the last line. When Nicolaus sang, *"die Sterne im Himmel schauten unten, wo er den,"* she and Erin concluded, "the little Lord Jesus, asleep on the hay."

Erin soon went to sleep on a blanket in front of the fire.

"Thank you, Nicolaus, for making this such a wonderful day for Erin. She'll never forget it." Then she added slowly, "And neither will I."

Comfort roused Erin and sent her to bed, then peered out the window. "It's snowing again." The window was frosty, and wind gusts whistled around the house. "Your assignment is going to be miserable tonight," she said to Nicolaus.

He shook his head in dismay. "I'm not concerned about the weather, but it's frightening that Colonel Rall and the other officers are taking our position here for granted. The majority of our soldiers are already drunk. We'll not be a fit army to defend ourselves in case of any attack. Some of us requested additional pickets, but the commanders laughed at us. 'Armies don't fight in this kind of weather,' was the answer we received."

Giving Nicolaus a hot mug of cider, Comfort said, "I took the liberty of making you a gift. You've served our family well this week." She handed him a pair of mittens. "I hope they aren't too small for you."

Obviously pleased, he put on the mittens, which fit snugly. "Just my size. Thank you. I'll wear them tonight."

He walked into the back room and returned with the Nuremberg angel. "This is for you. I've enjoyed seeing it atop the *Weihnachtsbaum,* and I pray that it may decorate many more trees in the Foster household."

"But, Nicolaus," she protested, "this belongs in your family. I can't take it."

He closed her hand around the angel. "My father gave it to me, and I want you to have it. If I should fall in battle, the angel would become part of the plunder. I'll be happier knowing you have it."

"Why would you give me such a treasure?"

He laid a hand on her cheek. "Because you've become very important to me." His blue eyes shone, and his brow wrinkled in wonderment that echoed in his voice. "It's hard to believe that in such a short time I've learned to care so deeply for you, but there's no mistaking the message of my heart."

"Oh," Comfort said, breathlessly.

"If my term of enlistment ends while I'm still in America, I'll request parole in the Colonies. If I'm no longer a part of the British army, will you forget that I'm your enemy?"

Bravely meeting his gaze, in a tremulous voice, Comfort answered, "You've never seemed like an enemy to me."

Cupping her chin, Nicolaus bent down and brushed her lips with a soft kiss.

"Guten nacht. Frohliche Weihnachten."

"Good night and Merry Christmas to you too," she replied softly.

As he strode briskly toward the outpost in the cooper's house, Nicolaus wondered if he should have kissed Comfort, but she hadn't resisted his caress. He didn't regret his boldness, for his body still tingled from the sensation of the touch of her lips.

His excitement cooled immediately when he reached the outpost. His fellow soldiers were grouped around the fireplace in earnest discussion.

"Nicolaus," one of them said. "A loyal farmer brought word that the rebel army has crossed the Delaware to attack Trenton."

Nicolaus slapped his thigh in disgust. "I've had the feeling all day that something was wrong. Why didn't the colonel anticipate this?"

Leutnant Wiederhold, commander of the post, said sharply, "He should have. Small rebel parties have been crossing the Delaware and pestering our patrols for days. A cousin of mine was killed in one of the skirmishes."

"Surely the colonel knew that," Nicolaus said.

"*Ja*," Wiederhold said, "but knowing that Washington's troops are half-starved and exhausted, he didn't figure they'd march during this harsh weather. Herr Trittenbach, go warn the colonel and return here as soon as you can."

The cold wind chilled Nicolaus in spite of the heavy coat he wore over his uniform. Freezing rain coated his musket with ice, and he tried to shield the weapon beneath his coat as he quickly retraced his steps into Trenton.

He heard the celebrating soldiers before he reached Rall's headquarters in the stone barracks on King Street. When he hurried into the anteroom, he was greeted with cheers. One soldier, mug of ale held high, saluted him.

"Where've you been, Nicolaus? You're missing all the fun."

The roistering soldiers sickened Nicolaus, but he didn't have the authority to tell them to prepare for battle. "I have a message for Colonel Rall."

Laughing and cheering greeted his remark as another soldier delivered a toast. Nicolaus strode outside, uncertain what to do until he saw Ludwick's bakeshop across the street. The baker was working at his ovens with only one Hessian on guard when Nicolaus entered. The soldier seemed sober, and Nicolaus asked him quietly, "Where's Colonel Rall?"

"At the home of Abraham Hunt. That's the big brick house down the street."

"Thanks," Nicolaus answered and waved to Ludwick, who watched him curiously. Outside, he was greeted by another onslaught of snow and sleet.

Nicolaus had admired the Hunt mansion more than once as he'd patrolled the streets of Trenton. He approached the rear of the mansion, and when a servant answered his knock, he asked for Colonel Rall.

"Mr. Hunt and his guests are playing cards, and they are not to be disturbed."

Playing cards when his whole contingent of men might be captured! Nicolaus considered shoving the servant aside and breaking in on the party, but he knew he'd be punished if he barged in on his superior officer.

"Will you take an urgent message to him?"

"I can take him a note when I go in with food and drinks."

"May I step inside to write the message?"

Nicolaus was shown into a small room, where he found paper and a quill pen. He hurriedly scribbled in German, "Washington is bringing his men across the Delaware. They're approaching Trenton." He started to add, "The troops need to be rallied," but he didn't go that far. All he could do was sound the warning—the rest was up to the commander. Nicolaus thanked the servant and rushed back to his post.

The two dozen Hessians at the outpost didn't relax their vigilance all night. By daylight the snowfall had intensified, and their vision was limited to a few yards. The howling wind kept them from hearing the approaching column led by Washington until it was almost upon them.

Nicolaus heard shots, rapid footsteps, and a sentry's cry, *"Der Feind! Heraus! Heraus!"*

"The enemy! The enemy! On your feet!" The Hessians

rushed toward the Americans, but when *Leutnant* Wiederhold saw the weaving line of Colonial soldiers, he shouted, "Men, we're outnumbered. Fall back and join the other troops."

Nicolaus retreated with his comrades, trying to fire his musket, but his gunpowder was wet. He thought of Comfort and Erin, wishing he could warn them of the impending battle, but a Hessian soldier couldn't help them today.

Chapter 7

Comfort learned of the Continental advance when her father rolled out of his blankets to answer an imperative pounding on the door.

"Comfort," Father called, and she hurried to the top of the stairs. He motioned for her to join him.

"That was Marion. The Continental army is attacking. Take Erin and go to the root cellar."

"But, Father. . ."

"Do what I say," her father demanded, interrupting her protest. "Immediately."

Hurrying to obey him, she asked, "Will you keep me posted about what's going on? The enemy could burn the house over our heads."

"Washington's men will keep the Hessians too busy for that. Fortunately, the enemy soldiers are disorganized. I'll bring you word when I can, but you must hide. I don't know what I'll face today, and I can't be worried about you and Erin."

Comfort dressed Erin in a heavy layer of clothes, put on several of her own garments and wrapped woolen cloth around their legs and shoes. She handed Erin a jug of milk to carry. Toting a basket filled with bread, cheese, and some candles, she hurried her sister along the stoop to the cellar door.

The cellar was damp, but not much colder than their attic bedrooms. The frigid weather had entered every nook and cranny of Trenton; and thinking of the soldiers fighting in the streets, Comfort knew she should be thankful for shelter of any kind.

Erin was crying, and Comfort put her arms around the child.

"Don't fret. We won't be here long. General Washington will soon drive the Hessians out of town."

"Nicolaus?" Erin said. "Will they drive him away?"

"Probably so," Comfort answered, a cold sweat breaking out on her body as she suddenly realized what a personal calamity it would be to never see Nicolaus again. How could he have become so important to her so quickly?

Throughout the morning, they heard intermittent firing and the sound of many footsteps sloshing along snow-covered Queen Street. More than once Comfort was tempted to peer out and see what was going on, but she knew her father was right. A battleground was no place for her, and she was responsible for Erin's safety.

About noon, their father opened the door and called down, "We're still safe here. Most of the fighting is on King Street. Are you all right?"

"We're awful cold, Poppy," Erin whimpered.

"It's cold everywhere. I'm sorry, but you'll have to stay hidden a little longer."

By midafternoon, their father called again. "It's safe enough now, I think, but you must still be cautious."

Comfort's feet felt like blocks of ice. She could hardly climb out of the cellar, and Father had to carry Erin up the ladder and into the kitchen. Comfort unwrapped Erin's feet and took off her shoes so the child could extend her cold toes toward the fire blazing on the kitchen hearth.

"The Colonials have apparently won the battle," their father said. "I don't have many details, but it seems that Colonel Rall has been killed and the Hessians have surrendered. I'm going to find out what happened. Don't open the door to anyone until I get back."

"What about Nicolaus?" Erin said through chattering teeth, asking the question that trembled on Comfort's lips.

With a quick look at Comfort, Father said, "I don't know."

The afternoon dragged by, but Comfort kept busy. She went into Nicolaus's room and stirred the fire, cleaning the room as she always did. Even to herself, she couldn't admit that she'd never again hear Nicolaus's firm step on the threshold. She walked into the back room and looked at the Nuremberg angel atop the tree. Was that all she had left of Nicolaus?

She pared carrots, onions, and potatoes, mixed them with the leftover goose, and placed the stew in an iron skillet over a bed of hot coals. She heated the oven and prepared loaves of bread for baking.

Darkness had fallen when their father returned with a jubilant Marion. "We got rid of the dirty foreigners," he shouted. "The cowards! The whole battle didn't take much more than an hour."

"Son," Father said, "it is a great day for the Colonies, but the outcome would have been a lot different if the Hessians had been prepared. When Colonel Rall learned of the attack, it was too late to rally his troops. If he'd heeded the warning he received last night, we might be mourning instead of rejoicing."

"You mean he was warned?" Comfort asked.

"Some soldier took a message to Colonel Rall," Marion said, "but he stuck the note in his pocket without reading it. It was unopened when he died."

"I'm not discounting the bravery of our troops," his father said, "but you'd have been no match for the highly skilled Hessians if Rall had heeded the warning and been waiting for you. Don't gloat over your victory."

But Marion was heedless to his father's opinion. "Forty Hessians killed, including Colonel Rall, about that many wounded, and we've captured nine hundred more. We're going to win this war."

Their father darted a quick glance at Comfort, and she knew he was aware of her interest in Nicolaus. She was pleased that the Continentals had won, but her heart was divided.

What had happened to Nicolaus? Was he dead, wounded, or a prisoner?

"Well, you don't look overjoyed," Marion said to Comfort. "Don't we get any thanks for releasing the citizens of Trenton from the cruel Hessians?"

"It's been a long day for me, Marion, worrying about what was happening. I have a meal ready for you—that should be thanks enough."

Erin looked at her brother, a slight pout on her mouth. "Nicolaus wasn't cruel to us. He taught me lots of things about his country. Hessians are Christians just like we are."

"You wouldn't think so if you'd see the way they fight," Marion said testily. "And who's Nicolaus—that scoundrel who forced his way in here?"

"Nicolaus Trittenbach wasn't a scoundrel," Father said. "He was courteous and served our family well. I agree with Erin. Some of the Hessians might be cruel, but it's un-Christian to judge all the soldiers by those who haven't been merciful. Let's change the subject."

Comfort stood by the fireplace and nibbled at a bowl of stew. Although she'd had very little to eat that day, she had no appetite. As soon as she washed the dishes and put away the food, she left her father and Marion before the fire talking about the battle. As she took the sleepy-eyed Erin upstairs, she heard her father say, "Marion, listen to me. This is only a symbolic victory for the Colonials, and I'm sure General Washington realizes that. Winning one battle won't end the war—we still have a long way to go."

Marion left before daylight to join Washington's troops. By then, Comfort had come to a decision. Through the long, sleepless night, she'd decided that, with or without Father's permission, she was going to search for Nicolaus.

When her father came from the hospital for his breakfast, Comfort had once again assumed the disguise that transformed her into a middle-aged woman. Father surveyed her appearance, but he asked no questions.

"Washington's army is retreating across the river," he reported. "His troops aren't fit to fight—they've gone for days without adequate sleep, food, or clothing. But they captured enough Hessian stores to provide food and clothing for awhile."

"So Trenton is without any protection?"

"Some Hessians escaped to join General Cornwallis's army north of here, so I suppose we're still at the mercy of the British if they advance on our town. As soon as the Colonials have rested, they'll attack the British again."

"When Erin has eaten her breakfast, I'm going to find out

what happened to Nicolaus."

"That's no job for a woman," Father protested. "I'll do what I can."

"No," Comfort stated flatly. "I'll do it. Erin can sit in your office."

"I'm going to be busy, for I have several new patients—the ones wounded yesterday."

"Erin won't need much supervision, but I don't want to leave her alone in the house until I return."

"Daughter, what is this man to you?"

Comfort evaded her father's stern gaze. "I don't want him to go out of my life, never knowing whether he's dead or alive."

"If you choose him over your countrymen, you'll be considered a traitor."

Comfort didn't answer, and her father sighed deeply. "It's times like this when I miss your mother. When I don't understand women's emotions, how can I advise you?"

"I'm not asking for advice, Father. Just a little understanding."

Her father pushed back his chair and rose from the table. "I'll keep an eye on Erin," he said as he left the kitchen.

When Comfort stepped out on Queen Street an hour later, she hardly knew which way to go. Nicolaus could be dead, wounded, a prisoner, or he might have escaped from Trenton. In her disguise and carrying a basket over her arm, Comfort hoped she'd appear as a housewife buying supplies.

She went to Ludwick's bakeshop first. He was loading his ovens into a wagon, preparing to follow Washington's army.

"Great news, Fräulein," he shouted when she entered the building. "So why are you sad? Is there trouble?"

"I'm concerned about your cousin, Nicolaus. He and Erin became friends, and she's worried about him." She hoped that wasn't being deceitful, for Erin was fretting over Nicolaus's absence.

"I don't know what happened to Nicolaus. He's a good man. I hope he's safe."

"Do you know where the prisoners are? Or the wounded?" She couldn't bring herself to ask where the dead Hessians had been taken.

Mr. Ludwick motioned his pudgy hand to the barracks across the street. "The wounded Hessians are in that building. Washington took the other prisoners with him into Pennsylvania. I'd help you, but I'm ordered to join the Continental army."

"Do you have time to see if he's among the dead?" She took his hand. "Please do that for me. I must know. I'll check among the wounded."

An hour later, Comfort came out of the barracks, enraged and disappointed. She'd had to fight her way past the Continental soldiers guarding the barracks to look at the faces of forty or more wounded Hessians. Nicolaus wasn't among them.

Mr. Ludwick was fidgeting from one foot to the other, apparently eager to be on his way, when Comfort emerged from the building.

"Did you find him?" he asked.

She shook her head. Nicolaus must not be among the dead either, or Mr. Ludwick would have known she had not.

"I will send you word if Nicolaus is with the prisoners," he promised. He started to climb aboard the wagon, but with one foot on the wheel, he paused and stepped back to the ground. Looking around, he said slowly, "I should not tell you this, but I've heard that some escaped soldiers are hiding in the old

Webster barn outside of town. Webster is sympathetic to the British. But you should not go there alone."

His words brought a ray of hope to Comfort. Her depression lifted, and she experienced the unerring conviction that she would find Nicolaus at the Webster farm. She waved good-bye to Mr. Ludwick and started the long trek along Princeton Road. The sun was shining now, glinting off the icy snowdrifts. She pulled her scarf more tightly around her face and stuck her hands in her pockets for warmth. For encouragement, she repeated over and over a favorite verse from the Bible, "For He shall give his angels charge over thee, to keep thee in all thy ways."

Two hours later, she topped a small rise and saw the Webster farm before her. Should she try to sneak into the barn or walk boldly up to the Webster home and state her business? She'd seen Mr. Webster a few times, and she hardly thought he'd harm a woman; but if he saw her sneaking into his barn, he might shoot first and ask questions later. The long walk through the slippery snow had sapped her strength, but Comfort took a deep breath and headed directly toward the residence.

A woman with unkempt gray hair opened the door cautiously. Her brown eyes shifted uneasily as Comfort introduced herself. "A Hessian soldier is a friend of my family, and I've heard that some Hessians are hiding on this farm. Will you tell me if the man I'm looking for is among them?"

"I know nothing," the woman said and started to close the door. Comfort stuck her foot in the opening.

"Ma'am, I appeal to you as one woman to another. Have you ever lain awake all night wondering if your loved one was dead or alive? If you have, you'll know why I'm concerned. I'm a Patriot, but when you love a person, it makes no difference which army he serves."

Comfort gasped in surprise. She'd told this stranger a fact she had barely admitted to herself. But it was true; she *did* love him.

"I'm not going to betray you, and I'm not interested in anyone else in your barn. If you tell me that Nicolaus Trittenbach is not here, I'll be on my way."

"Let her in," a deep voice said. The door widened enough for Comfort to slip inside to be confronted by Mr. Webster, holding a musket. He looked Comfort up and down, perhaps trying to determine her sincerity.

"Don't let her leave the house," he said to his wife and exited through a rear door.

Comfort's legs wouldn't hold her any longer. She leaned against the wall and slid slowly to the floor. Resting on her haunches, she dropped her head to her knees.

"You can sit on a chair," Mrs. Webster said in a kindly voice.

"I'm all right. I've walked all the way from Trenton without stopping, and I can't stand any longer."

"Do you want something to eat?"

"Yes, please."

Mrs. Webster soon handed Comfort a thick slice of brown bread, generously spread with preserves. She accepted the food with thanks and ate it swiftly.

"War is harder on womenfolk than it is on our men," Mrs. Webster commented. "They decide to fight; women sit at home and worry. It melted my heart to know that you laid awake all night. I haven't slept for two days, wondering if the rebel army will come and get my husband."

"I understand the Continental army is west of the Delaware

now, so he's probably safe for the time being." Comfort hoped she wasn't giving away important information to the enemy, but the woman had been kind to her. The wait seemed interminable. Comfort decided she must have dozed, for she was startled when Mr. Webster appeared before her.

"Trittenbach is out there, and he wants to see you, so I guess you're all right. God forgive you if you betray those men."

Offering a silent prayer of thanks that Nicolaus was alive, Comfort said, "You have nothing to fear from me."

Chapter 8

Nerves tingling, Comfort followed Mr. Webster down an ice-covered path. He motioned her inside the barn and stood guard at the door, his eyes surveying the surrounding countryside.

The scent of animals and hay stung Comfort's nostrils. When her eyes adjusted to the dark interior, she saw Nicolaus lying on the dirt floor. Rushing to his side, she dropped to her knees beside him. He lay on an improvised stretcher—a blanket tied around two long poles. He managed a weak smile.

"Nicolaus, are you wounded?"

"My leg," he said. "I can't walk. My friends plan to carry me with them, but I'm trying to persuade them to leave me behind. I'll just delay them."

Comfort pulled back the thin blanket that covered him. His uniform had been cut away below his left knee, and the leg was swollen to double its size. He felt feverish to her touch.

She looked up at the tall soldier beside Nicolaus. "You can't take him like this. He'll die of exposure."

He said something in German, and Nicolaus translated. "He says if I stay behind, the Americans will take me prisoner."

"Not if I can help it. Father will tend your wound."

"*Nein,*" Nicolaus protested. "You'll make trouble for your whole family."

"Nicolaus," she pleaded, "let me take care of you." She called to Mr. Webster. "Will you help me take him into Trenton? My father is indebted to him. We'll shelter Nicolaus until he's able to walk."

"I want these men out of my barn right away," Webster said testily. "I'm in enough trouble with the rebels. If they find out I'm harboring enemy soldiers, they'll burn me out."

"You may already be in trouble for sheltering them, so one more act of kindness won't make that much difference. If you'll bring Nicolaus into Trenton after dark tonight and help me smuggle him into our house, these other soldiers can go on their way now. Will you agree to that, Nicolaus?"

"Why are you taking such a risk?" he asked her.

"You'll die if you try to escape with these men. And if you're captured, you'll be living out in the open without any medical attention. You're safer at our home until you get well."

"Why are you taking such a risk?" he repeated.

She turned her eyes away and wouldn't meet his gaze, but her face flushed with embarrassment. What must Nicolaus and these other men think of her pleading for him to go home with her?

Nicolaus reached for her hand and squeezed it tenderly. "*Danke.* I'll stay behind." He turned to his friends and spoke to them in German. Comfort assumed he'd told them to leave, for they saluted, picked up their weapons, and hurried from the building.

Mr. Webster still hadn't said whether he would help or not, so Nicolaus turned to him. "I have some gold in my pack at the Foster home. If you'll provide transportation into Trenton, I can reward you for your services."

"What's a good time to bring him?" Mr. Webster asked.

"Two hours after nightfall. My father will be at the hospital, and the Continental soldiers are exhausted. No one is apt to see you."

Webster wasn't wholehearted in his agreement, but Comfort thought he would keep his word. She told him how to access the Foster home without being detected.

"You know where my pack is," Nicolaus said. "There's a bag of coins inside it. This is a risky move, and I won't blame you if I'm taken prisoner."

She bent forward to kiss his feverish cheek, but he moved his head suddenly, and her caress landed on his lips. His eyes twinkled a bit when she drew back quickly.

"You tricked me," she said, but her lips parted in a smile, taking any sting from the words. "Try to rest this afternoon."

She made final plans with Mr. Webster and started the long trek home, but the journey wasn't nearly as difficult this time. Nicolaus was alive!

Comfort reached Trenton in late afternoon. She went to the hospital and called for Erin. Her father followed them to the house.

"Did you find him?"

"Yes."

"Alive?"

"Yes, but I won't tell you anything else right now. What about Marion?"

"He's on the western side of the Delaware River, but I expect the army to return as soon as the men have rested. If Washington doesn't push forward, he'll lose the advantage he gained at Trenton."

"Will the Continental army return to Trenton?"

"Probably—I don't know."

That information concerned Comfort, and she fretted the rest of the day about the best place to put Nicolaus. With his wound, she couldn't get him upstairs. And how would her father react to having Nicolaus occupying his room? Would he refuse to treat Nicolaus if Comfort was successful in smuggling him into the house?

With these problems flooding her mind, nightfall came before Comfort was ready for it. After they'd eaten, Father gave Comfort a long speculative look before he returned to the hospital. She read Erin a Bible story before hustling her off to bed. She started a fire in the bedroom and took two gold coins from Nicolaus's pack to pay Mr. Webster for his trouble.

Bundling into heavy garments, Comfort monitored the progress of the town crier. When two hours had passed, she slipped out of the house and headed into the darkness. Would Mr. Webster keep his word? She breathed a sigh of relief when she rounded the side of their barn, heard a horse snort, and sensed the outline of a wagon.

"Mr. Webster," she called softly.

"Here," he answered.

"Nicolaus, are you awake?" she whispered, moving close to the wagon.

"Ja," he answered, and a moan escaped his lips. "It's been a rough ride."

"Can you walk to the house if Mr. Webster and I support you?"

"I didn't agree to nothing except bringing him to town," Mr. Webster complained.

"You'll get paid when he's in the house. If you're quick

about it, you can leave soon."

Nicolaus slid to the edge of the wagon.

"Mr. Webster will hold your right side, and you can put your hand on my shoulder."

"*Nein.* I'm too heavy to lean on you," he protested.

"I'll just support you. Drag your wounded foot and walk on the other one."

Nicolaus slipped once in the snow, almost pulling Comfort and Mr. Webster to the ground. The farmer swore, but after that near mishap he held Nicolaus more securely. Progressing slowly, they kept at it until the wounded soldier lay exhausted on the bed, his breath expelling in guttural wheezes.

Comfort handed Mr. Webster the two coins. Since hard money was scarce in the Colonies, he seemed pleased with his reward. He hurried from the room, and Comfort turned to Nicolaus and touched his face. His hot, dry skin was feverish.

"I have some herbal tea brewing. It's good for fever and contains a light sedative for pain. I'll bring it in, then I'll call Father to treat your leg."

"It's broken, I think."

Comfort brought the mug of tea, and Nicolaus leaned on his elbow to drink it.

"Tastes good," he said. "Can you tell me what happened? A few of us were separated from the rest of our troops during the fighting, and when the main body of Hessians surrendered, we escaped."

"If reports are to be credited, the Continental army took nine hundred prisoners, and when the Patriots moved across the river to rest, they took the prisoners with them. The river was partly frozen and very treacherous. I'm glad you weren't with them."

"What will happen if I'm discovered here and taken prisoner?"

"I don't know, but I hope we can keep you hidden until you're able to walk."

When he finished the tea, over his protest, Comfort knelt by the bed and removed his heavy shoes. "Now take off your coat and cover yourself with this quilt. I'll go tell Father you're here. If you hear an explosion coming from the hospital, you'll know he's displeased. If not, he'll come and check on your injury."

Still wearing her disguise, Comfort hurried across the backyard. Seemed as if she'd spent most of the past month running back and forth between the hospital and the house.

The patients were resting, and when she didn't see her father in the ward, she entered his office. He sat dozing, his chin on his chest. He looked so tired that Comfort hesitated to awaken him, but Nicolaus needed immediate attention.

She touched him lightly on the shoulder. He straightened, his eyes glazed with sleep.

"I have Nicolaus at the house."

"Are you out of your mind? Washington's army will be back in Trenton within a few days."

"Come and look at his leg," Comfort insisted. "I think it's broken."

With a resigned look, Father notified his helper that he was leaving for a few minutes and followed her into the house.

"I'm better off not knowing how you happened upon Nicolaus, but I took an oath to heal the sick in spite of circumstances, so I'll check on him. But he can't stay in this house. Some American soldiers are unscrupulous, and they might burn the house if they hear an enemy soldier is lodged here."

"Jesus said we were to love our enemies."

"Yes, but I doubt He was speaking of the same kind of love you are," her father said dryly.

"Nicolaus," Comfort said. "Father is here."

"*Danke schön*, Herr Foster."

Father pushed the quilt aside and gently massaged Nicolaus's leg. Nicolaus's muscles tightened with pain, but he didn't make a sound.

"It's broken a few inches below the knee. With so much swelling, I can't tell if the fracture is a clean break, but I think it may be. It's going to be very painful to fix it, for it should have been set right away, but you could lose your leg if I don't act immediately."

"Two legs are a necessity for a soldier," Nicolaus said with some humor. "I trust you. The decision is up to you."

"First, we'll have to find a safe place to hide you."

"Isn't this room safe enough?" Comfort asked.

"Daughter, use your head. If Marion comes home and finds Nicolaus, you know what a commotion that will cause. And he can't stay in the house without Erin knowing it. He has to hide."

"I don't want to make trouble for your family," Nicolaus stated through clenched teeth. His face was the color of ashes.

"There's no one in the isolation room at the hospital," Father continued. "If Nicolaus gets rid of his uniform and puts on other garments, he can pass as an American. His command of the English language will be in his favor."

"That's a good place to hide him," Comfort agreed. "But where can we find garments big enough for him?"

"I'll find some clothes for him, but, Nicolaus, we'll have to move you to the hospital where I have my equipment. I'll help you take off your uniform. Find a blanket to wrap around him, Comfort."

Nicolaus clenched his teeth as they moved him. When his leg hung down, it was apparent that he was in great pain; but leaning on Comfort and her father, he made the trip into the surgery room. He was barely conscious when they laid him on the table.

"Now, Comfort," Father said, "you're going home, and you will stay there."

"I want to help."

"No. You've done your part—the rest is up to me."

Nicolaus lay with his eyes closed, and a pulse beat rapidly in his forehead. While Father prepared the bandages and splints for the fracture, Comfort touched Nicolaus's hand, and his long fingers curled around hers so tightly that she winced.

"I'll be praying for you, Nicolaus. You're in good hands. My father received his training in Philadelphia, and he's been practicing for years."

Looking to be sure her father was occupied, Comfort leaned over quickly and kissed Nicolaus's cheek. Without opening his eyes, his lips parted in a tender smile, and he whispered, *"Guten nacht."*

"Good night," she answered softly.

"He's sleeping now," Father reported when he came for breakfast. "He bit on a bullet while I set the fracture, bandaged the area, and placed the wooden splints on it. He didn't make a sound, but when I finished, he was sweating like I'd thrown a bucket of water on him. I dressed him in a large pair of trousers and a blouse that another patient had left behind and gave him a small dose of opium that should keep him sedated most of the day."

"Thank you, Father. I hated to involve you, but I don't want him to die."

Her father encircled Comfort's waist with his left arm and drew her to his side. "You've only known the man a few weeks, but I guess time doesn't matter that much. *I* knew the first time I saw your mother walking along a Philadelphia street." He pushed back his thin hair. "But go slow. Times are too uncertain to make lifelong decisions."

That evening, her father allowed Comfort to visit Nicolaus. "He's alert and not in much pain, so you can see him. But after this, I want you to stay away from the hospital. If you visit a lot, the other patients might become suspicious. I'll sit with Erin until you get back."

Comfort had shed her disguise again, but she pulled a shawl over her face as she hurried through the general ward of the hospital into the private room that was reserved for very sick patients. She carried a pumpkin tart and a bowl of stew in her basket.

Nicolaus lay on his side with the injured knee half bent on a pillow.

"Good evening," she said. "You look better."

"I am better, but according to your father, I won't be walking much for several weeks."

"You can stay here until you're well. To avoid suspicion, Father says I can't visit again, but I'll send food each day. Can you sit up to eat?"

"Yes," he said, scooting to a sitting position with the injured leg stretched out on the bed. "I'm to keep the knee on a pillow as much as possible to take pressure off the fracture, but

I can change positions."

Comfort tucked the pillow under his knee and watched as he ate heartily.

"Let's have a prayer together and thank God for saving you," she said, and God seemed very near as they clasped hands and offered their thanks.

A few days later, when once again Washington led his bedraggled army across the Delaware, Trenton braced for another battle. The British were marching southward under the command of General Cornwallis, who was under strict orders to defeat the Continental army.

On the second day of the new year, Cornwallis's troops reached Trenton. Her father warned Comfort to stay hidden, for he expected another fight in town. But Washington tricked Cornwallis by circling the British army during the night. The next morning the Colonials attacked other British troops at Princeton, eleven miles to the north. By the time Cornwallis organized his troops and returned to Princeton, the Americans had won another battle.

After two defeats in less than two weeks, the British command decided to relinquish the territory along the Delaware and withdrew eastward. Before they did, they stopped in Trenton to release Hessian prisoners.

Father feared the British might take vengeance on the citizens for their defeat at Princeton, so he ordered his daughters to stay inside. Comfort was terrified when a tall Hessian appeared at the door, reminding her of the day, almost a month earlier, when Nicolaus had stood there. But this man also seemed courteous, no more of a threat than Nicolaus had been.

"I'm Conrad Holstein," he said in broken English, and Comfort thought he said, "I was here as *Belsnickel*. I'm Nicolaus Trittenbach's superior. I want to see him."

"He isn't in our home now," Comfort said truthfully.

Again Comfort found it difficult to interpret his words, but she decided he'd said, "Do you know where he is? I have checked the names of prisoners, and Nicolaus is not listed."

Why did this man want to see Nicolaus? If she told him where Nicolaus was, would he take Nicolaus with the retreating army? Comfort didn't want Nicolaus to risk injuring his leg by traveling, but did she have the right to keep him hidden from his comrades?

She shifted from one leg to the other, getting colder as snow whirled into the room.

"Will you come in? I must talk to my father," she said. She handed the Hessian a cup of cider and left him sitting before the fire.

The swelling on Nicolaus's leg had reduced considerably, and Comfort's father was tightening the bandage. Comfort closed the door behind her and blurted out the news about their visitor. She looked from Nicolaus to her father. "I didn't know what to tell him."

Oliver motioned to Nicolaus, indicating the decision was up to him.

Nicolaus rubbed his forehead. "I'm not any good to the army this way, and I don't want to fight against the Colonies anyway. I believe if I talk with Conrad, he might arrange for me to be paroled here in the Colonies. He's a reasonable man."

"You can't bring him to the hospital," her father said. "I

won't risk having my other patients imprisoned."

"I've been walking very well with the crutch you gave me," Nicolaus said. "I can make it over to the house."

Oliver replaced the splint, and Nicolaus stood gingerly, holding on to the wall until he got the crutch under his arm.

Looking her father straight in the eye, Nicolaus said, "If I am paroled here, I'd like your permission to marry Comfort."

Oliver's eyes gleamed humorously. "But does Comfort want to marry you?" He turned piercing brown eyes on his daughter.

Her face flushed, and she refused to meet his eyes. "I think so," she whispered faintly.

"Well, I won't give any such permission! You haven't known each other long enough to make a decision about marriage, but I will permit you to court Comfort. Will you both agree to trust my discretion in the matter?"

"Ja," Nicolaus said. "We couldn't marry soon anyway. The only profession I know is soldiering. I'll need a means of livelihood before I can support a wife."

"Go talk to your superior officer, then," Oliver said. "I won't insult you by asking you not to betray my patients, but I'm trusting you to be discreet."

Nicolaus rested his hand on Comfort's shoulder to balance himself as they went to the house, but it was still painful for him to jostle the leg. *Leutnant* Holstein stood quickly as they entered the kitchen and reached for Nicolaus's hand.

"Danke Gott, you still live, Nicolaus. I feared you were dead."

"Only wounded, Sir. I've been well cared for by Comfort and her family." Nicolaus spoke slowly in English so Conrad might understand and as a courtesy to Comfort, so she would know what they were saying.

Conrad said that the British were leaving Trenton the next

day and asked if Nicolaus could travel with them.

"I'd be a liability to the British now, for I won't be fit to fight for several months. And I don't really want to fight against the Americans any longer. Can you arrange for me to be paroled?"

Conrad looked from Nicolaus to Comfort, smiled slightly, and spoke in German.

Nicolaus smiled and translated for her. "He said, 'I'm not sure I want to return to Germany either, and I may stay here after the war is over—especially if I have the same incentive you do.'"

Comfort blushed and lowered her eyes.

Leutnant Holstein spoke in German again, and Nicolaus raised his hand. "If I am paroled in America, I swear that I will not take up arms against the British in their current conflict with the rebel Americans."

After promising that the parole paper would be delivered the next day, *Leutnant* Holstein clicked his heels together and exited the room with a salute. With a nostalgic twinge in his heart, Nicolaus returned the gesture. It was sad to part with the past, but he turned to Comfort—his future—put his arm around her, and drew her into a tight embrace.

"I'm committed to America and to you. *Ich liebe Sie*—I love you, Comfort. *Heiraten Sie mich?*"

"I love you too, and if your question means 'will I marry you?' the answer is yes. But I agree with Father that we should wait, at least until you find employment."

Nicolaus laid his crutch aside and sat at the kitchen table. "Christopher Ludwick asked me to join him in providing bread for the army. If I work with him, I'd not be fighting against the British, but I would be helping the Colonists win independence—a cause I believe is just."

Comfort put her arms around Nicolaus's shoulders and

leaned her head against his face. "That sounds like a good opportunity, but it means you'll be on the move a lot. I won't like that, Nicolaus, but it will be several weeks before you're able to walk. That will give us time to become better acquainted."

"*Danke Gott,* that He brought me to America or I wouldn't have found you."

"Yes, I thank Him too. Who knows, perhaps Father will relent and let us marry before you join Christopher."

Nicolaus's eyes brightened at the possibility, and he pulled Comfort down on his uninjured knee. His mouth covered hers hungrily, and Comfort responded to the touch of his lips.

Nicolaus had come to this house as an enemy, but the perilous experiences of the past few weeks had plunged them into an intense friendship that was blossoming into a satisfying love. He knew that for the time being, Comfort would shove aside her concern about the days when they would be separated. War still loomed on the horizon; but tonight, they were together, with no storm clouds to threaten their love.

IRENE B. BRAND

Irene is a lifelong resident of West Virginia, where she lives with her husband, Rod. Her first inspirational romance was published in 1984, and presently she has more than twenty-five novels published or under contract. She is the author of four nonfiction books, various devotional materials, and her writings have appeared in numerous historical, religious, and general magazines. Irene became a Christian at the age of eleven, and continues to be actively involved in her local church. Before retiring in 1989 to devote full time to freelance writing, Irene taught for twenty-three years in secondary public schools. Many of her books have been inspired while traveling to forty-nine of the United States and thirty-five foreign countries.

Dearest Enemy

by Pamela Griffin

Dedication

Dedicated to the loving memory of
my maternal grandparents,
Ludwig Boerner and Vera Zipperer Boerner,
and my paternal grandparents,
John Trampel and Karolina Fütterer Trampel.

For the abundant aid I received on this project,
I give heartfelt thanks to family, friends,
and helpers too numerous to mention.
Special thanks to my German relatives
Ingrid Truxa and Gerhard Heck and his family,
for the many questions they answered.

I also dedicate this book, with much love and thanks,
to my Lord and Savior, Jesus Christ, Who,
even when I didn't know Him,
never once regarded me as His enemy.

*"Therefore if thine enemy hunger, feed him;
if he thirst, give him drink."*
ROMANS 12:20

Chapter 1

Engelheim, Germany, 1918

B rigetta Linder climbed the mossy path, her gaze rising to the castle built into the rocky cliff. Engelturm. Towering dark firs and spruce of the Black Forest surrounded the citadel like guards watching over their king. Beyond that a steep drop-off led to the twisting River Wurm.

When Brigetta was a child, her *Oma* filled her head with countless fairy tales. Yet the stories Brigetta repeatedly begged to hear from her grandmother were the true ones regarding the sandstone fortress. Through the years, Brigetta had visited the structure often and dreamt a thousand dreams, an enjoyable pastime that hadn't lapsed now that she was a woman of seventeen. In her imaginings, the castle was as it had been in days of old, towering and strong, and she the lovely countess fighting for justice. Her count was handsome with a pure heart, doing good for the people. Everything a countess must have in a count. . .

A scrawny German shepherd turned on the path ahead and barked, as if telling her to hurry. "Hush, Wolfgang," Brigetta softly scolded, "you will wake the entire village."

In reality, such a chance was slim since her family's cottage was situated away from the township and up the hill, closer to Engelturm. Her *Opa* had become a hermit after his Eva died, built a cottage near the abandoned castle, and kept to himself making clocks. Upon his death, he left Brigetta's father the cottage, as well as the tools of his trade. Yet Brigetta didn't mind being isolated from the village of Engelheim, especially when it brought her close to her beloved castle.

The rose-tinted ivory tower soared above the treetops, beckoning to Brigetta. It promised escape, enticing her to forget about the war that seemed never to end. . .to forget that starvation lurked everywhere—an evil beast with sharp fangs ready to shred the life from a man. . .to forget that her cousins were fighting on the other side of the Rhine, in France, and might be dead even now.

Wolfgang barked, startling Brigetta from her morose thoughts. Shaking her head to clear it, she continued up the overgrown path, using a walking staff to aid her over the steeper places. Thorny bushes pulled at her calf-length skirt and thick stockings, but she ignored them, moving ever higher. She must hurry. Often she woke early and visited her castle in the gray predawn mist. Yet swirls of pale rose were already starting to filter the sky beyond Engelturm. Soon her mother would awaken and expect Brigetta's help with the morning chores and breakfast—what little of that there was.

At last Brigetta broke through the dense foliage. Inhaling an awed breath, she surveyed the magnificent castle—her castle— as she always did when she made it to this point. To see it so close moved something deep inside her. She wondered if perhaps hundreds of years ago there had been a young woman like Brigetta, dreaming her dreams as she peered from Engelturm's many arched and slit windows.

Growling, Wolfgang came to attention, his scraggly gray and white ruff bristling. His pointed ears pricked forward, then lay back against his head. He barked and ran over the make-shift bridge spanning the dried-up moat, toward the crumbling outer wall.

"Wolfgang! Halt!"

Instead of obeying her command, the dog disappeared through the opening. The blood drained from Brigetta's face. He never disobeyed unless there was a threat. Had a wild boar or wolf found its way inside?

Overcoming the impulse to turn and run, Brigetta a proached the stone edifice, wielding her stick over her shoulder like a weapon. She'd come too far to turn back now, to be deprived of her sojourn. The intruder must go—and she would see to it.

Carefully she stepped through the narrow opening, over the crumbled rocks, and moved across the courtyard toward the north wing of the abandoned fortress. Wolfgang was nowhere in sight, but his loud barking pierced the moist air.

Brigetta followed the sound and crept through what must have been a gallery. A long line of faded rectangles along the walls looked as if they'd once held portraits. Slowly she made her way past an arched door leading to the great hall and moved farther down the corridor. Here dawn's light didn't penetrate, and Brigetta entertained fear of the unknown as the clammy darkness moved to suffocate her.

Over Wolfgang's barking, Brigetta heard the unmistakable shuffling noise of loose rocks rapidly sliding over the ground, as if the intruder were trying to escape. Tightening her grip on the stick, praying under her breath that the good heavenly Father would protect her, she crept through the chapel entrance into the lower part of the tower. An agate altar glimmered below a broken stained glass window. Three rows of stone benches lined either side.

Wolfgang cornered the intruder, who'd pushed himself as far against the wall behind the altar as he could go. In the dim light seeping through the arched multicolored window, Brigetta could discern the brown uniform of the blond man who lay on his side, his watchful gaze never leaving the dog. She gasped as realization sank in.

An American soldier. Her enemy!

Mind reeling, Joseph Miller eyed the barking dog, vaguely aware someone had moved into the round room. Looking up, his gaze met the frightened brown eyes of a young woman with a halo of dark curls. He tried to make sense of everything but couldn't think straight. She held a stick as if she were going up to bat in baseball. Hot—he was so hot.

A hazy recollection of the past days flickered through Joseph's mind, playing tag with his memory, but the thoughts were disjointed. Rushing to obey an order. . .grenades and machine-gun fire exploding all around him. . .capture by enemy soldiers. . .somehow he'd been taken across the Rhine and into German-occupied territory—on foot? In a vehicle? He remembered running, getting shot, then running some more. Had he escaped? Or was he in a prisoner-of-war camp? But such places didn't have rosy-cheeked angels, did they?

Bracing his hand on the ground, Joseph tried to sit up. Burning pain seared his ribs. He inhaled sharply, curling inward and clamping a hand to his torn shirt and the cloth tied around his side. The dog growled.

"Wolfgang," the girl said tersely. Her command silenced the

animal, though she still held the long stick over her shoulder.

Joseph licked dry lips. "Water," he croaked. "Thirsty."

She looked at him, her brow crinkled in puzzlement. *"Was es das? Ich verstehe nicht."*

German. She spoke only German. Of course. And thanks to his grandmother, Joseph knew the language. *"Wasser, bitte. Durstig."*

Her mouth dropped open in shock. "You speak German?" she asked in her language.

"A little." Another pain stabbed his side, and he groaned. His eyes closed as he fell backward, letting his head knock against the stone floor.

"You're hurt!" She closed the distance and fell on her knees before him. The stick clattered to the ground beside her. "Where are you wounded?"

"Ribs. Left side." A dull heaviness invaded his head, separating him from reality. She put her hands to his shirt and tugged it up, inflicting worse pain.

"Aaahh!" His eyes flew open as he harshly reentered the world. Her head bent low, her gaze lowered to his bare chest. A becoming flush touched her face—or maybe it was the strange rosy light coming from above.

"The wound isn't too deep, but it looks infected." A pause. "How were you injured?"

"Bullet. . .from a German rifle."

Her head jerked up, and their gazes collided. Joseph saw fear return to her eyes. She snatched her hands from his chest and stumbled backward to her feet as if she'd just remembered who he was.

A film descending over his mind, Joseph watched his beautiful enemy back out from what would surely be his tomb, then turn on her heel and run away. Closing his eyes, he prepared to die.

Brigetta scrambled down the hill, coming to her senses when she was halfway home. Gasping for air, her lungs on fire, she stopped and looked back at the castle tower etched against the rosy clouds in the lightening day.

Could she really leave a man to die, foe or not? Her mother had raised her to be kindhearted to all God's creatures. Yet whether that lesson extended to enemy soldiers, Brigetta was uncertain. What would the Lord have her do?

She knew the answer to that as surely as she knew her name was Brigetta Linder. With a resigned sigh, she started to retrace her steps.

"Brigetta! Wait! Are you going to Engelturm?"

Six-year-old Ludwig came running up to greet her. Moss covered his knees underneath his *lederhosen* and a few fir needles stuck out from his blond hair.

Making an effort to mask her tension in front of her curious brother, Brigetta affected a stern gaze. "Do *Mutti* and *Vatti* know you are up and about, Ludwig Wilhelm Linder? Just look at you!"

He inhaled a large gulp of air, catching his breath. "I fell. *Mutti* sent me to find you. You are to care for me and Hilda while she goes to the village. Can I go to Engelturm with you?"

She ignored his question. "The village?"

"*Ja.* To visit Aunt Olga. Have you forgotten, Brigetta?"

She had forgotten but didn't want to admit it. "Come, and I will make breakfast."

Her heart twisted when he scrunched up his nose at the

mention of the tasteless millet gruel. She couldn't blame him. Oh, what she wouldn't give for a taste of her mother's *Streuselkuchen* or *Obsttorte!* Ludwig had never tasted such sweet treats as the crumb cake or fruit torte. All such delicacies ceased when Germany first went to war and trade had been closed off to them. Ludwig had been two at the time.

He slipped his small hand into hers. "Have you seen the doll *Vatti* carved for *Graf* von Engel's clock?" he asked, pride in his little-boy voice as he spoke of their father. "He finished it last night. It is ever so nice. One day, I'm going to be a clock maker, just like *Vatti*."

"And you'll be just as fine a clock maker as *Vatti*."

Brigetta smiled sadly at the child, who'd puffed out his thin chest at her remark. Her mind traveled down a path it had visited often this year. Would that day come? Or would they starve to death, as some had in their country? Despite reports of a coming armistice, there was still no sign of peace.

Because her mother's brother was a farmer, Brigetta and her family had a portion of potatoes, beets, and other vegetables but no sugar or seasonings of any kind. Her father bartered his clocks for millet or wheat when he could. Her mother kept a small patch of vegetables near the cottage, though her ability to grow them was sadly lacking. And as for meat? Even with Russia's surrender earlier this year, the meat shortage continued. Still, the turnips and withered carrots her mother grew, as well as the other sources of food, were more than many had.

Brigetta supposed she should be grateful for their questionable bounty, but she was mad. Mad at the *Kaiser* and his aides, mad at Great Britain for the naval blockade on overseas supplies, and most of all, mad at the Americans who'd entered the war only months before and turned it around in France's favor. And one of them lay in the castle on the hill. Her castle.

"Are you angry with me, Brigetta? You have such a fierce look on your face."

Forcing her facial muscles to relax, Brigetta attempted a smile. *"Nein, Liebchen.* I'm not mad. Let us return to the cottage."

And the wounded American? Brigetta refused to think about him. It was only then that she realized Wolfgang had not come with her from the castle.

Chapter 2

Brigetta whisked the plank floor free from dirt with a broom. Though her hands industriously set the cottage to rights, her thoughts were up on the hill, in the chapel room of Engelturm.

"Brigetta, I'm tired of writing my letters. Can we go to Engelturm?"

Ludwig's plea startled her, and she accidentally hit the carved leg of the hutch with the broom, setting a china shepherdess to rocking.

"Not today, Ludwig," their father said from his chair in the area where he often worked. Hazy afternoon light brightened the window behind him. His right foot, permanently damaged when a barrel had fallen on it years ago, rested on a cushioned stool. With a small knife, he meticulously carved a piece of wood, producing the beginnings of a doll the size of Brigetta's index finger. "You must do your lessons, *ja?* You must learn well and grow up to be smart, like all German boys."

"*Ja, Vatti.*" Disappointment clouded his blue eyes, but like all children in the village, Ludwig was polite and respectful toward his elders. That is, toward all of them except Brigetta.

Her mouth twisted in wry amusement. Ludwig argued

with her incessantly and tested her patience numerous times, probably because he thought her merely his sister and didn't classify her as an adult.

"What is the matter, Ludwig?" ten-year-old Hilda asked as she walked into the room with a basket of clothes. Her blond braids were wrapped in coils around either side of her head like their mother wore hers. "Are you not grateful the school has closed and Herr Rottingham went to fight in the war? I am! He scared me. His pointed beard and beady eyes reminded me of *den Teufel*, himself!"

"Enough, Hilda," their father remonstrated. "You shouldn't compare any person to the devil. *Gott* loves Herr Rottingham, no matter his appearance or behavior."

Hilda's brow creased in remorse. *"Ja, Vatti."*

Brigetta noticed her father's face had clouded at mention of the war. Like most Germans at the outset of the war, her father had been supportive of the German army. Now he just wanted the fighting to end, as they all did.

She went to perch on his chair arm, looping her arm around his neck and bringing her head close to his graying one. "You look tired. Does your foot pain you? Would you like me to bring you something? Or perhaps read to you from my book of poems?"

"Not now, *meine kleine Träumerin,*" he said quietly. "I must finish *Graf* von Engel's clock in time for his daughter's wedding."

Brigetta smiled at the special endearment he used for her: my little dreamer. And she was, like her father, a dreamer; whereas Hilda was more like her mother, sensible. . .down to earth. She kissed his temple and rose to finish her chores.

"Is *Mutti* coming home soon?" Ludwig asked as he etched his letters.

"Her sister is very sick," their father said. "She wants to spend time with her."

Ludwig looked up from his work in shock. "Will Aunt Olga die?"

"*Mutti* takes her food from our own portion," Hilda answered matter-of-factly. "Aunt Olga won't starve."

"Your *mutter* is a good woman." Their father looked at each of his children in turn. "We must always share with those who have none."

"Even our enemies?" Brigetta bit her lower lip after blurting the question, as surprised as the others, who'd all turned to look at her.

"What enemies do you have, Brigetta?" Ludwig asked. "Do you mean the butcher's daughter, Henrietta? Is she your enemy?"

Brigetta moved to tousle his hair. "Six-year-old German boys should not be so curious," she teased, hoping to change the subject and still her rapidly beating heart. "Or they might get eaten by a hungry wolf."

Ludwig laughed and thumped his chest. "I will eat the wolf!"

"Father Zimmerman says we should help our enemies," Hilda inserted wisely. "He said we should be like the Good Samaritan. Do you remember that story, Brigetta?"

"*Ja.*" Wanting to hide her hot face, Brigetta moved to the center of the room and began wiping off the sides of the round black stove with a wet cloth. The Samaritan had not only found his enemy on the roadside but tended his wounds, gave him drink, and took him to a place where he could receive care, even giving his own money to see to it.

Brigetta sighed, feeling convicted. Deep down, she knew she should do the same. Her gaze went to the kettle on the stove with the gruel left inside.

Again she thought about Wolfgang's presence at Engelturm, and a shiver of worry coursed up her spine. Though Wolfgang was the family pet, he was vicious toward strangers, as well as being half starved. Yet Brigetta couldn't depart from the cottage without a plausible excuse. It would seem odd for her to leave when she'd so recently returned.

Her mind a receptacle of frightening thoughts, Brigetta looked out the window to the dense forest and beyond, to the castle tower.

Joseph awoke, his ears swimming with a strange hum. His body felt as if it were on fire, yet at the same time he shook with chills and his teeth chattered. He opened his eyes.

Two slanted fierce orbs behind a long snout stared back. The growling started.

Even in his fever, Joseph recoiled from the vicious animal, realizing the danger. His eyelids slid shut. *Lord, help me. I'm so weak. . . . If I must die. . .don't let it be at the jaws of this beast.*

The next time Joseph awoke, the room was dim. Outside he heard the whir of insects. An owl hooted. A cool breeze touched his chest, likely coming from the broken stained glass window above him. It was then he realized the blood-soaked rag had been removed from around his middle and his shirt lay open. Something stiff covered his side. A bandage?

Curious, he moved his arm to investigate. Scorching pain blistered his ribs, and he groaned. Maybe he should just lie still for now.

A pitiful whine startled him. Hesitantly, he turned his head, noticing it lay pillowed on something soft. The same German shepherd sat on his haunches and stared back, only this time with its head cocked as if trying to figure him out. Joseph understood how he felt. Nothing made sense.

A gas lantern, the flame low, sat on the ground next to the dog and cast a pale light on the closest surroundings. An altar of some kind of glittering stone stood behind the animal. Joseph could see no one else in the room.

"So tell me," he said to the dog, his voice coming out raspy and weak, "are you my guard? Is this my prison?"

The dog barked, this time sounding almost friendly. His tail thumped the stone floor.

"Well then, Herr Guard, mind telling me where I am?"

The dog whined again, stretching out on his belly and laying his muzzle on his paws.

"Guess not." Joseph coughed, wincing at the pain this produced. "Oh, I get it. You're a German dog. You know only German." He repeated his questions in that language.

Footsteps echoed from nearby. "Do you always talk to canines and expect them to answer?" a feminine voice asked in German, a thread of amusement evident in her tone.

Joseph shifted his gaze upward, trying to see who was there. A dim figure approached and stepped into the pool of light. The young woman wore a black dress and blue shawl. Thick, dark ringlets just hit her shoulders. Her cheeks were rosy in her thin face, and the light reflected in her eyes.

Joseph blinked. An angel? He had a dim recollection of seeing her once before. He swallowed, keeping his eyes on the vision. "Where am I?"

Setting a pail on the floor, she sank to her knees beside him. She pulled a dipper from inside the bucket and slipped her hand underneath his neck, propping his head up. "Drink this."

"What is it?" Joseph tried to pull back but was surprised at how weak he was. His body wouldn't obey what his brain told it to do.

"Water," she said, tipping the dipper next to his mouth, "from a spring on the hill."

The cool liquid trickled over his cracked lips and down his stubbled chin. When Joseph tasted that it was indeed water, he gulped it down. Although his parched throat begged for more, she pulled the dipper away and let his head sink back to the pillowed cloth.

"You mustn't drink so fast. You will choke," she scolded, replacing the dipper in the pail.

He sucked in his bottom lip, trying to retrieve any moisture there, and assessed her. "Where am I?" he asked again. "And who are you?"

"This is Engelturm. And I have been taking care of you."

Engelturm. . .Angel Tower. Then she must be an. . . His heart skipped a beat. "Are you an angel?"

"What?" Her eyes widened. At this proximity he noticed a mislaid dimple under the corner of her mouth, next to her chin.

"An angel," he repeated, beginning to feel foolish. "You said this was Angel Tower."

"Ah, I see. You must still be a little delirious." She pulled up the wool blanket that rested near his legs, covering him to the chin. "I am but a simple woodcarver's daughter. I live on the same hill as this castle."

"Castle?" His surprised gaze swept the room. "We're in a castle?"

"*Ja.* Engelturm. My castle." Her face flooded with color, and she looked away.

"Your castle? You own this place?"

"*Nein. Graf* von Engel does, but nobody has lived in Engelturm since the Seven Years' War when the west wing was demolished." She stiffened and seemed to withdraw into herself. "I must go."

"Wait!" Joseph swiftly withdrew his arm from beneath the blanket in his panic to stop her.

She shrank backward, sudden alarm in her eyes, and put the soles of her shoes to the floor as if she would shoot up and run.

He coughed, the action sending ribbons of fire through his side. "Please. Don't go yet. You said you've been taking care of me. How long have I been here?"

She hesitated, as though undecided, then relaxed. "Three days you've been feverish. I tended your wound and put on a paste to draw out the infection." She bit her lip. "You almost died, I think, but the fever turned last night."

Joseph tried to absorb the information. Almost died? Three days? Weariness overtook him, and he closed his eyes.

He heard the rustle of her skirt and the scrape of her shoes on stone. Yet there was one more thing he had to know before she left. Without opening his eyes, he asked softly, "Why did you do it?"

A pause. "Do what?"

"Take care of me. I'm your enemy—an American soldier. Why didn't you leave me to die?"

A longer pause. "*Gott* tells us we must do good to our enemies and to those who spitefully use us and persecute us," she all but whispered. "Because of that, I could not let you die."

Before his tired brain could fathom a reply, she was gone.

Brigetta hurried down the hill, the American's question eating at her soul. At one point, she would have gladly let him perish, and remembering that made her feel terrible. Enemy or not, when a man was wounded and on the brink of death, he deserved care. And God must want this soldier to live.

Three days ago when she'd first returned to the castle to tend her patient, Brigetta had been surprised to see Wolfgang sitting placidly by the soldier, as though watching over him. The dog had looked up and whined, but otherwise hadn't moved. As if that weren't shock enough, each day she'd urged him to return to the cottage, without success. The first time Wolfgang refused to leave, Brigetta had lifted her chin and looked down at him, muttering, *"Varräter."*

But what was she? Was she also a traitor in giving aid to an enemy of the Fatherland? Would it not be better for her to contact the German army and inform them of the soldier's presence? Or at least shouldn't she tell her parents?

Yet Brigetta felt the still voice of God urge her to remain silent. Then, too, she was anxious concerning what might happen should she reveal the truth. Was it the voice of fear she heard and not of God?

The questions tortured her the rest of the evening, and she kept quiet, eliciting curious stares from her family as they ate their turnip soup. Later, Brigetta fell to her knees beside the bed she shared with Hilda. But her lips couldn't articulate her usual evening prayer. She dropped her forehead against clasped hands.

Sweet Jesus, help me. I know not how to pray. . . . I'm so afraid of the future. What will happen if someone finds out about the American soldier and that I helped him? Will they put Vatti and Mutti in jail? Will they take me? She lifted her face to the ceiling's wooden beams. *Yet I feel as if I must help him. Please show me Thy will, Lord.*

Hilda clambered up into the loft. *"Mutti* wants you."

Releasing a sigh, Brigetta rose and climbed down the ladder. Near the kitchen stove, the only source of heat in the cottage, *Mutti* sat in a rocking chair, mending a dress. *Vatti* sat across from her, whittling on a doll. At her entrance, they looked up.

"Brigetta," her mother started, her dark eyes concerned. The hand that held the needle lay still in her lap. "Ludwig tells me you've been visiting Engelturm several times a week—and twice have not returned home until after dark."

The little sneak. Brigetta kept her face expressionless. "I go there to escape my problems."

"To pray?"

"Sometimes."

Her mother shook her head. "I still don't like it. I cannot see why you should want to waste your time visiting a decaying fortress. It is a dangerous place. One day it might fall down around you."

"Nein, Mutti—only one wing is in ruins. And only because of the French invasion centuries ago. The rest of the castle is sturdy—"

"Hush, Brigetta. Do not talk back to your *Mutter.*"

She lowered her eyes. "I'm sorry, *Mutti.*"

The fire in the stove crackled and popped, filling in the ensuing silence. "As long as Brigetta sees to her chores and comes home before dark," her father said, "I don't think it would be such a bad thing for her to visit the castle, Karolina. Brigetta is right. Engelturm is safe. It has stood for centuries."

Brigetta raised hopeful eyes.

Her father smiled, his gaze soft. "If I were not a cripple, I might even be tempted to join her," he added wistfully. "I remember being a boy and playing there. Liam, Friedrich, and

I were the ones who built the wooden bridge across the dry moat. . . . *Ja,* we vanquished many an enemy in those days."

Brigetta held her breath, waiting.

"Ach, I don't know!" Her mother swiftly raised her hands, palms up in disgust. "It is trial enough to live with one dreamer, but to endure two in the family. . ."

Brigetta noticed for all her harsh words, her mother's lips had curled up, and hope whispered to Brigetta's heart. Bless her dear *Vatti. Mutti* always yielded to him. All German women were taught from girlhood to show submission to their husbands.

Before her father could reply, frantic scrambling of footsteps sounded on the loft's ladder. Hilda rushed toward them, her eyes wide. "Ludwig is gone!"

Chapter 3

Gone? What do you mean 'gone'?" *Mutti* rose from her chair. "The boy isn't gone, Hilda. He is somewhere— likely playing a game of hiding. Ludwig! Come out this instant."

A search of the room did nothing to divulge his whereabouts. *Vatti* grabbed his cane. Brigetta hurried to the door before he could rise. It stood slightly ajar.

"I will go look for him," she said before whisking outside.

The frigid air sneaked up the opening of her nightgown and wrapper, chilling her legs. She should have brought a lamp. If there was a moon tonight, it was hidden by the dense firs surrounding the cottage.

"Ludwig?" she called. The darkness felt eerie, the nocturnal sounds of the forest intimidating, and her voice came out more softly than she'd intended. "Where are you?"

She crept to the back of the cottage, the cold marshy grass brushing against her ankles. There, on his knees and in his long nightshirt, was Ludwig, fiercely hugging Wolfgang's neck. He heard her swishing footsteps and turned, joy making his pale face glow in the night.

"You were right, Brigetta! You said he'd come back. I heard

whining and knew it was him. He must have gone off hunting. Just see how much better he looks!"

Brigetta smiled. Relief at finding her brother warred with worry—for did Wolfgang's presence mean the soldier had left Engelturm? In his wounded condition, he wouldn't get far. As she bent to rub between the dog's ears, at the same time putting a hand to her brother's bony shoulder blades, Brigetta scanned the towering, shadowy silhouettes of the firs, almost expecting to see the soldier leaning weakly against one of them. But all that met her eyes was darkness—thick and enveloping.

"Come, Ludwig," Brigetta whispered, as though the trees might overhear and stop her. "Let us go inside."

"May Wolfgang sleep with me?" Ludwig asked hopefully.

"You will have to ask *Mutti.*"

Their mother said no, but Brigetta placated Ludwig with the promise of a story. The boy nodded, resigned to let Wolfgang sleep in his usual place by the stove.

Ludwig's room in the loft was small, a cubbyhole on the other side of the partition where the girls' bed stood. The plank walls in his area boasted countless newspaper clippings and postcards of his flying hero, Baron Manfred von Richthofen—the Red Baron. The German had been shot down by a Canadian pilot months ago, but Ludwig never let his admiration for his war hero die, claiming that one day he, too, would shoot down as many enemy planes as the Red Baron. Their beloved cousin Pieter was also a German flyer, which only increased Ludwig's aspiration to be a fighter pilot. Brigetta shivered at the grim prospect, hoping such a day would never arrive.

"Now what shall it be?" she asked, tucking Ludwig into his small wooden cot. She snuggled the down comforter around his shoulders. *"Hänsel und Gretel? The Bremen Town Musicians?"*

"Tell me about Engelturm and the people who lived there."

The name brought back thoughts of the soldier, troubling Brigetta. "How about something else instead?"

"Nein! I want to hear of Engelturm." He shot up, displacing the quilt Brigetta had so carefully tucked around him. "Tell me of *Graf* von Engel and his lady Amelia and how he met her in Dinkelsbühl. And how later, the children saved the village from the mean old enemy colonel because his heart was softened by the flowers they threw and the pleas they gave."

Brigetta crossed her arms, studying him with raised brows. "It sounds as though you could tell me the story," she said, amused. "You've learned it well."

Propping his elbows on his knees, Ludwig laid his chin on balled hands. "Why was the castle named Engelturm, Brigetta? Was it because of what happened in Dinkelsbühl?"

"Nein. At sunset the castle glows as though it were aflame, and legends say that angels encamp around the fortress. After Christian von Engel traveled to Dinkelsbühl and met Amelia and God delivered them from harm—from that time forward, the name of the castle further served to remind all who see it of God's faithfulness and protection."

She settled back, drawing up one leg beneath the other. "And there are other times God has been a safeguard to those in the castle. During the Seven Years' War, the French used siege artillery to destroy the fortress, but it began to storm, rendering their weapons useless. In the heavy rain they could no longer see to attack, but the von Engels didn't have that problem. From within the castle, they sent a volley of cannon fire the soldiers' way, and the French scurried like wet mice who'd angered a sleeping cat."

Ludwig's eyes shone with excitement. "Will you take me there tomorrow, Brigetta? Will you show me the west wing? I do so want to see it! And what's left of the armory too."

Brigetta sobered and stood. "Some day, *Liebchen*. Not now."

"But, Brigetta. . ."

She kissed his forehead, bid him a soft *"Guten nacht,"* and hurried from the loft.

Standing on the threshold of the chapel, Brigetta stared, then rushed forward. The shawl she'd used to pillow the soldier's head was empty; the blanket lay wrinkled underneath the stained glass window. She scanned the area, with its many alcoves cut into the wall. He was nowhere in sight.

Setting the bucket of breakfast gruel down with a bang, Brigetta hurried from the room to search. Since Wolfgang's return to the cottage, she'd had an uneasy premonition something was wrong. Now she wished she would have slipped away last night to investigate.

Brigetta rushed through an archway leading outside and came to a stop in the inner courtyard, surveying its few crumbling statues and stone benches. Scraggly bushes and gnarled trees dotted the area. Weeds had pushed their way through crevices in the brown cobbles now colored with moss.

Why had the American left? Was it to escape or to hide? Had he thought a stranger lurked nearby and felt the need to relocate deeper within the fortress?

Seeing no sign of him, Brigetta turned and sped back toward the chapel tower to retrieve her lantern. Several rooms with only small windows were dim, and she would need light. Lamp in hand, she took the stone steps spiraling the side next to the chapel and ascended to the top—to a room now empty of whatever it once held. And empty of the soldier as well. Frustrated, she glanced through the slit window, to the tops of the firs and below to the tiny village, before she exited and hurried down the gallery to another part of the castle.

Brigetta entered the tower that once held the armory. A rusted suit of armor stood in one corner, and a few weapons in an equal state of disrepair hung mounted to the walls, though many of the black iron hooks were empty. A quick study of the place showed Brigetta the soldier hadn't come here either. She hunted through more rooms of the castle's north and south wings before turning her search to the ruins of the west wing.

A cool wind blew, but sunlight warmed her shoulders and back as she walked through the wreckage. Moving around a waist-high block of crumbling sandstone, she almost stepped on the soldier. She gasped and knelt on the rocky ground beside him.

His wound had opened, staining his shirt. The bandage was halfway off, and drops of dried blood spattered his pants and the ground by his side. Brigetta shoved his shoulder to wake him, but he only groaned. His breathing was labored. Putting a hand to his forehead, she understood why. His fever had returned. Foolish man! He'd likely fallen, reopened the wound on the jagged rocks, and spent the night out here. A thick fog had covered the hillside early this morning—and that certainly hadn't done his health any good. Foolish, foolish man.

Brigetta surveyed her surroundings. With her slight build, and judging from his height and well-developed physique, she couldn't carry him back to the tower. And dragging him was out of the question because of the uneven ground.

Brigetta hurried back to the chapel where she kept her

things, then returned to her patient. Pulling his shirt and bandage away, she grimaced when she saw the injury. Hurriedly, she cleansed it, applied a salve, and rebandaged his side. The wound was deeper than she'd thought the first time she had quickly peered at it; the bullet had taken away a good chunk of flesh. Again she wondered where he had come from and how he'd managed to make it to the top of the hill.

Her gaze traveled to his face, now easy to see in the light of day. Thick stubble covered his chin and cheeks, and she noticed his features were classic in appearance, like those of aristocracy. His golden-brown lashes flickered, but he didn't open his eyes. His mouth was slightly parted, the curve of his lips soft, the bottom fuller than the top. Brigetta had the insane urge to run her index finger lightly along their outline but clenched her hands in her skirt instead.

He groaned, slowly rocking his head from side to side. Furrowing her brow, Brigetta whispered a fervent prayer for God's intervention. She didn't know what more in her power she could do to help him. But of one thing she was certain. She would intercede for him and trust his care to her heavenly Father. For the greatest power came from the One above.

Behind closed eyelids, Joseph sensed light. He felt something tickle his face and moved his hand to brush it away. A vicious twinge tore through his side before he raised his hand past his hips. He moaned, letting his arm fall back to the ground.

Opening his eyes to white glaring sunlight, he squinted, then turned his head. The angel was back, kneeling beside him. She whisked her hand above his face, shooing whatever insect crawled along his nose. He managed a grin.

"*Danke.*"

Her face turned a light cherry red. "Why did you leave the chapel?"

Joseph stiffened. His motive had been twofold. After she'd left, quoting Scripture with trembling words of why she must help him, Joseph knew he couldn't stay here any longer and put this young woman's life in jeopardy. She could get into a lot of trouble for aiding a prisoner of war. Still, he hesitated to tell her this and gave the other reason instead. "Your dog started barking and ran off. I thought danger of discovery might be near when he didn't come back."

Her brows bunched in confusion. "So you thought to throw yourself over that steep cliff and into the River Wurm instead?" She motioned to a crumbling wall on her right. "That is the direction you were headed."

"I couldn't see well. There was no moon last night."

She nodded. "Wolfgang likely picked up the scent of a hare. When he arrived at the cottage, he looked as if he'd enjoyed a good meal." She studied his face. "No one has visited Engelturm in all the years I've come here—since I was a child. It is my hideout. You are safe." When she talked of the castle, her eyes sparkled and came alive. Sunlight glistened in her hair.

"What is your name?" Joseph asked quietly.

She jerked, as though taken aback. "My name?"

He lifted one corner of his mouth. "I can't call you 'my angel' forever—though it wouldn't be far from the truth."

Again she seemed flustered, looking at her hands, which plucked at her dark skirt. "Brigetta. My name is Brigetta."

"And I'm Joseph Miller."

The hands stilled, and she swiftly raised her head, her mouth falling open. Dark eyes full of puzzlement sought his. "But, that is a German name—isn't it? It sounds German."

"My paternal grandparents emigrated from Baden to America when they were young. That's how I know your language."

She rocked back on her heels. "Baden?" she exclaimed, shocked disbelief raising her voice a decibel. "That isn't many kilometers from here. Then. . .you are German?"

Joseph wished now he'd never spoken. "I'm American. Born in New York."

"But you have German blood—you said so." She grew upset. "The men you have killed in this war may be your own kin. Does that not bother you?"

It bothered him more than he would ever let on. Yet when persecution of his family had increased in his hometown the longer the war progressed, Joseph had known he must do what he could to prove himself a loyal American. And so, he'd enlisted in the army not long after President Wilson declared war—after Germany invaded neutral Belgium and later destroyed ships carrying American citizens.

"Maybe if the kaiser weren't so power-hungry, there wouldn't be a war," Joseph muttered, suddenly angry.

Brigetta's mouth tightened, and she clutched her skirt. "And maybe if America would mind her own business and stop interfering in others' affairs, the war could have been over long ago. And many of our people wouldn't have starved."

"France is our ally. We're committed to helping them."

"Even at the expense of killing your own?"

Her emotional query ripped his heart, making it difficult to remember the words that had been drummed into his head by the sergeant during army training: *Death to the kaiser and the Huns! We must put an end to their greed and win this great war!*

Joseph closed his eyes and swallowed. "War is hard. No war in the history of the world has ever been fair. Everyone suffers, Brigetta."

Her name on his lips halted any reply she might have given. Something strange fluttered through her heart, and her face grew hot. If his eyes hadn't been closed, she would have turned away in confused embarrassment. What was wrong with her?

Studying Joseph's face, Brigetta noted lines of strain bracketing his mouth and creasing his forehead. He was obviously in a great deal of pain, and that thought brought with it remorse for her bitter words. He was in no shape to hold this discussion. She tenderly laid her hand on his clammy forehead. His eyes flew open in shock.

"Your stay out here last night has brought the fever back, though it isn't high," she explained. "Before I go, we should move you back to the chapel. The broken window doesn't keep the weather out, as you know, but it does have a roof."

He opened his mouth as if he would speak, then closed it.

"I will get my walking staff," Brigetta said, starting to move to her feet. "By using that and leaning on me, you should be able to get there, and I can take better care of you."

Before she could stand, he grasped her wrist—his grip firm. She looked at him in surprise.

His eyes were steady, serious. "I don't want you to get in trouble for helping me, Brigetta. Just go home and forget you ever saw me. When I'm stronger, I'll leave. No one need ever know about my stay at Engelturm."

Confused by the unexpected despair his low, intense words produced, she shook her head. *"Nein,* Joseph, I cannot do that.

You see, I will know."

Slowly extracting her wrist from his grasp, Brigetta rose and went in search of the walking staff.

Chapter 4

Brigetta sat on the stone floor, her chin propped on up-raised knees. Hands clasped tightly around the hem of her skirt at her ankles, she studied Joseph, who sat nearby. "Tell me, I've often wondered. How did you come to Engelturm?"

He had improved in the week since she'd found him in the west wing's ruins, though he wasn't ready to strike out on his own. He still needed aid walking—using both the staff and her shoulder—but his steps weren't as unsteady as they'd been.

With his back against the wall underneath the chapel window, he stared across the room, his expression grave. "The trenches were hell on earth. Think of the worst place you've seen, and you might be close. Sometimes, after battle, the leaders on both sides would declare a moment's peacetime, and enemy and ally would go to the no-man's-land in between boundaries and collect the wounded, working side by side." He shook his head, closing his eyes. "War is crazy."

Brigetta was in complete agreement. "But how did *you* get wounded—how did you escape the German army?"

"I'm getting to that." Joseph hesitated, then looked at her. "One day a new sergeant had the idea to post a full-frontal attack.

The result was carnage. I got caught in the middle and fell, though I wasn't wounded. A German soldier approached me—just a boy, really—and I lifted my hands in surrender. I'm not sure why he didn't shoot. I thought he was going to, since he'd raised his rifle to my face. Instead he took me across enemy lines, along with a few others who were captured."

Brigetta felt Joseph's horror as though it were her own.

He tipped his head back and looked at the ceiling. "It was at night, while three of them were transporting us to a prisoner-of-war camp, that I found my chance to escape. Something went wrong with their vehicle, and the lieutenant started arguing with the driver. The guard watching us turned to see. One of the prisoners struck him in the throat with his elbow. Another put the lieutenant in a headlock, and another grabbed the driver's gun. I rolled off the back and ran for all I was worth. Gunfire soon sounded behind me, and just before I reached the cover of the trees, I felt myself being hit."

"But if you were hit, how could you run?" Brigetta shook her head. "How did you get away?"

Joseph's smile was grim. "When your life is at stake, you'll find you can do a great many things you didn't think you could." He raised one knee, winced, and went on. "I zigzagged like crazy in the dark through those trees, praying all the while I wouldn't be found or shot down. That's another thing. My Christian convictions had faltered after the persecution my family endured—but when a man comes up against such odds, suddenly things like prayer and God are extremely important."

Brigetta nodded. She'd heard of close brushes with death bringing people to the Lord.

"I found a river and waded in. Ran as far as I could in that freezing water in case they used dogs to try to find me, then I got out on the other side. When I couldn't go any farther, I hid. At one point I heard men rustling in the bushes, but they never found me."

"So you walked all this way?"

"No, I traveled by night and hid by day—less chance of anyone catching me. I ate nuts and berries when I could find them. I stumbled across a village and found a farm with a horse cart loaded with hay. No one was around, and I was exhausted, so I burrowed deep inside. I have no idea how long I slept, but when I woke and emerged from the hay, it was late evening and I was in a different place—surrounded by tall trees. Here—in the Black Forest."

"Engelheim?" Brigetta asked.

"I'm not sure. By then the infection had set in, and I couldn't think straight. All the events after that are just a haze until I got to this place. But it took days. I remember the moon was full, and I looked up and saw the white stone of your Engelturm glowing in the night. In my fever, I somehow knew I had to get here to find safety, so I struggled up the hill. I rested often, sometimes passing out and then coming to again. I don't have any memory of how I finally reached this chapel."

"*Gott* was watching over you," Brigetta said, her voice quiet. "He guided your steps."

Joseph's eyes were steady. "I have an idea you're right about that," he said just as softly. "And He sent an angel to help me."

Heat rising to her face because she knew he meant her, Brigetta unwound from her position and stood, grabbing the bucket. "Before I go, I'll bring more water."

"Brigetta."

The low word stopped her as effectively as coming up against a rock wall. She turned.

His expression was tender. "I know I have said this many times. . .but thank you. You really are my angel."

Offering him a feeble smile, Brigetta hastened from the room, flustered, confused. She realized that at some point during these past weeks, she'd come to desire more than Joseph's gratitude. She wanted his friendship—and his love. Drawing her brows together and shaking her head at the impossibility of such an occurrence, Brigetta hurried down the hill and to the fresh-water spring.

Joseph watched her go, wondering if he shouldn't have spoken. This past week when Brigetta visited, they had often talked and for longer periods of time. He had listened in amused fascination to the little girl inside the woman, who possessed such a love for the castle. Her face brightened when she spoke of Engelturm, of the people who'd once lived here, and of her immediate family. Joseph felt he knew them all well, based on her descriptions alone. And he wished he could get to know Brigetta better. . . .

A wry grin quirking his mouth, he turned to the German shepherd snoozing near the altar. "What do you think, Wolfgang? Should I let sleeping dogs lie, or should I tell her how I feel? Would she be upset to learn an American soldier has fallen for her?"

Even as he said the words, Joseph knew the answer. There could never be anything between them. They were enemies, or at least he was hers. . . .

He sighed, remembering the chill that would suddenly frost her eyes when she spoke to him of her first cousins— Gustaf, Heinrich, and Pieter—fighting in France. A few times emotion would overtake her, and she would swipe at her lashes and escape the room, away from Joseph, apparently unable to bear even to look at him for what he represented: those who were shooting at her kin.

No, he must leave here soon. Leave her to enjoy what little tranquility she could find in this old fortress, without him there to remind her of the war.

Testing himself, Joseph inched to his feet. He inhaled a quick breath at the stitch in his side but forced himself to walk across the room, finally slumping to one of the stone benches. His heartbeat and breathing were rapid, and perspiration dotted his upper lip.

If only he had some meat broth or something more fortifying than the gruel and thin turnip soup she fed him, he might recuperate faster. Instant shame swamped him for the ungracious thought. He knew food was scarce in Germany, and sometimes he wondered if Brigetta were giving him her own meals. Her face seemed thinner than when he'd first seen her, her cheekbones more pronounced.

He heard footsteps and looked over his shoulder. A look of exasperation covered her face before she moved his way with the bucket and knelt before him. "You are worse than a child! You must keep still, or you may open the wound again. It probably should have been stitched, but I didn't know how. Here, drink this."

She brought the ladle to his mouth, cupping her other hand underneath to catch any liquid that might spill, and he gladly took a sip of the cool water. Joseph had reached the point where he could take the dipper himself but didn't want to tell her so. That might mean she would move away from him, and he wanted her close.

After his second dipperful, she replaced the ladle. "I should be going. . . ."

"Must you?" The words came of their own accord. She looked at him in astonishment, and he hastened to add, "There is nothing to do here all day. I'm too shaky yet to investigate the castle, and I don't sleep for hours on end like I once did."

A smile curved her sweet mouth, and the dimple near her chin appeared. "Ah, so you are bored? I will bring you a book to pass the time. Have you a preference?"

Joseph shook his head. The thought of reading appealed, though he'd never cared for it before. "Anything is fine."

"Very well. *Auf Wiedersehen*, Joseph." He thought he detected a mischievous glint in her eyes, but she turned away before he could be sure and was gone.

"Well, Daughter, what do you think?"

Brigetta gasped in awe. "Oh, *Vatti*, it is *wunderbar!*"

She stared at the wooden casing her father had carved for the cuckoo clock. It was indeed wonderful. Made of light wood and expertly crafted, the timepiece bore an amazing resemblance to Engelturm. At the beginning of each hour, a tiny set of double doors opened at the top of one of the gables, next to the chapel tower, and painted figurines of a man and a woman came from opposite sides to meet at the front, their wooden hands touching.

Her father had been able to procure the proper mechanisms for movement from his former employer. Not the standard copper ones required, since the blockade made it impossible to receive that metal, but rather a device made from pots that had been melted down. Before the war, her father crafted his clocks from home and sold them through the village's clock factory. Now the factory produced only war-related products. The commission of the count's clock had been a blessing to the Linders.

"I should be honored to take this to *Graf* von Engel," Brigetta said. "Come, Ludwig, let us go."

Together they crunched their way downhill toward Engelheim, marveling at the fairy-tale world God had created. Frozen, white lace coverings—as intricate as the trim on her father's cuckoo clocks—adorned trees and bushes. The overnight frost had lingered the past two days. Brigetta deeply inhaled the crisp, icy air, letting it fill her lungs, and released it in one cloudy puff.

As often happened, her mind went to Joseph. Shyly, she'd given him a pair of *Vatti's* cast-off long woolen underwear, though she knew the clothing must be much too short for him. And she'd found another old blanket to keep him warm during the freezing nights. She smiled when she remembered his face after she'd handed him one of her favorite books last week.

"Poetry?" His expression had reminded Brigetta of how Ludwig often reacted when given his breakfast gruel. Joseph easily read that one word on the cover, but when he opened the book and scanned the first page, his eyes widened, and he quickly shut it. "I can speak your language," he said, shaking his head, "but reading it is another matter. I've no idea what this says."

Brigetta tried to keep the smile off her face. She honestly did.

"You knew that, didn't you?" His eyes narrowed in accusation, though he grinned back at her. "When you offered to lend me a book, you knew I wouldn't be able to read it. Why you little minx. . . ."

Feeling flustered yet happy, she took the book from him. "Well, Joseph, it is fortunate for you that I not only like to read, but that I can read German," she teased. She innocently cocked her head and lifted her brow. "That is, if you would like me to read to you?"

"Please," he had said, his expression softening. "I would enjoy that very much, Brigetta."

"Brigetta!"

Startled out of her musings, she blinked and turned to Ludwig. Wolfgang panted at his side. "Did you say something?" she asked.

He shook his head. "You have been acting so strange since—since I don't know when. Even stranger than you usually are." He pointed to the left, to one of the large two-story structures in the distance, with its orange tile roof, window boxes, and brown trim diagonally slashing and rimming the white walls. "There is *Graf* von Engel's town house. Or did you want to go to Aunt Olga's?"

Embarrassed to see she'd taken the wrong path at the fork, Brigetta shook her head. *"Nein,* first we should deliver the clock." She ignored Ludwig's curious stare and joined him.

Once they arrived at the von Engels', Brigetta knocked on the ornately carved door, with its ferocious brass lion head knocker. After stern orders to Wolfgang to stay, they followed the servant to an elaborate parlor. Brigetta had little time to admire the splendid furnishings and oil portraits of sober-looking people she suspected must have come from Engelturm.

"Brigetta! Brigetta Linder! My, how you've grown," the count said. His broad face was wreathed in smiles, as was his wife's.

"Gross Gutt," Brigetta said with a nod, unable to shake hands since her hands were full of the clock.

"*Gross Gutt,*" he returned the familiar greeting. "And this is Ludwig? But it can't be!"

"*Gross Gutt, Graf* von Engel," Ludwig said politely in a most grown-up manner, while offering his small hand.

"And *Gross Gutt* to you, young Ludwig." Beaming, the count engulfed Ludwig's hand in his huge paw, then turned to Brigetta. "And now, let us see the clock."

Carefully she withdrew it from the cloth sack. The von Engels gasped with pleasure.

"It is Engelturm!" Tears filled the countess's voice.

"*Ja,*" the count said, moisture filling his own eyes. "Throughout the centuries the Linders have blessed my family with their fine woodworking abilities. Today is no exception. Hans Linder is a master of his craft—as good as Franz Ketterer ever was in his day."

Brigetta smiled. For her father to be compared to the seventeen-hundreds' gifted artisan and inventor of the cuckoo clock was high praise indeed. She turned the large hand on the round face to the start of the hour. Sweet music tinkled into the room as the doors opened and the painted dolls made their appearance. Again the countess gasped with pleasure.

"Emma will love it. She is marrying a fine German *Leutnant,*" the count said proudly. "A young army officer."

The count presented Brigetta with a small bag of coins, while the countess surprised both Linders with a sand tart.

"*Danke!*" With round eyes, Ludwig stared at the treat before nibbling a corner—then shoved the entire thing into his mouth, forgetting his manners. "Is *gut!*" he exclaimed, his mouth full of the cookie.

Brigetta took more time with hers, savoring each sweet, crispy bite. After more polite conversation, brother and sister made their good-byes and hurried away, Wolfgang trailing.

"Are we going to Aunt Olga's now, Brigetta?"

She looked toward the sinking sun beyond the frost-laden trees. If they didn't get home soon, it would be dark by the time she visited the castle, and she'd not yet brought Joseph anything to eat today. "Not this time, *Liebchen.*"

Relief covered Ludwig's face. Brigetta knew he feared their aunt, who had a reputation for being gloomy, and the dark furnishings of her house reflected her character. With three sons fighting in France, she had a right to be depressed, Brigetta supposed, but Aunt Olga possessed a dismal disposition even before the outset of the war.

Brigetta sympathized with Rolph, her twelve-year-old cousin who was shut inside such a house every day. Quiet and sullen, he'd adopted his mother's traits, though Brigetta occasionally witnessed a more cheerful side to his nature, like his brother Pieter's.

As they crunched their way up the frosty hill, Brigetta spotted their cottage's sloping roof through the trees and stopped, surprised to see the subject of her thoughts heading their direction. With lowered head, he swiped at his eyes with the backs of his hands.

"Rolph?" Brigetta stopped on the path and spoke to her cousin before he plowed into her.

His gaze shot up to hers, his teary blue eyes angry. "I hate the Americans and the French—and everyone else in this stupid war!" With a loud sob, he clumsily ran past Brigetta and Ludwig, down the path toward his home.

"Rolph!" Brigetta cried, alarmed. But he didn't stop.

"Brigetta," Ludwig asked fearfully, "what's wrong with Rolph?"

Forcing a smile, she took his hand. "I don't know, *Liebchen*, but let's go inside and find out. Hmm?"

As the two approached the cottage, an ominous feeling, like a dark cloud, settled over Brigetta's heart.

Chapter 5

J oseph awkwardly paced the room, trying to build up his strength, the pang in his side little more than an irksome bother now. The itching was far worse, and he had to clench his hands to prevent them from scratching at the bandage. Frowning, he sank to the bench, his gaze going to Brigetta's poetry book beside him and tracing the flowery letters on the cover. His stomach grumbled, and for what must have been the hundredth time, his eyes turned toward the chapel entrance. Still empty.

The irritation he'd felt earlier, when Brigetta still hadn't come with food, turned to worry. The sky was dark as pitch now. Had something happened to his angel?

Shivering, Joseph pulled the scratchy blanket closer around his shoulders. The castle room was dark, dank, chilling the very marrow of his bones; but both he and Brigetta had decided it would be too risky to start a fire for warmth. Someone from the village might see the smoke and associate it with Engelturm. At night that possibility was less risky, though Joseph had decided to start a fire only if absolutely necessary. He blew on his pink hands numbed from the cold.

It was absolutely necessary.

He grabbed the lamp and moved the blocks of ice his feet were fast becoming, forcing them to shuffle toward the wing farthest from the village. There, he knew, from his short tours of the castle, was a room with small arched windows—and a large fireplace.

Joseph pushed open the heavy door, wincing as the stitch near his ribs erupted into a painful twinge. Gingerly, he rubbed the bandage under his shirt and walked over the moss-patched flagstones to the stone grate, relieved to see what were probably old logs of spruce or pine inside. A thick layer of dust covered them, but Joseph was certain they would catch flame. He grimaced wryly. In fact, as brittle as the wood appeared, he'd be fortunate if he didn't set the entire castle wing on fire.

With the lamp and a dry rag Brigetta had used to tend his wound, Joseph started the fire on the first try. Loud, raspy crackling filled the room as the logs burst into flame. He jerked his upper body backward to avoid the spitting blaze of sudden heat.

The fire ate through the logs, a hungry carnivore feeding on its prey. Joseph wondered where he could find more wood. Perhaps in the dilapidated west wing?

Hollow footsteps on stone alerted him, and he swung around. Brigetta entered the room. Joseph's relief evolved into anxiety as he watched her wooden approach.

"Brigetta?" He rose to meet her.

Shadow and light played over a face devoid of expression. The only emotion lay in her inky dark eyes—simmering with hatred. She set down the pail she carried.

"Brigetta?" This time Joseph's voice came out hoarse, uncertain. "What has happened?"

"What has happened?" she repeated in a low, tortured tone,

turning the full force of her gaze upon him. Her hands clenched at her sides. "What has happened?" A maniacal laugh sailed from her lips, making Joseph cringe.

"Brigetta," he whispered, reaching out to touch her arm.

She jerked back before his fingers could make contact with her sleeve. "Don't touch me! Don't you ever touch me. You are one of them."

Feeling powerless, knowing he had no control over the situation—whatever the situation was—Joseph dropped his hand to his side. "Maybe we should sit and talk."

"Talk!" She shook her head, her dark curls bouncing and catching red highlights from the fire. "What good will talk do? Talk will not erase the past twenty-four hours. Talk will not bring Pieter back. Talk will not change the fact that you are an American soldier and I am German." Her voice caught, and tears washed her eyes, making them glisten.

Pieter. Her first cousin. One year older than she. Joseph felt something hard clench his gut. He didn't need to ask. He could see the answer in her eyes.

He took a step toward her. "Brigetta—"

"Nein!" Instead of retreating, she moved forward, striking his chest with the flats of her hands, trying to push him away, trying to punish. "There's nothing you can say! You are the enemy!"

Joseph grabbed her wrists, and the blanket dropped from his shoulders. She struggled to wrest her hands from him, but his hold tightened and he brought her close, dipping his head near her ear. "Then if you won't listen to my words," he whispered, "let me share your pain, Brigetta. I care that you are hurting."

She stiffened, but Joseph didn't let go. Gradually he felt her body give way, felt her forehead fall against him in defeat, felt the heat of her quiet tears as they scorched his collarbone.

"Oh, *meine liebste Feindin*," he whispered, "I wish I could make all the horrors of this war fade for you. I wish I could give you your idyllic childhood days at Engelturm again."

Brigetta drew a soft breath at both the feel of Joseph's warm lips near her ear and his strange endearment: my dearest enemy. Forcing her tears in check, she lifted her gaze to his in confusion.

His eyes were agonized, full of the same pain she'd carried since hearing news of Pieter. Brigetta tried hard to reconcile her thoughts to accept this man as her adversary. Yet the kind soldier she'd come to know, who looked at her now with sorrow in his eyes—sorrow not even his own—didn't match her idea of a foe. The fact remained, if she truly considered him her adversary, she never would have made the trip up here in the dark, once her mother had gone to stay with Aunt Olga and the family had gone to bed. Instead, she may have let Joseph starve or contacted the authorities. . . .

But she had needed to see him, needed his comfort and no other's.

Joseph's gaze went tender. He released one of her wrists to lay a hand against her cheek. "I care," he repeated. Bending down, he kissed her forehead.

Despite her grief, Brigetta's heart leapt. Wonder filled her. When he straightened, a sense of awe slackened his face. The rough pad of his thumb moved to trail over her quivering bottom lip. He swallowed, inhaled a shaky breath. "Brigetta, my dearest enemy. . ." Slowly, ever so slowly, he inclined his head.

In the brief second before his lips could touch hers, a strangled cry pierced the air. Startled, Brigetta broke away from

Joseph and swung toward the door. Ludwig stood on the threshold, his expression betrayed.

"How could you, Brigetta?" he whimpered, backing up a step. His gaze swung to Joseph, traveled over his soldier's uniform, and his eyes widened in fear. Whirling, he sped from the room, his footsteps echoing along the corridor.

"Ludwig!" Brigetta cried, fear and dismay lacing the word as it bounced off the clammy walls. She hurried to the entrance.

"Brigetta—wait!" Joseph walked her way, holding out the small lamp she'd brought with her. "Take this," he said, his voice low, repentant.

She accepted the offering without looking at him and rushed from the room and down the gallery.

Faint moonbeams filtered in through the windows overlooking the inner courtyard, but the bluish white light barely cut through the darkness, and Brigetta was thankful for the lamp's aid. She searched several chambers, but none of them contained her brother.

Oh, why had he picked this night of all nights to come? He must have had a bad dream and went looking for her, somehow knowing she'd be at Engelturm. He'd been quite shaken to learn Pieter's plane had been shot down, like his hero's—the Red Baron.

The dim outline of the huge brass-studded armory door came into view. It stood ajar. She didn't remember it being that way the last time she was here. Brigetta held the lamp high to fight back the shadows. Casting a cursory glance sideways at the mossy stone steps leading far down to the black cavern that was the dungeon, she sincerely hoped her search wouldn't take her in that direction.

She stepped across the threshold of the armory. Ludwig's sniffling reached her ears before she found him—hiding behind the old rusted suit of armor in the corner, his head lowered on upraised knees. Relief made her limbs shaky as she crouched beside him. She put out a hand to touch his hair. "Ludwig?"

His head snapped up, and he pulled away. In the soft yellow lamplight, his eyes accused. "How could you, Brigetta? I saw his uniform. He might have been the one who killed Pieter! How could you let him touch you?"

Brigetta pondered what to say. "*Nein, Liebchen*, Joseph didn't kill Pieter."

Ludwig lowered his head and rubbed his wet eyes with his fists. "He's the enemy!" He stopped, looking at her suspiciously. "You know his name?"

She nodded. "I've been taking care of him. He was wounded when I found him."

Ludwig's eyes widened. "And you didn't turn him over to the authorities?"

"*Nein,*" she said quietly. "Ludwig, do you remember the story of the Good Samaritan and the man he helped by the roadside? They were enemies, yet the Samaritan helped the Jewish man and tended his wounds. Jesus told that parable. So the way I see it is this: If Jesus thought the story important enough to use as a tool to teach others, He must want us to do the same."

Ludwig offered no response. When the silence became unbearable, Brigetta tried again. "Joseph is different than what I thought he'd be. He is kind, gentle—nothing like the cruel monster we were led to believe every American soldier is. And do you know, Ludwig, that in America they are told that the

Huns are bloodthirsty, barbaric fiends?"

"That isn't so! Pieter wasn't bloodthirsty. He was kind and funny. He made me laugh."

Brigetta nodded, feeling another wave of stabbing grief at the mention of her fun-loving cousin, who'd always had a smile on his face. *Ja*, Ludwig, you are right. My point is that each country has been told negative things about the enemy that may not necessarily be true." She paused, hoping her idea was the right one. "Instead of judging others based on what you've heard, why not make up your mind based on what you can see?"

"What do you mean?"

"Perhaps it is time for you to meet Joseph."

Ludwig's eyes widened, and he cowered against the wall.

"I won't force you. But, Ludwig, if he really were a bad person—why then hasn't he harmed me?"

Ludwig's brow creased in confusion. Obviously he had no answer.

"Whatever you decide, whether to meet Joseph or not, you must keep this our secret. Tell no one he is here."

His lips pulled into a petulant frown. "Because you don't want him caught?"

Ja, but also because I want to protect *Mutti* and *Vatti*. If Joseph were discovered, the authorities might decide our parents had something to do with his stay and put them in jail—even though they know nothing about his presence here."

Ludwig looked perplexed. "But, Brigetta, isn't it wrong to hide him? Isn't keeping a secret like this something like telling a lie?"

His soft query echoed the words that had plagued her for weeks. "I think," she began slowly, "that in times of war there are exceptions—especially when they save a life or more than one." She paused. "Joseph is not a bad man. He is a Christian. He probably would have died if the soldiers had taken him—he was very sick. I did what I believed *Gott* would have wanted me to do. And I will go on doing so. In the end, He is the One I must answer to. Not the German army."

"But you will have to answer to them too, if they find out what you've done," Ludwig insisted.

Brigetta nodded. *"Ja,* that is true. But do you remember, Ludwig, how in the Old Testament Rahab hid the enemy spies so they wouldn't be killed, even lying about their existence in the city? Do you remember that story? God spared her and her family for protecting His own. In light of that—and other similar Bible accounts—I believe God is pleased with Joseph being cared for at Engelturm."

Ludwig bunched his brows. "I suppose. But he is still an *American.*"

Brigetta smiled and held out a hand. "Come, Ludwig. Come and see the wolf you've feared isn't so horrific as you imagined. Sometimes, fear of the unknown is more frightening than the reality, I've come to discover."

Ludwig hesitated, then took her hand.

Joseph stood and stared at the dying flames. The fire was already spent, satiated from its meal of dry tinder. He listened to the faint pops and crackles. The pungent smell of old burnt wood assaulted his head and made it ache. Starting to feel dizzy again, he put a hand to the cold stone bordering the open hearth and whispered a prayer.

"God, to come to You and ask for something, after a year of ignoring You, probably isn't right. But for Brigetta I'll do it."

Joseph clenched his hand against the wall, the coarse stone grazing his fingertips and knuckles. He closed his eyes. "Help her family through this difficult time. And. . .I don't ask this for me, Lord. After deserting You as I did, I know I'm in no position to beg favors—though I thank You again for keeping me alive. But for Brigetta—for her, Lord—don't let my whereabouts be discovered. If I were strong enough to leave Engelturm, I would. I would find a way to get across the border and protect her and her family. Please strengthen my body so that I can leave this place. . . ."

"My sister says you are not a wolf to be feared," a faint childish voice spoke behind him. "Is that true?"

Heat raced up Joseph's neck and face when he realized he'd been overheard—and that he'd spoken in German. He took a moment to compose himself before turning. The child standing beside Brigetta, holding her hand, looked smaller than Joseph had thought Ludwig would be. Fair, with clear, blue eyes, he was a strong contrast to his sister's dark beauty. Joseph's gaze traveled upward to Brigetta.

Her gaze held his a scarce moment, then darted away. "After I found him, we talked, and I thought he should meet you."

Joseph nodded and looked at the child. "Hello, Ludwig."

Surprise lit his face. "You know my name?"

"I know a lot about you," Joseph said soberly. "You and I even have something in common. . . ."

"What?" Ludwig's brow wrinkled, as though he could not fathom sharing anything with a strange enemy soldier.

"We both hate breakfast gruel." Joseph grinned.

Ludwig's mouth flickered at the corners. "I sometimes give part of mine to Wolfgang when *Mutti* isn't looking," he admitted, his words tentative. "But he doesn't like it much either."

"Ludwig!" Brigetta exclaimed softly.

Joseph chuckled. "That Wolfgang is one smart dog."

"You know him?" The boy's eyes widened.

"Yes, I know him well. In fact, he and I share a number of secrets." Joseph wryly thought of the many times he'd foolishly confided in the German shepherd concerning his feelings for Brigetta.

Ludwig cocked his head to one side, as though considering. Slowly, he approached Joseph until he stood a few feet away. "Secrets? Like how you came to Engelturm?"

Joseph faintly smiled at the boy's curiosity, starting to feel weak again. "Tell you what, Ludwig, I'll answer your questions. But first, let's sit down. I'm still in recovery."

Brigetta flushed pink and grabbed the ladle, as if suddenly realizing he hadn't eaten yet. She spooned what Joseph figured to be turnip soup into a bowl.

Trying not to grimace from the dull throb that had started in his side, Joseph lowered himself to the cold stone floor. Ludwig did the same, sitting several feet away. The boy had relaxed, but Joseph sensed he still wasn't sure about him. By the dying embers of the fire, in the circle of pale lamplight, Joseph ate his soup and answered Ludwig's many questions.

In the middle of recounting his trek to safety, Joseph glanced Brigetta's way. Yearning filled the brown eyes fixed upon him. Stunned, Joseph stopped talking; but before he could say another word, she stood.

"Come, Ludwig. It is late. We must return to the cottage."

The boy let out a dismayed breath. "May I come again?" he asked Joseph hopefully as he rose from the floor. "To hear the end of your story?"

Joseph looked to Brigetta for approval. Their gazes locked.

A wide gamut of emotions barreled through him, threatening to knock him over.

"We shall see," she murmured. Looking suddenly flustered, she grabbed her brother's hand, pulling him with her to make a hasty exit.

Chapter 6

Brigetta stared out the window. Pale golden fingers of morning sunshine caressed the boughs of towering evergreens and bounced off the frosty ground to shimmer and dance in a spectacular radiance of light. Farther up the hill, the glowing tower of Engelturm beckoned. "I think I will visit the castle," she mused.

"Can I come?" Ludwig chirped.

"*Ja*, of course." Brigetta preferred to have her brother with her where she could keep watch over him—or rather over his mouth—as she had the past four days since he'd learned about Joseph. It wouldn't do for Ludwig to inadvertently let information slip.

"I'll get my coat." He shot up from his chair where he'd been scribbling something on paper and scurried to the loft's ladder.

Her father looked up from carving a clock casing. "You spend much time there, Daughter. Perhaps your *mutter* is right, and it is not such a good thing." His eyes were thoughtful. "You cannot always escape to the past to avoid the present. It isn't good to roam abandoned rooms of a forgotten time, day after day. To live with the ghosts of what has been."

"I know, *Vatti*, but it's not like that." Brigetta fastened her coat. "The castle makes me feel closer to God, and I've been inspired to work on my poetry while there." She had even read some of her poems to Joseph, who'd seemed to enjoy them.

Brigetta shot a rapid glance her father's way, then looked toward the door. The sound of creaking timber from the wind's mournful song seemed to magnify throughout the room.

"Is there something you're not telling me, Brigetta?"

Her cheeks burned. "Why would you think such a thing, *Vatti?*" she asked, wishing her voice sounded more natural.

The need to tell her father about Joseph rose within her, but she tamped it down. She couldn't—not yet. She must protect her family. And Joseph. Brigetta still wasn't sure that *Vatti* might not turn Joseph over to the authorities if he discovered the truth. Her father was a good man, but he was loyal to the fatherland. Unlike his errant daughter.

Swallowing hard, Brigetta went to the stove for the last of the turnip soup. She dumped the contents into a pail and covered the container with a dish towel. When the silence persisted, Brigetta didn't dare look *Vatti's* way. They were so much alike, and Brigetta was positive he could see through her to the truth she tried to hide.

"I'm ready!" Ludwig cried as he climbed down the ladder.

"Why are you taking the soup, Brigetta?" her father asked quietly when she turned to go.

She almost dropped the pail. He'd been so busy with his work in past weeks that he'd never noticed her take the food. Brigetta stood, her mouth parted, uncertain what to say. She had never outright lied and didn't want to start now. Yet what could she say to appease his suspicions?

"I was hungry last time we were there and asked for something to eat." Ludwig filled in the silence.

Surprised at her brother's reply, Brigetta shot him a glance. What Ludwig said was true, but she'd told him at the time they must save the food for Joseph, so he could regain his strength.

"Hmm," *Vatti* said, his gaze never leaving her face. She could feel red seep into her skin again. "Well," he said at last, "tomorrow there will be no visits to Engelturm. Thanks to *Graf* von Engel's generosity of giving me more than the price agreed upon for the clock, Ludwig will have a new pair of much-needed shoes. Take him to the cobbler tomorrow, Brigetta. And you must also stop in and see how things are with your *mutter*."

"*Ja, Vatti,*" Brigetta murmured, opening the door. "I will go after breakfast." She hurried out before he could answer.

Hilda crunched over the frost toward the cottage, her arms laden with sticks of wood for the stove's fire. "Off to Engelturm again?" she said, her pale eyebrows rising.

"*Ja.* Come, Ludwig." Brigetta pulled on his coat sleeve, anxious to escape more prying questions.

As they approached the castle, Brigetta analyzed her feelings for Joseph. She had so wanted him to kiss her the night that Ludwig had barged into the room. It made no sense. She shouldn't have feelings like that for the adversary—though she was coming to think of Joseph as her enemy less and less.

Puzzled, Joseph stared across the room. After giving him his soup minutes ago, Brigetta had moved away, exhibiting unusual interest in the cloth Joseph had stuffed in the hole of the broken stained glass window. She then eyed the furnishings—or what little of them there were. Furnishings she'd seen numerous times. Not once did she meet his gaze.

Ludwig filled any possible tension-filled silence with excited chatter, evidently having accepted Joseph as a friend. From the pocket of his coat, the boy produced a folded paper and handed it to Joseph. "I drew it this morning. It's for you."

Joseph unfolded the soiled paper to reveal a crudely drawn picture of an S.P.A.D.—or perhaps an Albatross. No logos were drawn on the airplane's wing or side depicting the country of the biplane.

"When I grow up, I want to be a clock maker, like *Vatti*," Ludwig said proudly. "But my second choice would be a pilot." He cocked his head as if a sudden thought came to him. "Perhaps I could do both—make clocks and fly planes."

"Perhaps you could," Joseph said and smiled. "Do you have another sheet of paper, Ludwig?"

"Do you want to draw an airplane too?"

Joseph chuckled. "I doubt you'd want to see me try. I have something else in mind."

"Brigetta, can we have some of your paper?"

Frowning, she turned. Her eyes were unfocused. "What? Did you say something?"

Ludwig blew out an impatient breath. "I need a piece of paper. Are you dreaming about the castle again?"

She didn't respond, only moved toward her poetry book that sat on the altar. Her lips a straight line, she snatched a folded paper packet from inside, pulled one away, and brought it to Ludwig. He, in turn, handed it to Joseph. Her brows went up at the exchange, but Joseph only smiled, setting the paper on the bench beside him.

Joseph could feel their curious stares as he deftly creased the paper into sections, making flaps and triangles. "I learned this from a guy who was a friend of the Wright brothers. American fliers—you may have heard of them?" Brigetta nodded, and

Joseph continued, "My friend lived in their hometown for five years. It seems the brothers, Wilbur and Orville, made models of this sort when they were investigating aerodynamics—or to put it in simpler terms—experimenting with how to get an airplane to fly."

Joseph made one final fold, then offered the paper creation to a wide-eyed Ludwig. "Why not give it a whirl and see if I remembered how to do it?"

Ludwig's brows bunched in confusion. "Give it a—whirl?"

"Here," Joseph said with a grin. "Let me show you." Holding the flap underneath with his thumb and two fingers, he positioned the pointed end toward the chapel entrance, brought back his arm, then sent it forward with a snap, letting loose his creation.

The paper craft sailed smoothly through the air, eliciting a gasp from Brigetta and a squeal from Ludwig.

"Oh!" he cried as he ran to pick up the paper missile that had landed a good twenty feet away. "Do it again!"

"Why don't you try?" Joseph said. "It's yours. Think of it as a thank-you for your drawing."

Joseph didn't think he'd ever seen a smile so wide on a child's face. "*Danke,* Herr Miller!"

The boy lifted his arm, mimicking Joseph's prior movements. He sent the plane zipping through the colored dust motes floating through the musty air and out of the room. With a victorious shout, Ludwig took off after his new toy, leaving Brigetta and Joseph alone. He looked her way. She averted her eyes and strode back to the chapel window.

Joseph watched her. "Now that I've sufficiently recovered, I plan to leave here at dawn—to find some way across the border and to locate my company."

233

Brigetta spun around. "Oh, but—you can't go! I mean. . ." She paused, blinking. "The weather has turned fiercely cold. We will have heavy snows soon. You will need a coat."

Joseph shook his head. If he were caught in civilian clothes, he could be mistaken for a spy and shot. "A blanket will do."

Furrows crinkled her brow. "But you cannot go out in this weather without proper clothing! There is a box, at the church, of cast-off clothes for the needy. I'll try to find something for you tomorrow—when we go to the village. Ludwig and I—to buy him shoes."

Her words came out rapid, jumbled. She obviously didn't want him to leave as much as he didn't want to go. Yet soon they would be left without an excuse either of them could concoct for having him stay. The thought was sobering. There must be some way to bridge the gap between them in the time they had left, some way to plan a future, uncertain as it was. It was time to confront reality, to stop pretending the truth didn't exist.

Ludwig's laughter and running footsteps faded down the corridor. Joseph rose from the bench and slowly approached Brigetta.

"That was kind of you," she said, a tremor to her voice. Her hands clasped and unclasped, fidgeting in front of her skirt. "Giving Ludwig that paper model, I mean. He's had no new toys for a long time."

Joseph said nothing, his gaze never leaving hers as he continued to cover the distance between them.

"*Vatti* spends his days making clocks—though few clock peddlers are traveling across Deutschland, and no one is going into other parts of Europe now—due to the war." She nervously licked dry lips. "They travel on foot with the clocks on their backs. An old peddler sometimes took *Vatti's* clocks for a small percentage, but he stopped doing so when war broke out. Still, there are those who can afford little luxuries like cuckoo clocks. *Graf* von Engel, for example. He is a well-respected man in Engelheim. This castle is his. Have I told you?"

Joseph came within a few feet of her. She gave a nervous laugh.

"*Ja*, of course I have. But my point is, *Vatti* hasn't been able to spare time to carve Ludwig a toy, though I know he wants to. You see, Ludwig's birthday just was—before *Erntedankfest*. Our Thanksgiving—in October."

Joseph stopped before her. "When are we going to end this pretense between us?" he asked, his voice low.

She eyed him warily. "I don't understand."

"When are we going to stop pretending we don't care for one another? That we don't dream about each other at night or count the minutes that we can be together again when we're apart?"

His blue eyes demanded an answer. Brigetta couldn't give him one, couldn't deny his claim, even if she were able to talk around the sudden lump in her throat. His hand lifted to her cheek, cupping it with tenderness.

"Brigetta, I love you. I don't want to live life without you. I want to marry you, to make you my wife."

Her heart lurched. She felt the same way about him, but she briskly shook her head. His hand fell away.

"Such talk is foolish, Joseph. We are enemies! Our countries are at war with one another."

"It won't last forever, and I've never once considered you my enemy. When there is peace between our countries again,

I'll come back for you and take you with me to America. If you'll have me."

"Away from Engelturm?" she asked, her heart sinking. "Away from my family and my home? Could you not stay here?"

What was she thinking? Her family would never accept him—not after what had happened to Pieter. And she doubted Joseph's family would accept her, despite the shared German blood flowing through their veins. So much bitterness had been aroused from this great war, bitterness she herself had felt before Joseph came into her life. Meeting him had changed her perspective on many things.

His expression sobered. "Before I left, I promised my father I would return and take over the family business, though deep down I've always wanted to be a concert pianist. I think I told you—my father owns a music store. I learned to play piano at my mother's knee when I'd barely learned to walk, and I continued my lessons—even composing my own music—until the day I enlisted." He gave a slight shake of his head. "But never mind all that. It's beside the point."

"Perhaps you could do both," she insisted, feeling safer with this topic. "Be a concert pianist and run a music store—like Ludwig will be both a clock maker and pilot some day." She offered a shaky smile.

Joseph lifted both hands to her cheeks, cradling her face like fine porcelain. "Tell me I was wrong, Brigetta. Tell me you don't care for me, and I'll leave before dawn's light. You will never see me again."

"You would freeze to death with only a blanket," she murmured, lost in his eyes. "You would never make it to the River Wurm, much less the Rhine."

His brow lifted in faint amusement. "Does that mean you

care for me? Even a little?"

What was the point of denying it? To do so would be to say good-bye to Joseph forever—and though Brigetta knew she would soon lose him anyway, she couldn't let him go thinking she didn't care.

Tears pricking her eyes, she gave a brief nod but kept silent concerning the whispers within her heart. Those words were too painful to utter, considering their hopeless situation.

Joseph's features softened in relief. He bent to kiss her forehead, then wrapped his arms around her and drew her close. Brigetta would have preferred for him to kiss her lips, as a man kisses a woman, having dreamt of him doing so many times. Yet she did enjoy the warmth of being in his arms, with her ear against his solid chest, listening to the rapid thuds of his heartbeat.

Light running footsteps slapped the corridor's stone floor, steadily growing louder. Brigetta tensed and tried to pull away. Joseph's hold tightened, his hand moving to cradle the back of her head. *"Nein, Liebchen.* If he doesn't accept me now, he probably never will. He's caught us in an embrace before. Let's see how he'll react this time, now that he knows me."

Brigetta didn't understand Joseph's reasoning about testing Ludwig's reaction but kept still, hoping it was the right thing to do. Perhaps Joseph was right. Perhaps it was time to see how the youngest member of her family would respond to their unspoken declaration of love. If Ludwig reacted favorably, there might be a chance that the rest of her family would accept her choice of a husband as well—when it would be safe to tell them. A glimmer of hope sparked within her, mixing with a flicker of fear.

The footsteps stopped abruptly at the entrance. From the

corner of her eye, Brigetta noticed Ludwig in the doorway. There were several seconds of interminable silence, then, "I made the folded paper do a loop—just like a real airplane! Will you show me how to make one, Herr Miller?"

At Ludwig's eager request, Brigetta felt Joseph's breath stir her hair in relief. Her smile was as wide as his when he pulled away and glanced at her before turning to her brother.

"Well, young Ludwig. . ." Joseph smiled, approaching the boy. "If the fair countess of yon castle allows us into her treasure trove for more of that paper, I'll help you make an entire flying corps." Joseph looked her way and lightly winked.

Pleasantly flustered, Brigetta hurried to retrieve the desired item. She'd been taught that a man's wink was considered insincere or rude. Yet Joseph's soft gesture, coupled with the adoring look in his eyes, produced only comforting warmth that uncurled deep within her stomach, spreading throughout her like eiderdown. She hugged herself, wishing she could bottle this feeling and bring it out on cold, dreary days.

As she watched the blond heads bent close, a phantasm of sudden fear crossed her heart. For no reason she could explain, Brigetta knew this idyllic day together was the last they would share.

Chapter 7

The next morning, Brigetta and Ludwig walked to their aunt's cottage. Aunt Olga lay abed, too despondent to rise. Rolph sulked in a corner, his nose in a book. Yet *Mutti* made up for any lack of welcome and hugged her children tightly, anxious for news of home. They talked in hushed tones and left hours later, their mother sending Wolfgang with them.

At noon, after the old cobbler had sized Ludwig's feet, promising a new pair of shoes for the boy in two days, Brigetta dragged her brother to the village church.

"Why are we here?" Ludwig complained.

"To see about getting Joseph a coat. Now hush." Repeatedly, she banged the flat of her hand against the huge door. Since pillaging had become a problem in Engelheim, the old priest regrettably locked the church between services. Brigetta's gaze traveled upward to the steeple, where the mammoth bell hung. Father Zimmerman had long been respected and feared by the villagers—young and old. Two years ago when soldiers threatened to take the bell down and melt it to make needed supplies, as many villages throughout Germany had been forced to do, the robust priest blocked the steps to the bell tower and told them they would have to kill him first, that he would not let them desecrate God's house. Surprisingly, the soldiers departed, and the bell had remained in its tower ever since.

The door swung inward, startling Brigetta out of her musing. The ancient face of Father Zimmerman appeared, his white hair ruffled over his cassock. *"Ja,* my child?"

"I–I have need of a coat," Brigetta hastened to say. "A man's coat." When the priest studied her with shrewd eyes, Brigetta fumbled with the button of her jacket. "I heard you have a box for the needy. It's for a friend."

He continued to stare, unnerving Brigetta until she was ready to blurt the truth. Father Zimmerman had that way about him. At last he nodded, opening the door wide. Before walking into the silent, musty-smelling church, she threw a look over her shoulder, expecting to see Ludwig. He had escaped her presence and now played with Wolfgang near a tall, round kiosk covered with war posters and bulletins. Signs were peppered throughout the village, on walls and doors, bearing the word *"Verboten!"* Yet it seemed everything was forbidden nowadays, and Brigetta felt assured Wolfgang would keep her brother out of mischief for the short time she would be gone.

She made quick work of selecting a suitable coat, thankful Father Zimmerman had left her alone. Fearful the priest might return and query her, Brigetta slipped outside the church door.

A ruddy-faced, plump boy stood near Ludwig, who threw a paper craft obviously made from a bulletin off the kiosk, sending it sailing like a multicolored bird into the pale gray sky. "See! I told you I could make paper fly." His proud voice carried over the still air. "My friend at the castle taught me."

"Ludwig!" Brigetta cried in alarm. She watched as a blond soldier, in the gray uniform and gold insignia of a German

Leutnant, stepped from the entrance of a nearby shop. He cast a sober glance her way, then walked toward the children.

Brigetta clutched the heavy wool coat to her breast with sweaty palms. "Ludwig," she called again, endeavoring to sound normal, "we must hurry home. *Vatti* is waiting."

Ludwig turned a fearful stare toward Brigetta, then watched the man approach. The German officer stooped down to pick up the paper airplane, moved toward her brother, and spoke. Ludwig shook his head, said something, and bounded toward Brigetta.

She grabbed his sleeve, noticing the officer watch them. Turning away, she tried to act casual. "Walk at a normal pace," she hissed to Ludwig. "Don't turn and look back for any reason."

"I'm sorry," he said and sniffled. "I–I didn't mean to say anything about Joseph. But Franz kept bragging about his brother marrying *Graf* von Engel's daughter—a–and said they would have roasted pig from the black market every night. That was his brother—the soldier."

At Ludwig's meek words, a cauldron of boiling fear spilled over inside Brigetta, seeping to every part of her being. "Hush! Don't talk. They may hear." To think that Joseph's life might be in danger because of Ludwig's pride filled Brigetta with rage, and she gripped his arm hard. Ludwig gave a muted yelp of protest but didn't utter a word.

When they returned to the cottage, it was Brigetta's intention to hurry to Engelturm and warn Joseph on his way, but her father had chores for her. Once finished, Brigetta grabbed the coat for Joseph, bundled it up, and opened the door. Thick white flakes swirled down from the darkening sky, and a freezing gust of air hurled itself against her.

"Close the door," her father ordered. "You may not go to

Engelturm in such weather. Besides, night approaches."

"But, *Vatti*—" She broke off at his fixed look and grudgingly moved toward the loft, ignoring Ludwig's pleading eyes. She hadn't spoken to him since their return. Nor did she intend to.

The snow didn't let up. That night as she lay in bed next to Hilda, Brigetta prayed that her fears lived only in her mind—but if not, that she could reach Joseph in time.

Brigetta groggily awoke to pounding on the door and daylight flooding the window. Upset that she'd grown weary and fallen asleep while waiting for *Vatti* to go to bed, when she'd intended to slip away to Engelturm, she grabbed her shoes and hastened from the loft. Her self-recriminations evolved into fear when she swung open the door to see German soldiers bearing rifles with bayonets. Instantly she came fully awake.

"Fräulein," the *commandant* said, clicking his boot heels together and giving a stiff bow. "We have orders to search the premises for an escaped prisoner of war."

Brigetta put a hand to her neck, affecting a startled pose. Her pulse threatened to burst from her throat. "It is only my father, my two siblings, and I, *Commandant*."

"What is going on, Brigetta?" Her father's voice came from behind.

She turned, hoping that puzzlement and not guilt showed on her face. "Soldiers, *Vatti*. They are searching for an escaped prisoner."

Ignoring the sharp glance her father cast her way, Brigetta opened the door wide for the men. Their search of the tiny cottage was quick. Afterward, the *commandant* approached her while his men marched outside. "You said you had two siblings, Fräulein?" At Brigetta's uncertain nod, he motioned to Hilda, who'd just climbed down from the loft, her face paralyzed with fear. "Yet I see only one. Where is the other?"

Ludwig! Brigetta's mouth went dry.

A shout from one of the soldiers brought them all outside. "There are tracks leading to the castle." He pointed up the path.

Brigetta stood in the doorway and apprehensively stared at the small set of footprints in the fresh snow. *Oh, no, Ludwig. . .no.*

Before she could say a word, the soldiers tromped up the hill. Brigetta hurriedly slipped on her clunky shoes and grabbed her mother's shawl from a nearby hook to throw over her dress.

"Brigetta!" Her father's tone demanded answers.

She faced him. "I'll tell you everything, *Vatti*. Only not now—please!" With that she took off after the soldiers. Though she ran, the snow impeded her. The men were halfway up the hill before she caught up with them.

"Please—my little brother is up there with his dog," she panted. "He goes there often. The dog is vicious toward strangers. He might attack, and I don't want to see anyone hurt—or the dog shot."

The *commandant* stared at her with narrowed eyes, then grabbed her arm. "Perhaps then, Fräulein, you should come with us. Seeing you, the dog might not attack."

"Oh, but—you don't understand—"

He ignored her protests, forcing her up the hill. Brigetta's heart dropped as they broke through the trees and came upon Engelturm. *Run, Joseph,* she silently cried. *Run, my love!*

The *commandant* turned to one of his five men. "Stay with her. The rest of you come with me."

Brigetta watched as they marched across the rickety bridge

and disappeared beyond the crumbling wall, their weapons at the ready. She took a step forward. The intense pressure of a hand above her elbow stopped her before she could go farther. She turned her head to look into the warning eyes of the young soldier, whose finger rested on the trigger of a pistol aimed at her back.

"I would not recommend it, Fräulein. Keep still, and you will not be harmed."

Wolfgang's frantic barking staccatoed the air, followed by a child's frightened squeal. Brigetta closed her eyes, squeezing the sudden tears from them, and prayed as she'd never prayed before. *Gott, forgive me for hiding the truth from my parents, for putting those I love in danger. Please keep us safe. Protect Joseph, Lord, I love him so. . . .*

The church bell from the village began to peal, the gongs reverberating through the frozen air. Brigetta looked toward Engelheim in surprise. The soldier's face also registered shock as he turned his gaze that way. Only on Sundays did Father Zimmerman ring the bell. Today was not Sunday.

Soon the soldiers exited the castle and crossed the bridge, their gaze on the village where the bell still tolled. A loud rustle and snap came from the forest beyond. The soldiers whipped around, aiming their guns toward the noise.

Hilda broke through the trees, her face flushed from running. She stared in horror at the guns turned on her, then lifted anxious eyes to Brigetta. "Kaiser Wilhelm has abdicated! Revolution has broken out. The men of the village—are being summoned to meet at the fountain—in the town square." She darted a look at the soldiers, then dropped her gaze.

Silence cloaked them like a heavy mantle though the bell continued to clang, issuing its news. All knew what this meant.

Surrender was imminent. Germany had lost the war.

The *commandant* threw a sharp glance toward the village, his brow furrowing as though he were trying to make a decision. His steady gaze then swung to Brigetta for a few heart-racing seconds, before moving to the soldiers. "We must return to headquarters to receive our orders," he said soberly. Before moving away, he looked once more at the castle tower, shook his head, and departed down the hill with his men.

"Go home, Hilda," Brigetta urged. "I'll be there soon."

Brigetta didn't waste another moment but lifted her skirts and sped across the bridge into the castle. "Joseph!" she cried, the word echoing down the corridor. "Ludwig! Where are you?"

Ludwig appeared, and she threw her arms around him. Crying, she held him tightly, then pushed him away, clutching his upper arms. "You were naughty to come here. You could have gotten killed!"

"I wanted to warn Joseph so you wouldn't be angry with me anymore. They didn't see him, Brigetta! They looked right at him but didn't see him! The bell started to ring, and they turned away. I hid him *gut*. Wolfgang helped." He puffed his chest out proudly.

Brigetta drew him close for another swift hug, realizing she could have so easily lost him. "Joseph. . . ?"

"In the chapel."

"Run home to *Vatti*." Brigetta stood, her gaze going to the chapel entrance. "Tell him I'll come soon."

After her brother sped away, Brigetta hurried inside the chapel. Nothing was visible except for a pail lying on its side, water puddled on the stone floor. She walked toward the stained glass window. Wolfgang sat beside the altar, at the edge of a blanket that covered a lump. The sole of a man's boot peeked from beneath. No one could mistake that a person hid under the rough cloth. Had God blinded the soldiers' eyes?

Tingles rushed over Brigetta's arms and down her back as she knelt and removed the blanket. Joseph blinked at the sudden light.

"Why didn't you run?" she asked.

He gave a rueful grin, slowly pushing himself up on one arm. "I couldn't. Ludwig warned me the soldiers were coming, but in my haste to escape, I tripped over the water bucket and twisted my foot. Ludwig covered me with the blanket, and my faithful friend over there," he paused and nodded to Wolfgang, "kept watch."

Brigetta didn't know whether to laugh or cry. Tenderly, she cradled his face between her palms. "Oh, you foolish man," she murmured, her voice trembling. Heart brimming with love, relief, and gratitude, she kissed his cheek.

"Brigetta?" he said uncertainly, a catch in his voice.

"You need a wife to take care of you. If you want to live in America, then that is where we'll go. After today, I know I never want to be without you." She drew a shaky breath. "The bell—the reason it rings—the war is over, Joseph. The kaiser has abdicated."

Joseph sat the rest of the way up, wincing as he moved his foot. His stance was uncertain, but his blue eyes glowed. "I don't know whether to let out a whoop or comfort you. If it's wrong to want to shout to the hills for joy, knowing you'll soon be mine, knowing the fighting between our countries is over—then God forgive me."

He didn't shout but rather put his hands to her shoulders, brought her close, and kissed her temple. Impatient, Brigetta lifted her face, clutching the hair at the back of his head, and drew him down until their lips met. He stiffened, then slowly, ever so slowly, his mouth moved over hers. Heat sizzled through both of them, dispelling the cold. They pulled back at the same time and stared at one another.

"I knew it would be like that," Joseph murmured. "All along I knew God must have designed us for one another and led me to Engelturm—not only for refuge, but to find you. . . ." His expression sobered. "Brigetta, I must search for my company. I have another year left in the army."

"Then I will wait," she assured him, stroking his bearded cheek with her fingertips. "I will wait forever if I have to. I love you, Joseph."

"And I adore you," he whispered, inclining his head. Again his warm lips touched hers, gently, experimenting with this newfound level of their relationship. She wove her fingers through his hair and pressed closer, never wanting this moment to end. . .knowing it must. For soon—very soon—he would go.

As if suddenly realizing the same thing, he tightened his hold around her and hungrily deepened the kiss. Heat spiraled through her, sending every nerve ending into awareness. When she didn't think she could stand the sweetness of being in his arms any longer, Joseph broke away.

"I'll come back for you," he said hoarsely. "I promise. But for now. . ." His gaze lowered to her lips. Briefly he closed his eyes and released her. "You should go."

"Will I see you again before you leave?"

He hesitated, then gave a slight nod. "I'll stay another day or two until I can walk well. If you could bring me food until then, I'd appreciate it."

Her body trembling, she nodded, shaken by the intensity of her feelings for this man. Knowing that in one emotion-ridden moment, she might have gladly given herself to him. She was thankful he retained the presence of mind to prevent such a thing from happening, something that could sully their love for one another and for God. And in that moment, Brigetta loved Joseph more than she'd ever thought possible. She gave him a hasty peck on his cheek and rose, quickly exiting the room.

Epilogue

Erntedankfest was in full zenith, the Thanksgiving harvest festival a huge success. Dancing and merrymaking went on all around Brigetta. Deep in thought, she stared at the table of food.

Offerings of grain, fruit, and vegetables had been presented in artistic arrangements before the church altar earlier that morning, a symbol of the villagers' gratitude to God. Afterward the food was distributed to the needy, something for which both Hilda and Brigetta volunteered. It had cheered Brigetta to see hope in the impoverished people's eyes and receive their smiles and thanks.

Later, at the parade, she'd watched as decorated carts trundled by, bearing sheaves of grain tied in bunches to resemble animals and people. Recognizing her uncle's cart laden high with plump, orange pumpkins, Brigetta chuckled at the absurd sight of blue bows tied around the burly oxen's necks.

Now she stared at the abundance of food and chose bratwurst and sauerkraut. An array of desserts tempted her from the next table. Ciders and wines flowed freely, and several villagers looked to have imbibed just as freely.

With disbelieving eyes, Brigetta observed eight-year-old

Ludwig devour his second plateful of food in under three minutes and head to the heavily laden dessert table. He gave her a cheeky grin and piled pastries high on his plate.

Cousin Pieter came up beside the boy. Glancing Brigetta's way, Pieter gave a friendly grin and wave, then focused on stacking a few slices of *Lebuchen,* the popular honey almond cake, onto his overloaded plate.

Brigetta smiled as she watched her jovial cousin. Everyone had been shocked and grateful to learn that the report of Pieter's death was false. Though her cousin had been shot down behind enemy lines, he was only wounded and later cared for by American missionaries in Paris. Now he was home, as were his two brothers, looking as hearty as ever with an appetite to match.

A hopeful suitor caught Brigetta's attention, one of three men who'd asked for her hand. Her smile evaporated as thoughts that had troubled her earlier returned. Not wanting to dampen everyone's jubilant mood, Brigetta set down her plate and left the crowded festival, needing to be alone for awhile.

Now that she was nineteen, everyone expected her to marry. Yet she'd made a promise. And even without that promise, her love had never died, as his must have done. Why else had Joseph stayed away? Next week would be the two-year anniversary of the morning she'd found him lying wounded on the chapel floor. And now she was the wounded one, her heart stricken by the blow of rejection. She didn't understand. She had prayed so often for God to bring them together again and believed He would. Had Joseph's love not been as strong as hers?

The faint sound of instruments and merriment carried up the hill as Brigetta remembered those last days. Her father had been upset to learn about Joseph but insisted he be brought to the cottage. With the aid of a walking staff and Brigetta's shoulder, Joseph limped down the hill and stayed with them two days until the war officially ended on November 11. Before he left, he held Brigetta close under the tall spruces and vowed his love. Their parting kiss had been bittersweet—but his eyes had held promise.

Brigetta's gaze drifted upward. The setting sun struck the ivory-pink tower of Engelturm, causing it to glow amid the dark firs. Without making a conscious decision to do so, Brigetta took the path to the fortress. Whether it was misplaced sentimentality or simply a need to visit her hideaway, she didn't know—but when she broke through the foliage and stood in front of the citadel, she knew she'd made the right decision.

Whispers of clouds in rose, gold, and lavender streaked the blue sky like brilliant banners adorning her fairy-tale castle. Shimmering with the luminescence of a rosy pearl, the fortress took Brigetta's breath away, and she wondered if this place must indeed be inhabited by angels, as legends told.

"Brigetta?"

The cool breeze carried the soft word to her ears. Her heart skipped a beat, and she turned in disbelief.

Joseph stood at the edge of the forest. Brigetta closed her eyes, wondering if she were hallucinating; but when she opened them, he was still there. How many times had she envisioned such a scene?

Civilian clothes replaced the uniform, the blue of his shirt matching his eyes. His hair—glowing red-gold in the setting sun—was shorter, his jaw clean-shaven. Faint lines indented the area between his eyebrows and ran alongside his nose to his mouth, as though he, too, had suffered.

"I had a feeling I'd find you here," he said quietly. "You look more wonderful than I remembered. With Engelturm behind you like that, you look almost ethereal."

Heart beating fast, Brigetta glanced at the dark *dirndl* and embroidered apron she wore for festivals. An uneasy silence elapsed, broken only by twittering birdcalls and the muted sounds of celebration from the village.

"I probably shouldn't have come," he said at last, his voice resigned, "but I had to see you, had to know for sure. . . ."

When he said nothing more, Brigetta looked up and frowned. Know what? Wasn't she the one entitled to an explanation? "Why didn't you return after your time in the army?"

"I explained in my letter."

"Letter?" Brigetta's heart made a crazy skid. "I received no letter."

His eyes widened with disbelief, then hope. He took a few steps toward her. "I sent it at the beginning of this year. I assumed you didn't respond because you didn't love me as you'd thought, that you couldn't leave this place. . . ."

Incredulous, she slowly walked his way. "I never stopped loving you, Joseph. And *ja*, I shall always treasure this castle with its memories. But, as lovely as it is, Engelturm is only an edifice. You are my life."

He stared for a moment in shock, then, releasing a stunned breath, quickly closed the short distance that still separated them and took her in his arms. "I should've known the letter was lost, but I grew to think you no longer cared for me. You were so young when we met," he explained. "I wrote and asked you to come to America. After my father had a stroke, I had to take over the music store. He's okay now, but I couldn't leave then, and I was determined to think of another way of bringing you to me. I told you I'd send money for your ticket. When you didn't answer—I thought that was your answer."

"Never." Brigetta shook her head against him and tightened her hold around his waist. He still cared for her! A troublesome thought abruptly pricked her joy. "But what of your parents? They might not like me."

With thumb and forefinger, Joseph lifted her chin. His eyes shone with reassurance. "Once I told them about you—and how you risked your life to save mine—they already loved you. My mother, especially, is eager to meet you."

She wrinkled her brow. "But, Joseph—I don't know any English!"

He grinned. "Then I will teach you. We'll start your lessons while I'm here. Since my brother is helping Father run the store, I can stay in Engelheim for a spell." His smile faded. "But will your family approve of me?"

Brigetta laughed, her heart light. "Oh, *ja! Vatti* has often said he wished he could have known you better. *Mutti* too."

"Really?" Joseph's brows lifted. "Your father was a good host those two days I stayed at your cottage, but he seemed more than happy to see me go."

Her mouth parted in surprise. "But of course—I haven't told you—Pieter is alive! Americans nursed him to health, as I did you."

"That's great news!" he softly exclaimed.

Her smile matching his, she nodded. "My entire family feels much kinder—and grateful—toward your people."

"Who, I hope, will soon be your people too." He cradled her face, his expression becoming determined. "Never again will I leave you, Brigetta. I love you. If only you'd gotten my letter and our reunion hadn't taken this long. . . ."

A startling thought broke through her cloud of bliss. "Joseph—what if I wasn't meant to receive your letter? What if it was *Gott* Who waylaid it?" At his obvious bewilderment, she explained. "Had I received the letter when you sent it, I cannot say how my family would have reacted. *Gott* has worked in their hearts much this year, and the news of Pieter has helped. My family and I have had many good conversations about you."

His eyes widened with the revelation. "You know, you may be right. Though we wanted to be together sooner—only God knew the best time for everyone involved. It was only during the last two months that I strongly felt I was to return to Engelheim."

Awed, she stared at him, at last beginning to understand. As He had with all who'd lived here throughout past centuries, the Lord had proven Himself faithful in His protection of their lives. . .and their love.

Joseph's expression softened. "If your parents approve, I want to marry you before I take you with me to America. Say you will, my angel."

"Ja, I will." Her happiness overwhelming, Brigetta could barely speak. "And I know they will consent—especially when they see for themselves how wonderful you are."

Joseph took Brigetta in his arms and kissed her, sending her heart soaring amid the rosy clouds. The church bell began to peal, and Brigetta was certain even the angels of Engelturm rejoiced with her over her reunion with this man: once her dearest enemy. Forever her dearest friend.

As for God, his way is perfect: the word of the LORD *is tried: he is a buckler to all those that trust in him.*
PSALM 18:30

PAMELA GRIFFIN

Pamela is a native of central Texas and is the mother of two sweet boys, Brandon and Joshua. She divides her time between family, church activities, and writing. Her first novel, *'Til We Meet Again,* came out with **Heartsong Presents** in the spring of 2000; since then she has contracted three more novels and six novellas. She fully gave her life to the Lord Jesus Christ in 1988, after a rebellious young adulthood, and owes the fact that she's still alive today to an all-loving and forgiving God and to a mother who steadfastly prayed and had faith that the Lord could bring her wayward daughter "home." One of Pamela's main goals in writing Christian romance is to help and encourage those who do know the Lord and to plant a seed of hope in those who don't. She invites you to visit her website at: http://members.cowtown.net/PamelaGriffin/

Once a Stranger

by Gail Gaymer Martin

Dedication

To my mom, sister Jan, and brother Dan,
who traveled with my husband, Bob, and me
to Europe enjoying the lovely city of
Dinkelsbühl and the Black Forest.

Love ye therefore the stranger:
for ye were strangers in the land.
DEUTERONOMY 10:19

Chapter 1

Maddy Johns dug a spoon into the whipped cream topping of her chocolate ice cream and slipped it between her lips, letting the cold dessert melt on her tongue. She scanned the scenery and sighed. This was the life.

After six years of college, Maddy had graduated from the University of Michigan with a master's degree in history, and today she was relaxing in the quaint German village of Dinkelsbühl, bathed in the warm July sunlight and the charm of the twelfth-century village. The pleasure lay as sweetly on her heart as did the creamy treat on her lips.

Looking past the ornate buildings and the Lion Fountain, she focused on the children gathering in groups along the street near the *Wörnitz Tor,* one of four town gates that surrounded the walled city. Curious, she stretched her neck, looking for a waiter to ask about the occasion. With none in sight, she settled back and noticed a pleasant-appearing man sliding into a chair at the next table. He smiled, and she smiled back.

He studied the sweet shop menu, eyed her ice cream sundae, then returned the menu to the table.

Curious about the children, Maddy wondered if he spoke English and scuffled to organize her German sentence properly.

When she felt confident, she leaned toward him and asked, *"Bitte, sprechen Sie Englisch?"*

He tossed his head backward with an amused laugh before answering. "I'm American."

Heat, not caused by the sun, rose up her neck, and her laughter joined his. "Then, you probably couldn't answer my question."

"Try me." He slid his chair closer and focused his russet-colored eyes on hers.

Maddy gestured with her spoon. "The children," she said. "I wondered why they're gathering beyond the fountain."

"Rehearsing," he said. "Next week is the *Kinderzeche.*"

She grinned. "I got the *kinder* part. . .but—"

"It's a children's festival. About a hundred years old, I think."

"Ahh," she said, turning back to her melting sundae.

"Looks good," he said.

Maddy lifted her eyes to his again. "Pardon?"

"The sundae. Might have one myself while I wait."

Wait? Curiosity jiggled through her. She eyed his friendly face and pushed her reserve aside. "Would you like to join me?" she asked.

"Sure," he said, rising. "I'm Jacob Bruckner."

"Madeline Johns," she said. "Most people call me Maddy."

As he slid into the chair facing the children, the elusive waiter came through the doorway. Jacob placed his order, then folded his hands across his stomach and leaned back. "Vacationing?" he asked.

She nodded. "You too?"

"No, I live here."

Surprised, she straightened her back. "Right here?" she asked, swinging her spoon in front of her in a wide arch.

He ducked. "Whoa! You wield that spoon like a weapon."

Grinning, she dropped it on a napkin. "I've been told I use my hands too much. Too enthusiastic, they tell me."

"*They?*" He arched a brow and gave her a wry grin.

"They. . .you know, people, my folks and friends. When I get excited, everybody ducks."

"Thanks for the warning."

The waiter appeared and placed an identical sundae in front of him.

"*Danke schön,*" he said in thanks.

The waiter nodded and moved off, wiping tables and adjusting chairs as he headed back inside.

Jacob dipped his spoon into the ice cream, captured some chocolate syrup, and raised it to his mouth. Licking his lips, he tapped the sundae dish. "Good."

"So tell me, why do you live in Dinkelsbühl?" Maddy asked.

"Can you think of a better place?"

At the moment, she couldn't. The past couple of days had been wonderful. She shook her head in agreement.

"For four years when I was in the army, I was stationed a few miles from here, and I loved this city."

"I can't blame you," she said. "So who are you waiting for?" In a flash, a wife came to mind.

"A few kids from the orphanage."

With that, he'd caught her attention, and she felt her eyebrows lift.

"During my stay here, I volunteered at the orphanage between here and Nuremberg. . .and found it one of the most meaningful experiences of my life."

"Really? And that's why you're staying here?" *Doing charity work?* Maddy could hardly imagine that being motivation for anyone.

He laughed. "Well, I have to admit that with the name Jacob Bruckner, I have roots in Germany." Like a German, he pronounced it "Yacob" and rolled his R in Bruckner.

She grinned. "Me too, but I'm a mutt," she said. "A little blend of everything." This man amazed her. He seemed to find pleasure in the simplest things. She liked that attribute as well as his warm smile and easy manner. But his compassion awed her. "What did you do at the orphanage?"

He licked the spoon and rested it on the edge of the dish beneath the stemmed glass. "All kinds of things. Lots of my army buddies went with me. We painted, did repairs, helped in the garden. The orphanage is run by a missionary with limited funds, so our donated time meant a lot to the staff and the children."

"You're a Christian, then?"

"Absolutely," he said. "Jesus said, 'Suffer the little children to come unto me, and forbid them not.' I consider those words a Christian mission."

"That's wonderful." A tingle of guilt rattled up her spine. Coming from a well-to-do family, she'd always lived with luxury and never thought about volunteering for a cause. Her education had been her focus for most of her twenty-seven years.

He looked at her quizzically. "You're not a believer?" A serious expression dimmed his smile.

"Oh, yes, I've gone to church. . . ." Church, yes, but nothing else. "I just never—"

He touched her arm. "Don't feel bad. A lot of Christians don't do volunteer work. Not even for their own congregations."

"I guess some of us take our faith for granted."

"It's never too late to begin," he said, his voice encouraging.

"That's true." She wanted to know more about the orphanage but didn't want to pry.

Jacob dug into his ice cream, and she turned her attention to the children farther down the street. They appeared to be organized in sets of eight, like square dancers. Recorded music drifted up the street, and she watched them skipping and gliding to a lovely folk tune.

"You don't think I'll let you off that easily, do you?" Jacob said.

She pivoted toward him and studied his face. "What do you mean?"

"I told you about me. Now, it's your turn."

Let me off that easily? The comment had flustered her for a minute. She'd assumed that he might ask her to visit the orphanage with him. When he didn't, disappointment edged through her. The emotion surprised her. The man was a total stranger. Why would he ask her to go with him? She pushed a pleasant expression to her face. "What do you want to know?"

"First, why are you in Dinkelsbühl? Are you here with friends?"

"No, I'm alone."

His eyes widened. "Really. Most people travel with a friend or two. Why not you?"

"I was stood up." She grinned. "My girlfriend was offered a job she couldn't refuse, so she had to cancel." She picked up her spoon again and stirred the melting ice cream. "So here I am, alone."

"Too bad."

Maddy wasn't sure it was so bad. Since arriving, she'd changed her itinerary and spent time where she wanted with no one else to consult. "The trip is a gift from my folks—for completing my master's degree."

"Whew!" He rubbed his neck. "My folks couldn't afford a bus ticket to the next state. . . . But that never mattered. I love them just the same."

"Mine can afford it," she said, then wished she hadn't. It sounded snobbish—not at all the way she felt.

He seemed to ignore the comment and continued. "So how do you happen to be sitting at Café Rohe on a sunny July day?"

"Same as you, I suppose. I love the town. When I arrived, I'd planned to follow the Romantic Road, so I headed straight for Würzburg. My plan is to go all the way to Füssen. It's two hundred and eleven miles."

"You aren't even one-third down the Romantic Road, you know."

"I know. I've decided to stick around here for awhile. I have the whole summer." She lifted her head at the sound of the children's voices and glanced down the street. "You don't see things like this just any old place."

"You don't," he said. "Let me catch the waiter, and we'll walk closer so you can really hear the children. If you're staying another week, you'll be in Dinkelsbühl for the fest—costumes, parade, children's band, and all."

Excitement spread across his pleasant face.

"I'd love that," she said. "Tell me what it's about."

He looked heavenward a moment and frowned. "Let's see if I can get this right." He returned his gaze to Maddy. "It reenacts a time during the Thirty Years' War when the Swedish colonel Sperreuth marched his army into the city and attacked it for weeks. The city's three mayors knew they couldn't resist, so they decided to surrender; but instead the watchman's daughter gathered the town's children and led them to the enemy, where they confronted the army and begged them to withdraw from the city."

"So they did?" Maddy asked, caught up in the tale.

Jacob nodded. "Sure did. Tradition says that the colonel had recently lost a young son, and so he gave in to the children, and that's how they saved the village."

Maddy gestured toward the activity near the *Wörnitz* gate. "You mean, the kids act out the whole story."

He nodded. "I'll get the bill, and we can head down the street and watch for awhile." He rose and went inside.

Maddy watched him go and tried to imagine being excited about a children's festival or volunteering to help the needy. The idea seemed alien to her, but each time he talked about those things, a smidgen of guilt poked at her conscience.

When he came out, he beckoned her to follow. He bounded to the street, and she hurried after him.

She caught up with him near the *Löwenbrunnen,* one of the village fountains surrounded by half-timbered houses. In the center, the statue of a majestic lion sat on his haunches circled in flowers.

"What's my share?" Maddy asked.

"Share of what?"

She realized he knew what she meant, but she played the game. "Share of the bill."

"Zilch. All ice cream sundaes are free today."

Seeing no sense in making a scene, Maddy gave him a quiet thank you but felt uncomfortable accepting the gift from a stranger.

Jacob clasped her arm and guided her through the crowd, his warm hand sending a tingle up her limb.

"Is this okay?" he asked, motioning to the location.

"Wonderful," she said, amused at the two children who inched their hands upward to send him a shy wave.

He chuckled and waved back. "Gretchen and Henri," he said.

"They like you." *Like* was an understatement. From their gleeful grins and delightful waves, Maddy knew they loved him. She sensed he was real—no pretentiousness, no hidden motives, no negativity. Jacob seemed like a lovable man.

Intrigued by the children, she watched their intricate dance patterns. With eyes focused on Jacob, the boy named Henri missed his step. With apprehension, Maddy followed his awkward stumbles until he righted himself.

"You seem to distract children *and* adults," Maddy said, thinking of herself latched to his side.

"I'm the Pied Piper."

"I hope not," she said. "Didn't he lead the children away from the village to get even with the city fathers?"

He shrugged. "Bad example, I guess. Maybe I'm more like the ice cream man."

She grinned, finding that most appropriate since they'd met over a sundae.

The dancers moved to the side, and a children's band lifted their instruments and played a final tune. Within seconds, Jacob was surrounded by seven smiling faces speaking at once in German.

His patience awed Maddy, and in a mixture of German and English, he introduced her to the children. They chattered and laughed while she tried to remember each one's name.

Jacob covered his mouth and whispered, "I'd better get these kids back before Brother Karl thinks I am the Pied You-Know-Who."

He took a step backward, and Maddy had to rein in her desire to latch onto the children's hands and go along with him. Something about Jacob filled her with pleasure. His kindness and gentleness? His tenderness with the children? Maybe his unique spirit? Whatever it was, he could "pipe" her away in a minute.

"Thanks," she said, sad to see him go. She dug into her pocket and pulled out some bills. "I'd really like you to take this for my sundae."

He shook his head. "No, it was my treat."

"But I have no way to pay you back. We have no chance for it to be my treat." The words flew from her mouth before she could stop them.

"Well. . . ," he said, "how would you like to go with me to the home on Saturday?" He tilted his head and waited while the children chattered and tugged at his hand.

"Schokolade," they sang out in chorus.

"Chocolate," Jacob said with a shrug. "They love the stuff."

"Could I bring some on Saturday?" she asked, wondering about her good sense. But despite the warning in her head, her heart sensed she'd made the right decision.

"Bring all you want," he said as the children pulled at his sleeves. "You'll come then?"

"Why not?" she asked. "Can you think of a better place to be?"

"That sounds strangely familiar," he said as he tried to gain his footing instead of being dragged off by the eager children. "Where can I pick you up?" he called.

"On *Langegasse*. I'm at the *Goldenes Lamm*. Do you know where it is?"

"Golden Lamb, huh? Suits you. I'll see you Saturday around nine."

"See you," she said.

She wondered if he heard her over the clamor of the children and the distance they'd accomplished with their exuberant tugging.

He gave a final wave, and she lifted her hand in good-bye. Turning away, Maddy headed toward her room, feeling a new bounce in her step. Today she didn't feel like a stranger in town. She had a friend.

Chapter 2

J acob looked at the attractive young woman at his side and wondered why she had agreed to come along—not that he wasn't pleased. From what he'd learned, Maddy came from a wealthy family, and seeing children living with the bare necessities in an orphanage didn't seem like something she would want to do while on vacation.

That morning, he'd easily found the inn where she was staying. Maddy had waited for him in the small lobby. Heading out of the village, Jacob had retraced his route, passing St. George Minster, the gothic church in the village center. Exiting by way of the *Wörnitz Tor*, he headed across the countryside toward Nuremberg. The Children's Mission lay in that direction near the city of Schwabach.

Looking at Maddy now, Jacob noted her expensive clothes and designer shoulder bag, a clue to her high-classed background. Still, her apparel wasn't the only indicator. Her polished manners and social awareness made it obvious. The way she spoke, the way she ate, the way she walked showed a woman of breeding.

Jacob stemmed from a blue-collar American family—a good Christian home. His father worked in a small factory and his mother was proud to be a housewife. Jacob's older brother and sister fell into the same family pattern of marrying young. Jacob wanted to be different.

"You're quiet," Maddy said.

Jacob glanced away from the highway and noticed her curious face. He sensed he should apologize for his distraction. "Thinking, I suppose."

"A *Deutsche mark* for your thoughts," she said.

He grinned and pondered if he should be honest. Finally he braved his decision. "I was wondering what a wealthy woman like you is doing with a plain old guy like me, heading for an orphanage to do volunteer work. It doesn't fit."

"My father is wealthy, not me," she murmured and turned her head to look out the window before returning her focus to him. "Maybe it's time I learn a little about how the average person lives. Experience *real* life, I mean."

She appeared uncomfortable and hesitant to say any more. Jacob pondered what to do. Should he apologize for his comment or let it pass? He needed to learn discretion and to keep his mouth closed.

"God has blessed me," she said, finally, "but if I call myself a Christian, you've helped me see that I should be concerned about people less fortunate. I've been thinking about this a long time."

Still, Jacob squirmed, knowing he had caused some of her discomfort. Maddy stared out the passenger window at the passing landscape, occasionally commenting about a distant castle on a hillside or a small village circled by an ancient stone wall, but the conversation strayed from personal topics.

When she spoke again, he heard a poignant ring to her voice. "Sometimes I feel guilty that I've been given so much and that I've given back nothing in return. Nothing for others."

Jacob's stomach twisted with his own guilt. "I didn't mean to upset you, Maddy."

"It's not you. Like I said, I've been questioning myself for a long time. Money rules the world, but just think if love was the standard. Can you imagine what the earth would be like?"

Her words wrapped around his heart. "That would be like heaven, Maddy. It's a great thought."

She nodded. "Just a thought. . .I know." She sighed. "Sorry, I seem to be a drag today."

"You're not a drag. I'm glad you came along. I enjoy your company. You've brought a little home back into my life."

She shifted in the seat to face him. "Speaking of the home, why'd you join the army? And why'd you decide to stay here? You could have done volunteer work in the U.S., so it wasn't the orphanage that brought you back."

Her questions jogged his thoughts. "I know why I joined the army. . . ." His mind worked its way back to the year he decided to settle in Dinkelsbühl. "But I'm not so sure how the other happened."

"Then start with the army. Tell me why you joined up."

She sounded interested, and Jacob struggled to organize his thoughts. "Maybe it was mild rebellion; I don't know. I wanted to be different. My mom and dad married young. My brother married his high school girlfriend and went to work in a factory like my dad. They have four kids now. My sister has three."

The thought settled uneasily in his mind. He was missing out on seeing his nieces and nephews grow up. "I felt as if I was expected to do the same."

Her face looked tender and concerned. "You mean like get married and settled down?"

He nodded.

"And you didn't want to. Did you have a high school girl-friend?" she asked.

Amused at her question, he glanced her way and saw a sly grin on her lips. "Sure. . .that wasn't the problem. Do I look like a guy who can't find a date?" He tried to sound witty, but reality reminded him that he felt inadequate at times in his youth.

"Goodness, no," she said. "You're a good-looking man—and fun to talk with." She chuckled. "I just wondered if you had a secret side I don't know."

"No secrets, just determined not to fall into the family syndrome of marrying young. I'm the first one in my family to make it to twenty-nine without being married."

She looked at him in surprise.

He wondered if she understood what he meant by young. "Everyone in my family married before they were twenty."

"You're kidding." Her eyes widened as if people with sense didn't marry young. "I'm twenty-seven and haven't considered marriage yet."

"No joke," he said. "That's what I mean about marrying young."

Seeing a faint flush on her face, Jacob assumed she felt embarrassed by her reaction. "I had other reasons for joining the army," he added, changing the subject and hoping to make her feel more at ease.

Her embarrassment seemed to fade. "Like?"

"Like I wanted a little adventure, and I wanted an education. My parents didn't have money for my college education without struggling, and I didn't want to add stress to their lives. I figured the army could give me both—adventure and an education."

"And did it?"

"Well, I traveled to Europe. That's adventure for a guy like me, and if you call carpentry an education, I think it did," Jacob said, wondering what she really felt about his blue-collar occupation.

"I'd say it's a great career if you enjoy it and if you're making a living. What more do you need?"

He shrugged at her comment, but he felt curious. How could a financially secure woman ask what more he needed? He wondered about Maddy. What made her tick? Why did she seem disconcerted by her family's wealth?

He let the thoughts sit in his mind as they entered Schwabach. Jacob wended his car through the narrow streets, and when he reached the outskirts, he pointed to the children's home and parked beside the stucco structure.

"This is it?" Maddy asked.

Jacob eyed the peeling paint, the drab surroundings and nodded. "They have a small playground in back. But this building is home to about forty kids."

Maddy sat unmoving, then shook her head and pushed open the passenger door. Remembering his manners, Jacob hurried around the car to meet her as she stepped onto the cracked concrete. Grass and weeds shot through the ruptured surface.

Children's voices carried on the air from behind the building, and Jacob smiled, thinking of the waifs who had fun doing the simplest things. Nostalgia shivered through him as he thought of his siblings' children.

Jacob guided Maddy toward the entrance, and inside he led her to the office where they would receive their assignments.

When he came through the doorway, Brother Karl, the head administrator, gave him a wave, and Jacob waited. After finishing his business, the man stepped across the room to greet them.

In a smattering of English and German along with a generous smile, Brother Karl gave Maddy a warm greeting, then suggested where their work would be most needed. Jacob hoped Maddy could handle the mundane task.

Heading for the door, Maddy halted, motioning to the box she carried. "I brought chocolate treats for the children."

Jacob turned toward the administrator to explain, but Brother Karl had caught enough English to understand.

"*Schokolade,*" he said, his face beaming. "*Die Kinder* will be *sehr* happy. You will eat *Mittagessen.* After, you can the treat give."

Maddy eyed Jacob with a questioning look.

"That will work," Jacob said. "*Mittagessen* is lunch."

"Right," she said, giving him a grin.

With that settled, Jacob opened the door as a staff member met them in the corridor and offered to guide Maddy to the sewing room. Jacob watched her go down the hall, the woman's broken English echoing against the high ceilings. Jacob prayed Maddy would fare well, then turned in his own direction to gather painting supplies.

Apprehensive, Maddy followed the woman into a small workroom. An old wooden table stood in the middle of the floor surrounded by a few chairs, and an outdated sewing machine sat against the wall. A cart beside the table had been piled with garments. "To mend," she said, pointing to the stack.

Maddy slid her candy box on the table and lifted a child's faded blouse, eyeing the tear beneath the arm. Next, she lifted a skirt with a torn hem, jeans needing a knee patch, and an unending pile of worn-out garments.

"Play clothes?" Maddy asked.

"Nein," the woman said, wagging her head, *"Die Schulju-gend."* She gave Maddy a bright smile. "School, *ja."*

"School." Maddy stared at the near rags. "You mean the children wear these, uh, clothes to school?"

"Ja." Her head wagged again, then she pivoted and pointed toward the sewing machine. *"Sie ist kaputt."*

"Kaputt? You mean broken?" Maddy struggled to keep her face from showing her concern.

The woman gestured toward the table. Maddy eyed the objects; she spied the needles, pins, and thread that she was to use.

"Mit der Hand naehen," the woman said, acting as if she were sewing.

Der Hand. Maddy understood that. "Sew them by hand," Maddy said to let the woman know she understood.

The young woman nodded, then backed toward the door and retreated into the hallway while Maddy sank into a chair, facing hours of mending clothes too worn to be repaired.

Her chest tightened when she thought about the children. In her travels, she'd noticed that clothing seemed very expensive in Germany, so dressing forty children would certainly exhaust a limited budget. Maddy's own high-priced clothing soared into mind, but they were costly by choice, not necessity.

Her heart ached as she thought of the school-aged boys and girls facing classmates in their patched garments. Along with the ache, guilt rifled through her, and her mind snapped with ideas, thinking of her next visit and how she might help the needy orphanage.

Pulling the pastel garments from the stack, Maddy threaded a needle with white thread and went to work. Time seemed to fly as her fingers created tiny stitches while her mind created larger possibilities.

When the door swung open, Maddy jumped in surprise.

"How's it going?" Jacob asked from the doorway.

"Okay." She gestured to the pile still needing work.

"Sorry you came?" He stepped toward the table, his gaze on the folded garments beside her.

"Not at all." She gestured to the stack. "See what I did today."

"Better than I did. I couldn't begin to paint until I did some patch jobs. This place needs too much." He beckoned to her. "Ready for lunch?"

"Sure," she said, setting her sewing on the table and rising. "I wonder how they keep this place going."

"Prayer and donations."

Maddy nabbed her package and trudged beside him down the corridor, weighted with concern. Instead of the dining hall, Jacob led her through a doorway into the sunshine. She drew in the fresh air and looked toward the glowing sun, needing something to brighten her day.

Outside, the children's chattering voices carried on the breeze. While some children played on rusted swings and slides, others were circled in small groups. Games, Maddy assumed. Older children talked and joked in scattered groups, and their laughter lifted into the air.

"I thought you said lunch," Maddy said with a grin.

He grinned back. "They'll ring the bell and bring everyone inside."

"The sun feels good," she said, feeling her stomach rumble, yet struggling with more concern about eating the children's food. "Should we go somewhere and pick up a snack?"

Jacob frowned. "No, this is their way of paying you for your kindness. If we leave, we'd appear rude."

"Don't want to do that," she said as the bell sounded.

The children forgot their games and conversation and hurried to the door. Jacob and Maddy waited, then followed them inside and listened while the children sang a lovely song that served as their blessing.

Following the prayer, a savory aroma drifted from kettles, and soup was dished into large bowls and served with bread. When they'd finished, Brother Karl announced their dessert treat, and Maddy handed him the box filled with bars of chocolate. After Brother Karl doled out the candy, the children rose and headed for the exit, clutching their own small bar. As they filed past, many paused beside Maddy, sending her a smile and thank-you.

Gretchen, the child Maddy remembered from the festival rehearsal, darted to her side with a grin. *"Schokolade,"* she said, *"Danke."*

"Bitte schön," Maddy said in reply, giving a pat to Henri as he scooted past, waving his treat.

Maddy's chest tightened with emotion as she watched the children's exuberance over a chocolate bar. What could she do? What could anyone do to help these little ones?

Jacob's voice lifted in her memory, the day he sat on the porch of the ice cream shop and spoke about his work at the orphanage. " 'Suffer the little children to come unto me, and forbid them not,' " he'd said, quoting Jesus.

Tears pushed behind Maddy's eyes as she compared her own lush childhood with the day-to-day difficulties of these children. Yet, they were not unhappy. Instead, she heard laughter and joyful voices to go along with their bright smiles. Maddy knew she'd been guided here for a purpose. What would God have her do?

Chapter 3

Maddy locked her room and headed down the inn staircase. When she stepped outside, she crossed the cramped street and sat on a bench waiting for Jacob, who had invited her to dinner in the village of Donauwörth on the Danube. The thought of enjoying a meal while admiring the famous blue Danube thrilled her.

Today, the town had become crowded with tourists who had come to see the *Kinderzeche*. Though she'd seen the rehearsal, she planned to watch the program some afternoon while Jacob worked. Out of her room window, she had seen children heading toward the *Wörnitz Tor* dressed in colorful seventeenth-century costumes.

Looking down the lane, Maddy watched Jacob's car turn the corner. When he pulled alongside her, she opened the door and slid into the passenger's seat.

Leaving the lane, Jacob turned the car toward the *Nördlinger Tor.* "I thought we'd go this way to avoid the crowds."

Though she'd been in the town two weeks, Maddy still gazed with admiration at the fairy-tale buildings standing out of line along *Nördlinger Strasse,* narrow, brightly painted houses with steep roofs and window boxes overflowing with colorful flowers.

On the highway, Jacob indicated the cities as they drove through them; and within an hour, they reached their destination, the medieval village that was first settled on a delta where the Wörnitz River meets the Danube. On the main street, once the Imperial Highway, Jacob guided Maddy to a charming café in one of the renovated merchant houses.

After ordering, Maddy admitted her heartache over the children's plight. "I want to do something. I don't know what exactly." She hesitated, staring at the stressed wood of the restaurant table and wondering what her contribution might be to help the facility.

"Do what? You're only here for a vacation, Maddy. What could you do for these children?"

"I don't know, but I feel driven to help them."

"You have, and you're welcome to go back again if you really want. Volunteering is a big gift to the small staff."

She sighed. "If I lived here, maybe I could do that every week too, but I don't."

When the words left her mouth, a stranger feeling of sadness washed through her. Reality was that she would have to leave one of these days. Her stomach knotted. What about Jacob and what about the beautiful country? "Sometimes I wish I could stay here forever."

"This place is a fairy tale, Maddy. But you have to face reality." A look of sadness filled Jacob's eyes. "Soon you'll have to return home. There's your family. . .and career."

"What about you? You have family," she said.

"But that's different. Mine is. . .well, they're used to me being away. I'll go back one day. One day when I'm ready, but now I can enjoy the family that I have here in Germany."

Her pulse did a double step. "Your what?"

A grin settled on his face. "Guess I forgot to mention that."

"Forgot?" Apprehension shivered through her, wondering if this could be a wife that he'd forgotten to mention. "The day I met you, you commented about having roots in Germany, but I thought you meant *roots*, not living plants," she said, forcing herself to be lighthearted.

A deep laugh shook his shoulders. "It's some very distant cousins. . .on my mother's side. Engels."

"Engel is their last name?" she asked.

He nodded. "Yes. It means angel in German."

Her heart warmed, seeing his enthusiasm. "Do they live in Dinkelsbühl?"

"No, the Black Forest. The Engels lived in a castle. It's still there. *Engelturm*. It means Angel Tower."

"I'm intrigued. I'd love to own a castle. . .who wouldn't?"

"Me, I suppose," Jacob said. "What would I do with a castle?"

"I could think of a million things," Maddy said. "But now I know why you're so wonderful with the children, why you give so much of yourself. It's your family name, Jacob. You're an angel."

"This time you assume wrong. My mother's the angel. I'm far from it." He slid his palm across the worn table and captured her hand. "But maybe that's what you are. You're nearly a stranger in this country, yet you want to help the children's home."

"I'm no angel either. I'm just gaining some wisdom. A new life experience. Whatever it is, I'm a different person from when I arrived a few weeks ago."

While Maddy sipped her apple juice, Jacob studied her, sensing she was serious. He didn't see a difference, but then he barely knew her. Yet something deep inside discerned that she was right about one thing. God had sent her here, and Jacob hoped that he was part of God's plan.

Before the conversation continued, the waiter arrived with their meals on large platters. Jacob dug into his sauerkraut and wurst and watched Maddy sliver off a piece of her *Rouladen*. When she tasted it, she smiled. "It's delicious."

"Good," Jacob said. "I thought you'd like this place. I've always enjoyed the food here. When we're finished, we can drive down to the Danube and take a stroll."

For awhile, they ate in silence until Maddy pushed her plate aside. "You've really intrigued me. Tell me more about your family in the Black Forest—and about the castle."

Between bites, Jacob told her about the small village in the southern edge of the forest. "It's called Engelheim on the River Wurm. The castle is on a hill overlooking the river. Now, it's overgrown with trees; but back in the sixteenth century, the trees were cleared away for safety. No place for the enemy to hide."

"Did you know all this before you came to Germany?" Maddy asked.

"No, my sister's a genealogy buff, and when she bought a computer, she started looking into the family tree. I knew we had relatives somewhere in Germany, but no details until she located a family member who'd left the area. He lives in Frankfurt and filled her in on the family left in the Schwarzwald."

"That's so exciting. Have you met them?"

"I've been there several times. They're warm, kind people, but poor. Very different from here. My family makes their living by wood-carving—cuckoo clocks and forest animals. Some religious statues. Anything they can sell to shops in the tourist areas."

"They'd do better economically if they had their own shop," Maddy said.

"True, but they don't have money to start their own business. You'd understand if you went there." The words lingered in his thoughts and a plan settled in his mind. "Would you like to go with me?"

"To the Black Forest?"

"Sure, why not? It's a two-, maybe two-and-a-half-hour drive. The scenery's nice, and you'd see another area of Germany."

"And the castle?"

"It's pretty much in ruin now—except for a few sections—but we could hike up there. You'll have to wear comfortable shoes."

Her face brightened like the sun. "Jacob, I'd love to go. When?"

His plan sank like a weight, remembering his two-day commitment at the orphanage. "I promised Brother Karl I'd work this weekend to get that painting finished." Looking at her face, he read her thoughts. "I suppose you'll be leaving before I have time to make the trip."

She looked away and didn't speak for a moment. Then she turned to him. "No, I'll be here. I'm not going anywhere right now. If my parents' gift money runs out, I have my own. I don't need to hurry back to the U.S. when I have a castle to investigate and children's clothes to mend."

"You're sure?" Teasing, he arched a brow but wondered if she were serious.

"If you have to spend the weekend, I'm sure they can keep me busy too."

"No question," he said, excited that she was willing to spend more time with him. "We could attend worship with the children on Sunday. . .if you'd like."

"I'd like," she said. "I'd like to very much.

Leaving the worship service on Sunday morning, the children scampered past Maddy with shy waves and giggles. She'd brought them chocolate again on Saturday, and today, Brother Karl had agreed to her big surprise.

Maddy had spent Saturday evening searching the markets for graham cracker–like wafers. Along with them, she bought bags of marshmallows and more chocolate bars. Tonight, they would have a bonfire in the back of the property and make s'mores treats like those Maddy had enjoyed as a child.

Since she'd met Jacob, Maddy's life seemed full, spending time with him as well as the children and the small staff who cared for them. God had blessed the caregivers with giving hearts and a bounty of love, but they also needed money for building repairs, new clothes, and a truckload of toys. Maddy felt helpless.

"Ready to work?" Jacob asked as they left the chapel.

"Ready as I'll ever be," she said, wishing she were painting rather than sitting in the little room with her needle and thread.

When she said good-bye to Jacob, Maddy headed for the sewing room. When she opened the door, a young woman swung toward her, then laughed. "You scared me."

"You're American," Maddy said, pleasantly surprised.

She nodded. "Kansas. My husband's at the army base nearby, and we learned about the volunteer program. Are you from the base?"

"No," Maddy said with a smile, knowing how silly it sounded, "I'm on vacation."

"Vacation?"

Settling into a chair, Maddy proceeded to tell the woman about Jacob and her travels. The time flew by, and before she knew it, lunch blended into suppertime. The woman and her husband left before the evening meal. Maddy and Jacob joined the staff for dinner.

Knowing they had a special treat, the children hurried through dinner; and when they finally headed outside, someone had already started a bonfire. With the staff's eagle eye on the children, Maddy unloaded her supplies and introduced the children to the chocolate-marshmallow treats.

"See," Maddy said, popping a toasted marshmallow onto the cracker along with a square of chocolate. "Now wait a minute so it melts, and you have what we call in the U.S. s'mores."

The older children who had learned English in school followed her example and helped the younger children. Gathered in a large circle, some of the children joined in song. Not exactly campfire songs, Maddy decided, but folk songs that filled the coloring evening sky with music.

When all the chocolate and marshmallows were gone— except the ones on the ground covered in dirt or charred from the fire—the staff roused the children to their feet and herded them back inside for their studies and the younger ones for quiet play until bedtime.

The day seemed perfect. Maddy realized her heartstrings were tangled around the smiling chocolate-splotched faces that had beamed at her. Each day in Germany she seemed to learn something new about life and about herself. God was at work. She had no doubt.

As they turned toward the building, Brother Karl beckoned to them, and they met him near the doorway.

"Have you a moment?" he asked.

Maddy glanced at Jacob for his response. "Sure," he said. "Is something wrong?"

The administrator glanced over his shoulder, then nodded yes.

Maddy's stomach knotted, fearful that they may have done something to offend the kindly man; but Jacob seemed unconcerned. She followed them into the building and down the corridor to the administration office.

Brother Karl motioned toward two chairs, and Maddy crumpled into a seat, afraid to hear what he had to say. "Did we do something?" she whispered as she leaned closer to Jacob.

He shook his head, but a frown marred his good looks.

After Brother Karl sank into a chair, Jacob rested his elbows on his knees and bent forward. "What's wrong? Is it what we talked about?"

The man nodded his head. "Yes, as I feared."

Maddy's concern grew, hearing their cryptic dialogue. "What is it?"

Jacob shifted toward her. "The government recently did an inspection on the facility, and the building didn't meet the regulations."

"I'm so sorry," Maddy said, her heart sinking like an overturned boat.

"So what needs work?" Jacob asked the man, already knowing that many things needed repair.

Discouraged, he shrugged and lowered his head. "The roof needs repairing; we cannot meet some costly safety regulations, too much for our small budget."

"What will happen now?" Maddy asked, her heart weighted with fear.

"We will close our doors," Brother Karl said.

Chapter 4

Maddy stared into the darkness, hearing Brother Karl's words. *We will close.* Close? But the children? What would happen to them? The thought darkened her spirit.

On the way home, Jacob seemed thoughtful too; and although they talked about the children's excitement over the chocolate-marshmallow treats and what they'd accomplished during the day, neither mentioned the sad news they'd heard.

Maddy knew that God could work miracles. . . . An idea niggled at her. Maybe God had already begun to provide the solution by bringing her to this village and by guiding her to Jacob. She had sensed a calling since arriving in Dinkelsbühl, and now Brother Karl's message added to Maddy's own thoughts and touched her heart. She needed time to think, but she would do something to help the children.

The topic clung to her all week, and only the thought of visiting the Black Forest had kept Maddy from being downhearted. Dressing for the event, she'd remembered that Jacob spoke of hiking to the castle, so Maddy had slipped on her jeans and stepped into her most comfortable walking shoes. Now looking at the landscape, she regarded the heavy foliage and sloping vista of the Black Forest where the trees stretch to the horizon, and she was glad she'd worn them.

Rolling down her window, Maddy drew in the alpine air. Her gaze feasted on an occasional village in the distance, an occasional thatched roof, and cattle grazing in a nearby pasture. "This is wonderful. Fresh, clean air. Crystal streams. It has to be healthy here."

"Sure is," Jacob said. "This area is full of mineral water spas. For centuries, people have come here for rest and recuperation—especially nobility. The world seems to slow down in the forest."

"I love it," she said. "It gives me time to put my life in perspective."

He sent her a smile, then turned away to concentrate on the rolling highway.

Maddy relaxed and closed her eyes. Life in Germany had become calm and precious, so different from her fast-paced life at home. She loved the sense of timelessness and perfection that she found in the natural setting.

Sensing the car slowing, Maddy opened her eyes. "Where are we?" she asked.

"Engelheim."

"All I see are trees."

"We're above the village." He gave her an amused smile. "I thought you might like to visit the castle first before we get tied up with the family."

He stepped from the car and opened her door. "Ready?" He gestured toward the steep pathway.

"Never readier," she said, sounding more confident than she felt.

"I want you to remember what you said." With a wry smile, Jacob slid his arm around her shoulder and gave it a squeeze.

A warm tingle ran down her back, and she gave him a sidelong glance to see if he sensed her reaction. If he did, he hid it well.

Side by side, they trudged upward between the spruce and fir trees, the incline growing steeper as they ascended. A heavy pine fragrance filled the air. Maddy marveled at the clusters of wild roses and tall plants with upright dark green leaves and the fading vestiges of pale purple flowers nestled among the dark green limbs.

Farther on, another fragrance filled the air. She bent down to breathe in the deep purple fernlike foliage smelling like chervil. Closer to the road, berry bushes grew in large bunches, but the season was too early to taste the sweet fruit.

"Tired?" Jacob asked, sliding his arm around her waist. "If you need some energy, I can help." Teasing her, he pulled her forward.

Laughing, she hurried to keep up with him. "Slow down, Silly," she said, "and let me enjoy the sights." As the words left her lips, Maddy looked ahead of her through the trees and spied an outcropping of pinkish white stone. She faltered and stopped. "What's that?"

He grinned. "Engelturm. The tower."

"You mean we're here?"

Instead of answering, he took her hand and drew her forward. She loved the feel of his palm against hers as he guided her through the trees. When they came into a small clearing, Maddy released a gasp. Below, in the shade, vines climbed the base of the tower; but as she looked upward, the sun glowed against the stone like a heavenly aura.

"It is an angel tower," Maddy said. "In the light, it shimmers like it's gossamer."

"It's known for that," he said. "I'll have my cousin Heinz tell you the folklore of the tower when we get to the village."

"I'd love that." She eyed the structure. "Can we get inside?"

He nodded and led her along a weed-grown hollow beside the crumbling wall. *A moat*, Maddy decided. The farther they walked, the deeper the depression became until, in the distance, she saw a heavy plank bridge, weathered but still standing.

Awed, Maddy walked across the worn bridge and stepped through the partial walls of the castle. Inside the rounded entrance, once a tower, she imagined that years ago Jacob's relatives stopped in the same spot to climb from their horses and wrap themselves in a sense of security.

Jacob rubbed his hand across the pinkish white wall covered with lichen. "This is sandstone," he said. "It's amazing how it's held up through the years."

With her mouth agape, Maddy hurried through the shadowy entrance hall and out into another sunlit courtyard. "This is awesome," she whispered, imagining the many souls who called the place home.

"Over this way," Jacob said, heading across the open area. "The great hall is still standing, and the small chapel is only in need of a little repair."

Maddy hurried behind him through a long gallery, and when he pushed open the heavy plank door still hanging by one hinge, she followed him inside. Around the top, small arched windows allowed the summer sunlight to enter the room and spread bright golden patterns on the gray stone floor spotted with moss.

A huge fireplace stood at one end, and Maddy could almost see the lords and ladies, fans fluttering, lining the walls as couples danced folk dances—perhaps the minuet—or guests eating at long plank tables.

Eager to see more, she darted out another doorway into the corridor and, wandering farther, stepped through an opening that once must have supported a plank door but hung now only as scraps of decayed wood clinging to the rusted hinge.

The room appeared to be part of the tower with alcoves cut into the stone. A set of three crumbling benchlike stones faced a large slab of what appeared to be elegant agate, which stood against the far wall. Overhead arched a single window that once might have been adorned with stained glass. Awareness stifled her breathing.

Hearing Jacob's footsteps behind her, she swung around. "Is this—"

"The chapel," he said. "Some of the people in town have salvaged a few of the wood carvings from the castle. The workmanship is amazing. Maybe some came from these niches in the chapel."

"Really?" Her heart skipped at the thought of seeing the wonderful antiquity.

The sun shone through the arched window above the agate altar and sent sparkles glittering from the stone, though much of its surface had blackened with lichen. The dampness sent a chill down her back, and daunted by the cold, Maddy headed for the doorway leading to the warmer outside.

Stepping into the light, Maddy shielded her eyes for a moment until they adjusted. She wandered to the center courtyard, gazing at the decaying structure. "Can you imagine people coming here for tours—or seventeenth-century dinner reenactments in the great hall?" The thought thrilled her. "I could stay here forever," she said, pivoting in a full circle.

"If you do, you'll be alone," Jacob said, eyeing his wristwatch.

"Let's leave some exploring for another day. The family will wonder where we are."

Another day. The thought shuffled through her as soft and lovely as silk. She would love to spend another day at the castle. . .and another day with Jacob. He delighted her with his lack of pretense and gravity. His casual joy for life and his benevolent spirit would keep her content. . .always.

On the drawbridge, Maddy turned back to gaze at the awesome structure. Together they made their way to the path, and this time, Jacob wove his fingers through hers. They ambled hand in hand down the incline, talking about his family history and the people she would meet in town. Her heart reveled with his connection to the past and her hope for the future. A future that nuzzled in her thoughts like a prayer.

Returning to where they began, Jacob eased the car around and headed back the way they had come. At a crossroad, he turned, and within minutes, Maddy knew they had reached Engelheim. Though many half-timbered buildings stood along the street with orange tile roofs, smaller homes also dotted the roadway, a few with quaint thatched roofs. Men worked the ground in small gardens beside the houses, and young children played in the yards.

"Here we are," Jacob said, pulling in front of a cozy cottage surrounded by flower gardens. "This is where Cousin Heinz and his wife, Isa, live."

Before Maddy could step from the car, an elderly couple hurried from the house, arms opened wide. Jacob did quick introductions, and Maddy listened to their German conversation, only hearing an occasional familiar word.

Isa swung her hand toward the house. *"Herein,"* she said.

Jacob took Maddy's arm and steered her into the house.

The main room stretched across the front of the house with a large fireplace on one end with comfortable furniture. At the other end, a dining table had been set for a meal with a lovely bouquet of garden flowers in the center. A rich scent of herbs and meat filled the room.

"*Sitzen, bitte,*" Isa said, gesturing to the sofa.

Maddy nodded and sat against the arm, hoping Jacob would stay nearby to help her with the language. Isa went through the doorway while Jacob did as Maddy hoped and sat beside her.

"Some others will drop by after dinner," Jacob said finally. "Isa has made her Wiener schnitzel for dinner. You'll love it."

"I can smell it," Maddy said, feeling her stomach awakened by the savory aroma.

"I was telling Heinz about our hike to the castle. After dinner, he will show you a chest that's been in the family for hundreds of years."

"I'd love that," Maddy said, her excitement rising.

Isa called them to dinner, and following the blessing, Maddy delved into the delicious food—thin slices of veal served with lemon and homemade German dumplings. She watched the animated conversation, and occasionally Jacob would pause to explain what had been discussed.

After dinner, Heinz beckoned them to follow him. In their bedroom, he pointed to a chest that sat at the foot of the bed.

"This is the one I told you about. . .at the castle," Jacob said. "It's hand carved and has been in the family for centuries."

Maddy knelt beside the trunk and ran her fingers along the rich design. Though worn by time, birds and flowers carved with intricate detail adorned the dark wooden chest.

Jacob drew her attention to the hinges. "Look at these," he

said. "Handcrafted wrought iron."

"They're beautiful," Maddy said. "A piece of art by themselves." She moved her hand across the lid, touching the etched pattern, and faltered on the strange indentations. She examined the depressions, wondering what had once been embedded in the wood. "What are these for?"

Jacob shrugged a shoulder and asked Heinz before he could answer her question. "Family tradition says the chest was embedded with gemstones. Heinz says they were probably looted sometime during the Thirty Years' War. A chest is cumbersome to plunder. Jewels fit in a pocket or sack."

"It must have been even more beautiful." Maddy's imagination recreated the chest when it had been new. "You're very blessed to have it in your family," she said to Heinz and Isa, who was standing beside him.

Jacob repeated her words in German, and a sense of history and awe hovered over the room.

When they returned to the main room, Jacob asked Heinz to tell the story of the angel tower while he translated. Piqued by her love of history, Maddy listened, her delight growing as she heard Jacob retell the tale.

"The tower took the name from the family as you can guess. *Engelturm*. . .or angel tower in English. But a phenomenon of nature added to the meaning. At sunset, the cliff appears like it's glowing."

"The cliff?" Maddy asked.

"Where the castle is. It's harder to see now with the trees grown up around it. Maybe before we leave today you'll get a chance to see the effect."

"It sounds beautiful. . .like angels hovering over the cliff," she said.

He grinned. "A tale began that angels made camp on the mountain. The story added more meaning to the family name."

"I'm amazed at how fitting it is."

"But that's not all." Jacob took a lengthy breath. "The Engels have always been a religious family. When one of my early descendants knew the lore of the angels, he gave the castle a Bible verse from Psalms."

"Which one?" Maddy asked. "Although I can probably guess."

Jacob grinned as if he agreed that she could. "Everyone in the family memorizes this verse even to this day. 'The angel of the Lord encampeth round about them that fear Him, and delivereth them.'"

"It's wonderful and so appropriate," Maddy said.

"Especially for a castle. It reminds us that more than castle walls protects us from evil and danger. God sends His angels to watch over all believers."

Maddy's thoughts shifted back to the orphanage. The home needed more than walls. It needed God's mercy. She prayed that God would send angels to watch over the children and the staff until a solution could be found. The same niggling sensation filtered through her. What would God have her do?

Chapter 5

With the children's festival ended, Maddy walked through Dinkelsbühl, enjoying a more peaceful town. Though the village always attracted tourists, the multitude had moved on to another village and another festival.

Her thoughts settled for a moment on her wonderful day with Jacob at Engelheim—the castle, the village lore, the lovely antique chest, and the breathtaking sunset, just as the tale described. She had been mesmerized by the ethereal glow that shimmered against the cliff and sent sparks shooting from the sandstone tower.

A smile tugged at her mouth as she thought of the thrill of owning such a lovely castle. A foolish dream maybe, but it tickled her imagination.

Leaving *Segringer Strasse*, Maddy stood at the street crossing and gazed at the lovely gothic church, St. George's Minster. Drawn forward, she strode across the street and stepped into the cool shadows of the interior.

When her eyes adjusted, she looked down one of the long aisles, marveling at the nuance of light that shone from the high tracery-headed windows and spread over the forest of twenty-two pillars that supported the barrel vault ceiling. She stepped forward and sank onto a pew, wrapped in the silence.

Her life back in the United States slid into Maddy's thoughts. The family wealth and a life she'd taken for granted seemed unimportant as she weighed all that she had heard and seen in Germany. The orphanage's deep need and the poor economics of the Black Forest village only accentuated her guilt that she had been so unaware back home. The rich often involved themselves in charities—but many times for a tax write-off rather than pure benevolence.

Maddy contemplated the grandeur of the church with its elegant carvings and intricate stone masonry, knowing that people had gone without their own needs to create this magnificent edifice honoring God.

In her own life, a modern, practical building served as her family's church, while their home publicized their wealth with its expensive artwork, stately antiques, and posh surroundings. What had happened to her family's values?

Sadness wove through her, and she wondered why God pushed these concerns into her mind. With one last admiring look, she released a sigh and rose, heading back into the sunlight.

Coming through the doorway, she noted for the first time the belfry stairs. Calculating the steeple's height, she wondered if she were ready for the lengthy climb, but the view and curiosity encouraged her to step through the doorway and begin her long ascent.

When she reached the top, Maddy's heart thundered, not only from the climb but from the view. An extraordinary vista spread before her—the walled city with its fourteen towers, four gates leading out of the city, and the countryside beyond.

Feeling as if she could touch the sky, Maddy pondered the

diminutive scene below and wondered what man would look like to God. Small and finite, she imagined, to God's infinite might.

As the idea settled in her head, she lifted her eyes to heaven. *Heavenly Father, help me know my purpose in this place. Direct my wisdom to act as You would have me do. . .and, Lord, give me understanding about Jacob. I need Your counsel and guidance. I need to know if it's only my heart or Your direction. In Jesus' precious name. Amen.*

Turning from the magnificent landscape, Maddy began her descent back to earth with her thoughts. What would God have her do? The question had niggled her for weeks, and the answer came as clearly as if a voice had spoken in her head. The orphanage and town needed finances.

Maddy had a healthy savings and good investments. She'd been raised to know how to handle her money wisely. Today she knew what God would have her do—use her finances to help others. But which? The orphanage or the village?

Who could benefit the most? *Suffer the little children.* The answer came as strong as it had a moment earlier. The children. As she continued down the steps, Maddy's plan fell into place. She would contact her bank to make arrangements for a donation, then speak with Brother Karl. A few thousand dollars might help meet the cost of repairs and make a difference for the children.

When her feet hit the ground, Maddy's praise headed heavenward, thanking God for the awesome answer to her prayer. Now, only one question remained. Jacob.

"Why so quiet?" Jacob asked, heading for the Schwabach children's home. "I'm guessing that you have something on your mind."

Maddy pondered how he would accept what she planned to tell him. "Yes. . .I've decided. . .I'm going to help with the finances at the orphanage."

"Finances? You mean donate money." A frown settled on his face. "I'm not sure that's wise, Maddy. I know you want to be helpful, but bringing chocolate and mending clothes is the kind of thing most people do."

His expression concerned her—a look she couldn't identify.

"I'd do that if I lived here all the time, but I. . ." The thought weighed in her heart.

He reached across the seat and caught her hand. "I know. . . . You'll be leaving." His face washed with sadness. "But their problem is so dire, I don't know if your gift would help or only confuse their decision, Maddy." Along with gloom, stress tinged his face. "Give them false hope, you know." He squeezed her hand, then slid his own back to the wheel.

"I realize my contribution can't do everything, but I think it can help. I'm going to talk with Brother Karl about it today."

Jacob shrugged, and she wondered if she'd made him feel as if his contribution had been unimportant. That's not what she wanted to do. "You know, Jacob, a gift of money is easy for people who have it. Giving yourself and your time week after week is a great gift."

"But money is what they need now, not volunteering."

"Don't say that," Maddy said, turning as much as she could to face him. "Don't belittle people's gift of time. It's precious."

"I'm not belittling. I just mean that financially they need thousands and thousands. Your wanting to donate money is generous, but like I said, I don't know that a few dollars will accomplish that much except give them hope—and then they have to face reality again."

What did he mean by a few dollars? She tried to imagine what her contribution would be in *deutsche marks*. "I think it will help, especially with the exchange rate, and I've already contacted my bank."

Jacob's expression took on more than curiosity. "Your bank?"

"I don't carry that kind of money around with me," she said.

His eyes narrowed and a faint flush edged up his collar. "What do you mean?"

"I have a few thousand on hand, but I want to give more than that."

Jacob felt his jaw drop, hearing her response. He closed his mouth while embarrassment shot through him. More than a few *thousand* dollars? What had she planned? He found his voice. "More than that?"

"I called my bank to find out how much I have that's not tied up in investments," she said. "I figure I can spare forty. Maybe more."

Forty? "You mean—"

"How much would forty thousand be in *deutsche marks?*"

Jacob's stomach churned, amazed at her offer. He knew she was well-to-do, but forty thousand? "Maybe seventy thousand or more," he heard himself mumble.

"That would make a difference for those kids, wouldn't it?" she asked. "They'll need more, but it will help."

"I–I'd think so," he said, dumbfounded by the concept. "I've never known anyone like you, Maddy."

"You were just lucky," she said, a smile playing on her mouth.

Her comment made him laugh, and instead of thinking of himself, he thought of the children whom he prayed, with

Maddy's generosity, would not be uprooted from their home.

"I suppose," he said after much silence, "that I've been feeling like I lack something when I think about your finances and education. I don't have either, but today I'm thrilled by what you're willing to do for the kids."

She caught his arm. "Never feel that you're less than anyone because of material things, Jacob. You have more goodness and kindness in your heart than any man I've known."

He glanced at her face and saw the deepest sincerity in her eyes.

"Remember Jesus' parable of the widow's mite," she said. "The widow gave more with her small offering than anyone because she gave all she had."

Her words warmed his heart, and the shame he'd felt melted away. But Maddy had changed him, and today he'd experienced something that would alter him forever. "All my life I've tried to escape my family's simple ways, trying to make something special out of myself, and you know what?"

She shook her head, her honest eyes searching his face.

"It doesn't matter anymore. It's not what I do, but what is done for others—no matter who does it. What's fame and fortune anyway?" He sent her a grin. "Except it makes life a little easier."

"Easier sometimes," she said. "Sometimes it makes it more difficult to focus on what's important. I've had the same problem you have. I think we have trouble letting go of our own needs and asking God what He would have us do."

She'd said it perfectly. Jacob nodded, realizing that his and Maddy's accidental meeting—and their conversation that day at the ice cream shop—had been directed by God and would affect both of their lives forever.

Jacob watched Maddy's enthusiasm grow as they neared the Black Forest village. He'd been amazed at her donation to the orphanage. Brother Karl had been astounded and grateful. The money could correct the inspection violations and leave something extra for a few new toys and clothing. In Jacob's eyes, Maddy had become an earthly angel.

"So what do you think?" Maddy asked.

Pulling his mind from his thoughts, Jacob glanced her way. "Sorry. My mind drifted."

"About repairing only part of the castle. The great hall is in repair—sort of—and the chapel. That could be so beautiful for weddings. And don't forget tours. The townspeople could build a little shop near the drawbridge and sell their wood carvings. It's perfect."

Excited, her voice had risen in pitch, but she'd forgotten the major issue. Finances. Though generous to a fault, Maddy seemed to overlook that most people didn't have the assets that she took for granted.

Hating to destroy her fantasy, Jacob had to set her straight. "Funds. Backing. Did you look around the village, Maddy? They're wonderful people who've learned to live on bare-bones budgets."

Her face sank with his words but in a heartbeat, brightened. "That's the answer. You said it."

"I did?"

"Backing. We need to find backers. I wonder what it would take to start the renovations. Not the whole castle. The ruins will draw the tourists, but a few restored rooms could add to their interest and be used for other purposes."

Jacob had no words to respond. The thought was great, but. . .

"A Castle Feast. Can you imagine? People eating with their fingers on wooden platters. Begging the king for salt—you know salt was precious back then—everyone in costume."

She rattled on with her dream while Jacob smiled and nodded, but his own common sense said her ideas were pointless.

On this trip, Jacob bypassed the road to the castle and drove straight into town. At his cousin's cottage, Maddy bolted from the car as soon as he turned off the ignition. He felt grateful she couldn't speak German well enough to explain her ideas. When she solicited his assistance, Jacob would have to use careful wording to explain. No sense getting their hopes up for nothing.

Heinz and Isa greeted them at the door, and again the scent of food filled the cottage. Inside, Franz and Gerde rose from the sofa as they entered the room. Jacob hurried toward his cousins to greet them.

Maddy paused in the doorway, then recognized them from her last visit. Though enthusiasm had bubbled through her on the long drive to the village, looking around the humble home, reality nipped at her.

Her ideas for the castle and the community would be only a dream unless she found backing for the venture. People she knew marched into her thoughts, but who back home would take a chance for the amount needed to bring her plan to fruition? Her father came to mind.

She'd always been Daddy's girl; and though she wished on occasion that she didn't need her father's help, she often did. One day, Maddy hoped she could stand on her own two feet.

Her gaze shifted to Jacob, and while he conversed in German, she relaxed and watched him interact with his family, letting her mind wander. What would making it on her own really mean? Jacob certainly took care of himself. He lived in a small flat in Dinkelsbühl, paid his bills, and seemed happier than Maddy had at times in the U.S. Why? Because Jacob had a purposeful existence.

"Did you understand anything?" Jacob asked.

Tugging her from her thoughts, she grinned and shook her head. She'd been miles away.

"Isa suggested that we visit their son and daughter-in-law after dinner. Kathe and Herbert have a new baby girl. Nina's three months old and sleeps in a cradle hand carved by the Linder family hundreds of years ago."

Maddy's heart tripped. "I'd love to see both—the baby and the cradle."

"Good," he said, relaying her message in German. "Kathe and Herbert are younger and speak a little English."

His comment added extra incentive for Maddy. Eventually, Isa called them to the table for another wonderful meal. When she'd eaten her fill, Maddy poked Jacob's arm. "Will you tell them about my idea?"

His face told her how he really felt, but he did as she asked and presented the gist of what she'd told him.

Watching their faces, Maddy tried to decipher the mixture of body language and facial expressions until she tired of waiting. "What are they saying?"

"Sorry," Jacob said finally. "They'd thought about the idea for years, but finances were always a major problem. Now they have a new dilemma."

"Dilemma? What do you mean?" Maddy asked.

"Someone wants to buy the property, and if the Engels can't show ownership, the government will sell the castle."

Maddy's heart fluttered. "But they can't. You said the

property's been in their family for hundreds of years. Isn't that enough?"

"Not anymore. Now they need a deed," Jacob said.

"A deed? Did they have deeds back then?"

Jacob asked Heinz, then gave Maddy the answer. "Family tradition says a letter of ownership had been signed in the sixteenth century by Duke Frederick I of Württemberg, but they have no idea where it is—or if it even exists."

Maddy observed sorrow in their faces and wished she hadn't insisted Jacob tell them her idea. She'd only created disappointment and dredged up their troubles. Frustrated that she couldn't apologize, she asked Jacob to make amends for her, but she knew he hadn't.

Filled with questions, Maddy pressed her lips together, afraid they might escape. Had they searched the castle grounds? Would the original family have taken the deed with them when they abandoned the castle? Would they have left it behind? Where did people in the sixteenth century keep documents of value?

From their expressions, Maddy decided the conversation had drifted on to other topics, and soon they rose from the table.

"We're going to visit Kathe and Herbert," Jacob said.

She only nodded, afraid if she spoke she might say something else to put a damper on the gathering; but on the way back to Dinkelsbühl, Maddy knew she would pelt Jacob with her stifled questions.

Chapter 6

J acob drove up the mountain path for a look at the castle and hopefully another sunset. Maddy had been quiet since the situation at dinner, and he thought this might cheer her.

When he parked, Maddy left the car and looked into the sky, then drew in a deep breath. "I'm sorry, Jacob. I should have listened to you. Now I've stirred up their terrible situation and—"

"You didn't cause the problem. They had it before we arrived, and really there's nothing we can do to help. This is one of those situations, like you mentioned, where money won't solve the problem."

"Money can't solve every problem, but God can. We need to pray for them. . .and then use our heads."

Confused, Jacob peered at her. How would their heads help the situation?

"Why are you frowning?" she asked.

Jacob shook his head. "Because I can't see how our heads are going to solve this problem."

"First we talk with God, then we think about where the deed could be."

He rested a palm on each shoulder and looked into her eyes. "Burned during a looting in the war, moved with the family belongings when they left, buried under all the rubble. . ." He swung his arm in the direction of the castle. "We'll never find the deed."

"Ahh, ye of little faith," she said, a quirky smile tilting her mouth.

He laughed and slid his hands down her back, drawing her against his chest. "You're a wonder, Maddy. Let's head to the top. Maybe we'll see the angels."

"Good idea. I've never seen an angel."

Jacob chuckled, slipped his hand in hers, and walked beside her up the incline. Near the top, the golden sun had lowered in the sky, washing the castle in an eerie glow.

Maddy broke free and hurried ahead of him. Dashing across the drawbridge, Maddy clomped along the planks, her shoes resounding, until she reached the other side and vanished through the opening.

Jacob followed her inside the large courtyard. "Hold up. You'll break a leg running through here."

"Prayer time," she called, standing in the center and holding her hand out toward him.

Breathless, he reached her; and together they stood, their hands clasped, their heads bowed, while Maddy asked God for divine intervention. "And Lord," she said, "give us wisdom to find the deed. Guide our hands to the spot and bring peace and comfort to this little village. In Jesus' name. Amen."

Jacob echoed her amen but didn't release her hands. Instead, he pulled her closer. "You're a beautiful person, Maddy. You fill my life with. . ." The words seemed empty as he looked at her upturned face. Words couldn't offer the depth of his meaning. Only a kiss could do that.

Focusing on her lovely mouth, Jacob inched forward, praying

Maddy wouldn't pull away. Answering his prayer, she lifted her mouth to his as he drank in the sweet softness of her lips. The words "I love you" swirled in his head, but he knew better. Not yet. Not now.

He eased back, and Maddy's brooding eyes searched his own. A sigh escaped her throat, and he wrapped his arms more firmly around her while she rested her cheek against his shoulder.

When she lifted her head, he saw determination on her face. "Jacob, we have to search the grounds. We could ask the family to come up. What about the chapel? Wouldn't that be a place to hide something? Close to God?"

"It's too dark now. Maybe we can come back next week." He said the words but wondered if one day she would tell him she had to return home. "Next week?" he asked again.

"Early in the morning. . .so we'll have all day. And we'll pray each day, okay?"

"Together, each day?"

She nodded. "God is good. We'll find the answer. I am as sure of that as. . ." Her voice faded.

"As what?"

A faint flush washed across her face. "As—as—it doesn't matter. I'm just sure."

As sure as she knew that she loved him? Had Maddy been thinking of him? Jacob could only hope.

Maddy loved having Jacob's arm around her. In the pleasant evening air, a sense of comfort and rightness filled her as they walked back to her room after dinner. Light from a full moon shimmered over the rooftops, leaving the village washed in a silver glow.

In the silence, Maddy heard the beating of her heart. She'd struggled with her decision whether to forget Dinkelsbühl and return home or stay and help search for the elusive deed. What would be best for the villagers—and for Jacob? What would be best for her?

She'd fallen in love. She knew as sure as the sun and moon rose each day—as certain as a spring rain. Jacob at her side meant more to her than investments, a career, and her comfortable life in Connecticut. In this small village, for the first time, Maddy faced how finite life really was and how infinite God's grace and love were.

Spending time with the children and the humble people of Engelheim had helped her see how much she had taken life for granted. Tonight she wanted to tell Jacob. If she were going to stay, she needed to know what part she played in his life.

"You smell good," Jacob said. "I meant to tell you before. You remind me of my grandmother's cookies."

"Are you sure you're not just getting homesick?" Maddy asked, hiding her smile.

"Never, as long as you're with me," he said.

His response had not been what she'd expected, and it sent her heart on a breathless chase. "Vanilla," she said.

"Vanilla?" He tilted his head toward hers and arched a brow.

His face looked moon-kissed in the quiet night, and it sent a shiver of longing down her back. "The scent is vanilla. It's my new moisturizer. Like it?"

He stopped and turned her to face him. "I'm not sure."

Her pulse skipped as his hands rested on her shoulders, his playful eyes grinning at her. "Why not?"

He looked over his shoulder, then ahead of them before answering. "I need a taste," he said, lowering his lips to hers and lingering a moment before drawing back. "I love it. I don't think I'll ever get my fill."

"I could buy you a bottle. I bought it right here in town."

He shook his head and slid his arm around her waist. "It wouldn't be the same. It's a blend of warm summer skin and vanilla. It's you, Maddy. I'll never get enough."

She paused and looked into his face, watching a hint of sadness sully his loving smile. "Me neither," she admitted.

"Then what are we going to—"

She stopped him with the tip of her index finger. "Later." Tucking her arm in his, Maddy remained silent. They needed to talk but not on the street.

When they reached the *Goldenes Lamm,* she beckoned him around the back. "Let's go up this way. We can sit on the porch outside my room."

Jacob agreed, and she led him up the flight of stairs and along the walkway bordered with flower boxes to her second-story veranda.

"Nice," he said.

She motioned to a white bench covered with cushions, and Jacob sat, drawing her beside him. He draped his arm over her shoulder and drew her closer. "I think it's time we talk."

"It is," she said. "I've been thinking for the past few weeks about home. . .and here. . .and you." She covered his forearm with her hand and brushed the downy hair below his elbow.

"And did you come to a conclusion?" he asked. His hand captured hers, lifted it to kiss her fingers, then lowered it again.

"I have."

"So have I," he said.

Holding her breath, she waited to hear what he would say.

"I love you, Maddy. I suppose it's foolish. We come from

different worlds—in proximity and lifestyle. I have nothing to offer you, but—"

She hushed him, but this time with her lips. He had everything to offer her—if he could only understand. With gentleness, she delighted in his eager mouth; and when she drew back, Jacob captured and drew her back to his soft mouth. The warmth and intimacy aroused dreams of being with him forever.

He eased back and brushed his nose against hers before giving the tip a peck for good measure.

She thought her heart would burst with his tenderness. "I can't bear to hear you say that you have nothing to offer me, Jacob. You have everything to offer me: your time, your concern, your faithfulness, your love, yourself. . . . Who could ask for more? I never imagined loving anyone the way I love you."

"You love me too." Disbelieving, he searched her face. "Are you sure? I've dreamed of hearing you say this but. . .never thought it would happen."

"I am sure. As sure as. . ." She chuckled, remembering the day she almost told him at the castle that she loved him.

He grinned, apparently remembering the same moment. "God will answer our prayers as certainly as you love me. Is that right?"

"Exactly." She relaxed, nestling in his arm while feeling complete and satisfied.

"So what will you do now?" Jacob asked.

Maddy knew what he meant, and she didn't have the answers. Many decisions had to be made, but she would make them in time.

The summer sun baked down on the castle courtyard. Though

some shook their heads as if Jacob had lost his mind, members of the Engel family had joined Jacob and Maddy at the castle to explore the ruins for a clue to the missing deed.

"Let's separate into groups," Jacob said in German, pointing to the area where each should search for a secret cache or clue to a hiding place.

As the groups moved off in various directions, Jacob encircled Maddy's hand in his. "I think the picnic really got them up here."

She laughed. "After we crawl over these rocks for awhile, we'll be hungry and thirsty. I thought it was a good idea."

"You're full of ideas," he said, tousling her hair and loving every moment he spent with her.

She pulled away and ran toward the great hall and chapel. Jacob knew when dividing the area that Maddy would be disappointed if she didn't search those locations. He could still hear her determined voice. *That's where it is, Jacob. I know it.*

He hurried after her, and when he entered, Kathe and Herbert had already begun the task. Each of them tugged on stones in the floor and walls, probed for crannies, and searched the niches for a secret compartment. Undaunted, Maddy climbed the worn stone staircase that wound to the upper tower above the chapel. Now in ruin, the chapel contained nothing but crumbling stone, moss, and dead leaves.

With aching backs and blistered fingers, the family and townspeople gathered in the courtyard for lunch when the sun rose straight overhead. While Maddy unloaded a box of cold meat, cheese, and bread, Jacob filled plastic glasses with apple juice and bottled water.

The stories they shared were all the same. Nothing. No hint, no clue, no secret niche. As they talked, Jacob suggested other possibilities—along the cliff wall, on the drawbridge, and in the moat, but he sensed the truth. The deed was not on the castle grounds. Not anywhere perhaps.

As opposite as the sun to the moon, Maddy remained determined. "I might be wrong about the castle, but then it's hidden in something that has been in the castle. Somewhere. I feel it in my bones."

Jacob could only laugh at her persistence.

When they had finished for the day, the family gathered around Jacob below the castle to talk about strategy. Telling them Maddy's resolve, he suggested they persevere. "Tell me," he said in German, "what is still in the village that had once been housed in the castle?"

The family talked among themselves, murmuring items that had lasted through time still owned by someone in the village. Maddy seemed distracted, and in the midst of the inventory, she sighed.

"What's wrong?" Jacob asked.

"I'm frustrated."

He wrapped his arm around her shoulder. "I suggest we get back to town and see what we can look at today. What do you say?"

She nodded, and he gave the same advice to the others. Tired and sore, they climbed into their cars and made their way back to the village. When they reached Heinz's house, Jacob sat for a moment before facing the new search.

"I can barely think," Maddy said, leaning her head against the chair back. "But we only have a couple weeks before they need the deed. We can't stop now." She rubbed the back of her neck and stretched her chin downward as if to relieve the tension.

"I'm glad we decided to stay tonight," Jacob said, feeling

guilty that she had worked so hard for his family. "I hope you'll be comfortable with Kathe and Herbert."

"I'm sure I will," she said, flashing a grin. "At least they speak a little English." As if she'd gotten a second wind, Maddy sat forward. "So. . .what do you think we'll see?"

Jacob shrugged. "They mentioned different things earlier. Religious carvings from the chapel. . .a couple of clocks. Carved panels. Chairs. Who knows?"

"Too much," she said.

"Too much and not enough. . .if we don't find anything." He rested his hand on her tensed, scuffed fingers. "Promise you won't get discouraged, Maddy. I know you think the deed is somewhere in town. And I know we've prayed, but God doesn't always say yes. No is another answer." He watched sadness inch across her face. "Maybe it's not meant to be."

She pulled her hand from under his. "Faith, Jacob. What do you imagine God thinks of us, doubting His promise? Ask and you shall receive."

Her frown pinned him to the seat, and he closed his mouth. Somewhere along the way, they'd traded attitudes. When they first met, his faith had been strong and hers weaker. In the past weeks, he'd watched her change and grow in her trust and faith. He only prayed that if things didn't go as she planned, she wouldn't be disappointed.

When he'd eased his tired body, he rose, anticipating the job ahead. "We'll leave some things for tomorrow, Maddy. And if we find nothing. . ."

"We will find it, Jacob," Maddy said. "We will."

Chapter 7

A t the shop where she first met Jacob, Maddy dipped a
spoon into her ice cream, her thoughts flying. During
their last trip to Engelheim, she'd been more disappointed than she could remember. She had never been disappointed in God because she knew the Lord would eventually
answer her prayer, but she felt frustrated that they hadn't found
the deed the following weekend.

"We need to talk with the Linder family," she said when
she focused on Jacob.

He looked at her with doubt in his eyes. "You are the most
determined woman I know." A faint grin covered his skepticism. "Maddy, those carvings were done hundreds of years ago.
What can you tell anyone about something one of your ancestors did that long ago?"

"Nothing, but this is different." She licked her spoon, then
dragged her tongue over her lips.

"How? What makes this different?"

"Because. . .people here are proud of their heritage. They
focus on the past." She swung her spoon toward St. George's
Minster. "Look at the age of that church. In the States, they
tear down old buildings to make way for upscale modern ones.

Americans are too practical."

Jacob chuckled. "I still don't see what that has to do with anything."

"Next weekend, we'll go to Engelheim and give it one more try. . .please?" She sent him her most pleading smile.

Grasping her spoon-gripping hand, Jacob kissed her fingers and laughed. "One more time, but—"

"Look. I've been thinking. If we can find that deed, I'm going to call my father and get him over here. He trusts my judgment, and if anyone would invest in the castle, it would be my dad."

Jacob's eyes widened, and his eyebrows shot upward. "You're already saving a castle we can't even prove belongs to my family. Even if we found the deed, what makes you think your parents would want to invest in it?"

She released a stream of breath. How could she explain to Jacob that her father was a man who doted on his daughter— and one who liked speculation? He'd made millions playing the stock market, but she didn't want to say that to Jacob. "I just know," she said. "Sometimes Daddy likes to take chances. And he's usually successful. He'd love this idea."

She prayed that he would. It seemed a bit more adventuresome than taking a chance with the stock market.

"Getting back to the Linder family. What do you expect to hear when you talk with them?" Jacob asked, pushing his empty ice cream dish toward the center of the table. "I just can't understand how it will help." He fell back against the chair and folded his arms over his belly.

"Have faith, Jacob. God is good, and I believe the Lord wants to help us. . . ." She wished she could explain what she felt in her heart. "It's just in the Lord's good time, that's all."

"How can I doubt you, Maddy?" he said, a grin growing on his face. "Or the Lord. Ask and you'll receive. You've said it a hundred times. . .at least."

She poked his arm, knowing he spoke the truth. The words had become her invocation these past weeks. So many things had lived in her head recently. Staying in Germany was one. Maddy couldn't believe she'd been in Dinkelsbühl so long and had no desire to leave. The little room at the *Goldenes Lamm* had become her home.

The last she spoke to her parents, they had urged her to finish her vacation and hurry home, but she'd told them she wasn't ready. She'd heard a little concern in her father's voice, but he gave her credit for having good sense—until she told him about her donation to the orphanage and Jacob.

She cringed, thinking of her father's comments. But no matter what he said, Maddy knew she did have good sense—at least most of the time.

She lifted her eyes to the afternoon sun glinting off the red tile roofs and felt a warm breeze brush her face. Gazing at Jacob, Maddy knew he made her feel warmer and more caressed than any summer's day. She longed to be part of his life.

Gazing at his handsome profile, Maddy's mind drifted back to the Black Forest village. "Let's think," Maddy said. "If someone were to hide important documents, where would it be? In those days one war followed another, so they probably always worried about that. What hiding space would be the most likely to survive a mob of looters?"

As if in thought, Jacob stared downward, shaking his head. "Your guess is as good as mine. Let's do what you said. We'll go next Saturday and talk with the Linders."

Though his voice rang with skepticism, he'd agreed, and

that's all Maddy wanted to hear—except the other three words that sent her into the clouds: *I love you.*

"I'm not sure why the first Linder settled so far from town. Maybe he was a recluse," Jacob said as he trudged beside Maddy toward the Linders' hillside cottage.

"I'd love to hear the story." Maddy stopped and caught her breath, then grinned. "Maybe we should have asked a Linder who lives in town."

"Too late. He's expecting us. Anyway, I figured coming up here would give us a nice walk. . .if nothing more."

Maddy jabbed her hands against her hips. "Stop saying that, Jacob. You're so negative."

He laughed. "How about realistic?"

Giving him a swat with her fist, she chuckled. "I hope not. Even a little clue of where to look would help."

"If anyone knows, he'd be the person. Wilhelm's one of the oldest Linders in town." Jacob clasped her hand and encouraged her up the path.

Through the trees, a small cottage appeared. Jacob pointed. "See, the walk wasn't that bad."

She halted and gave him a dramatic huff and puff before continuing on.

When Jacob knocked, the elderly gentleman swung open the door. *"Guten Tag,"* he said, widening the door. *"Bitte, komme Sie herein."* He beckoned them inside.

"Wie gehts, Wilhelm," Jacob said in greeting and stepped aside to allow Maddy to enter first before he introduced her.

Inside, the decor could have been a showroom for the ancestral carvings. As Jacob gazed at the handcrafted chairs and tables, an elegant mantel clock chimed the hour.

"Sitzen Sie, bitte." Wilhelm motioned them toward a sofa, and when they were seated, Jacob explained the reason for his visit.

The older man rubbed his cheek and stared at the floor. *"Ach, es ist lange Zeit her."* He shook his head.

Jacob knew it had been a long time ago, but he hoped the man could remember something. Even a small detail.

Finally Wilhelm began. "If only my *vatti*, Ludwig, were here to tell you stories," the man said in German. "He was full of tales about his boyhood. . .during World War I. I remember his sister, Brigetta, *meine Tante,* found an enemy soldier—an American—hiding in the Engelturm chapel. He'd been wounded, and she nursed him back to health. *Tante* Brigetta took many chances."

Jacob translated, and Maddy's eyes widened as he retold her the exciting story. "What happened to the soldier?"

Jacob asked the question, and Herr Linder's wrinkled face broke into a smile. "They fell in love and married. She went away to America. She's been gone many years now, but she left behind five children—all Americans."

Maddy squirmed and strained closer as if getting nearer the elderly man would help her understand the language.

Jacob grinned at her useless attempt and encouraged the white-haired man back to their search. Wilhelm rubbed his neck in thought, then spoke of the castle and the Engels.

Jacob turned to Maddy. "He only remembers tales handed down through his family that his ancestors made furniture and carved panels for the Engels."

Wilhelm continued, and Jacob listened intently. "He says they mainly carved statues of saints and wooden panels for the chapel and great hall."

"Und die Uhren," Wilhelm continued.

"Clocks." Yes, they'd seen numerous clocks in town. *"Auch der trank und die Wiege,"* Jacob added, reminding the man of the chest and cradle.

"Ja."

"Ask him about secret compartments," Maddy said.

Feeling awkward with the question, Jacob harnessed his discomfort and did as Maddy asked.

"Ja. Ja," he said, rising. Wilhelm hurried across the room and returned with a small lidded box—like a coffer—and handed it to Jacob.

Jacob studied the box, seeing nothing unusual. He shrugged and handed it back to Herr Linder. *"Ich sehe nichts."*

"Schau her. Der boden is dicker." He pointed to the thicker bottom of the small container. *"Überwachen Sie mich!"* he said, asking them to watch. Jacob kept his eye focused as Wilhelm manipulated the carved edge. Pulling his hand away, the base of the box dropped downward, revealing a small hidden compartment.

"There," Maddy said. "See! We have to look at Heinz's trunk again. That's where it's hidden. Looters stole the jewels and left the chest because it was too cumbersome to carry off."

"Maybe. . ." But Jacob wondered. An elegant chest with jewels might have created a strong enough temptation to carry it along on a cart. Despite his question, he agreed that would be their next stop, and he gave Maddy's shoulder a squeeze.

After thanking the kind gentleman, Jacob rose and guided Maddy to the door. *"Auf Wiedersehen, und noch einmal danke schön."* Saying his good-bye and thanks, Jacob guided Maddy outside.

Wilhelm stood in the doorway and watched them retreat down the trail. Jacob turned around for a final wave, then hurried to the car and back to town.

When they reached Heinz's house, Jacob stopped to tell him what they had learned. Maddy hurried to the old chest, and Jacob followed, once again searching every nook and cranny. Nothing led them to believe the chest had a secret compartment. The chest walls seemed the same thickness. No loose panels. Nothing.

When Maddy rose from her spot on the floor in front of the chest, her shoulders drooped, her voice was downhearted. "I was so certain."

Jacob hated seeing her that way. "Don't give up, Miss Optimist," Jacob said, hoping to tease her from her sadness.

"I'm not giving up. I'm thinking." Maddy's eyes widened, and excitement built in her voice. "What about the cradle? Even the worst enemy might not disturb a cradle that held an infant—especially a sleeping one."

Maddy had a point. Earlier they'd examined the chest and the cradle and saw nothing—but he'd seen nothing different about the little chest Wilhelm Linder had shown him either. Maybe Maddy had the answer.

"We'll go to Kathe and Herbert's and check the cradle," he said, then explained their plan to his cousin. Confessing their curiosity, Isa and Heinz decided to follow.

Outside, Jacob breathed the fresh mountain air. Nothing seemed as pure and invigorating as the Black Forest countryside, and since Herbert's house sat only down the street, they walked. When they arrived, Herbert opened the door and greeted them with a smile.

Offering a quick explanation, Jacob paced until Herbert brought out the baby's cradle. Today Nina sat in a modern contraption and bounced as she gurgled and cooed.

Kathe removed the linens and mattress, and the family

gathered around, eyeing the cradle.

"The rockers aren't hollow," Jacob said, examining them thoroughly, "and the bottom doesn't seem to have any more depth than a normal crib—only a normal board's width. No hiding place."

Maddy hovered beside him. "I love the angels," she said, running her fingers over the beautiful wood carvings that adorned it. "Angels. So fitting for the family name."

A shiver ran down Jacob's back, and he stood back. "Angels. Engel. That could be an indicator, couldn't it?"

Maddy caught his arm. "Maybe. Or just coincidental." Her face sank, and her voice quaked with discouragement. "Don't be depressed," Jacob said, running his finger along her arm. "Angel. Engel. We have to find. . .something." He knelt and ran his hands along the wood, while Maddy leaned down to examine the delicate carving.

"Look here," Maddy said, caressing the cradle's side, her voice charged with enthusiasm. Her excitement riffled the air. "Here at the head and on the sides, the angels have their hands together as if in prayer. See." She pointed to each praying angel as they followed her around the cradle. "But look here."

Jacob stopped, surprised at her finding. "You're right, Maddy." On the foot of the cradle, an angel stood facing forward, the hands uplifted in praise. As he looked closer, Jacob held his breath, overwhelmed by his conclusion. "If you measure the end panel, I think you'll see it's much thicker than the head and side walls."

The family moved closer, and Herbert explained to his parents as they examined the foot of the cradle. Heinz measured the space using his knuckle to the end of their finger, then compared it to the sides. *"Ja. Ist dicker."*

"*Ja. Ja,*" Isa agreed.

"Something could easily be hidden inside the space," Maddy said, "but how can we see without destroying it?"

Jacob knelt on the floor and probed the carving, feeling the outstretched hands and hoping to find a trigger to open a hidden cache. Studying it more carefully, he noticed the inset of the carving seemed to have more depth in spots. "Herbert, do you have a thin knife or tool? Maybe this panel can be pried loose."

"*Ja,*" Herbert said and darted into the next room. He returned with an implement that Jacob had never seen before.

"*Hier ist* a carver's gouge," Herbert said.

A carver's gouge? The tool looked sturdy, yet very trim, as if it could fit into the groove of wood and be strong enough to pop open a panel. "Do you mind if I try it?"

Herbert shook his head. "*Naturlich.*"

All eyes seemed to focus on Jacob as he knelt at the foot of the cradle. With caution, he slid the gouge into the crevice, pushing in and down. Nothing. Sliding the tool along the cleft in the wood, he tried again. This time he sensed that the wood shifted.

He lifted his eyes to the others, seeing their intent faces following his every move. He tried again, forcing the tool deeper into the crevice and prying the carved panel forward. His heart skipped when the panel toppled to the carpet with a thud, revealing a hidden compartment.

Gasps filled the intense silence.

Jacob stepped back, beckoning his cousin to reach inside. With trembling hand, Heinz jutted his fingers into the gaping interior. His face flinched with emotion, and Jacob held his breath as Heinz withdrew his fingers and a folded paper.

"What is it?" Maddy asked, her voice hushed with awe.

Heinz carefully unfolded the document, then scanned the

page. With reverence, he nodded and offered it to Jacob, who eyed the document, noting the signature. "This is the letter."

Maddy moved beside him. "But it's not aged," she said, confused by its condition. "It's not even yellow."

"It's been sealed, airtight," Jacob said. "Unspoiled by time." His heart thundered with the discovery.

"Is that it?" Maddy asked. "Nothing else."

"Nothing else?" Jacob asked in German.

Heinz motioned for him to look inside.

Jacob knelt, peering into the opening, and slid his fingers into the darkness. He touched another document and drew it out. Again, he delved inside toward the base of the opening, and his fingers touched solid faceted shapes. Using his fingers as pincers, he plucked out an item into the light while gasps filled the room.

"It's a jewel—a gemstone—and there are more." He handed the gem to Heinz and, delving deeper, pulled out eight elegant stones—topaz, ruby, emerald. . . . Other jewels he couldn't identify by name.

"Thank You, Lord," Maddy whispered, squeezing nearer. "They are gorgeous and valuable I'm sure."

Heinz took another stone, held it to the light, feeling its shape. *"Von der Trank."*

"He's right," Jacob said, "they were pried from the chest."

Maddy peered into his hand. "Sure, for safety." Wonderment lit her face, and she pressed her hands together. "Do you know what this means?"

"I would guess they're worth a fortune," Jacob said.

"And might help to pay for the castle renovation," she added.

Jacob closed his eyes for a moment, overwhelmed by God's goodness and faithfulness. Not only had the Lord helped them find the needed proof of the castle's ownership, but the Lord had done so much more.

He looked into Maddy's loving eyes, praising another of God's miracles.

Chapter 8

M addy nestled into Jacob's shoulder as they leaned against the *Löwenbrunnen* fountain, watching the September sun settle over the Dinkelsbühl rooftops. She dipped her fingers into a bag of potato chips and shoved a couple between her lips.

"Now that you're settled in, do you like your new apartment?" Jacob asked.

"Can't you tell from the smile on my face?"

"You smile all the time," he said.

She chuckled, looking into his warm, loving eyes. "That's because I'm with you."

He gave her shoulder a squeeze, then dug into the bag to snatch a handful of chips.

"It works out nice with Mom and Dad coming to visit," Maddy said. "I can sleep on the sofa, and they can use the bedroom while they're here."

"And what if they. . ."

She looked into his face and saw it flood with concern. "You're worried they'll force me to go back?"

"No one can force you to do anything." He sent her a tender smile. "But. . .certainly, I wonder if you might want to go home."

"I won't, Jacob. I can't."

His head shot upward, and his gaze riveted to hers. "Because of the castle?"

She shook her head. "Not the castle. I'm thrilled that Heinz agreed to sell the jewels and they brought in so much money. That will give them a good start on renovating. I think my dad will invest if I encourage him. He'll see the potential. Besides, think how it'll help the village."

"Always thinking of someone else, aren't you," Jacob said, running his finger along her cheek. "Let's go for a walk." He reached for her hand and wove his fingers through hers.

Maddy followed as he headed around the corner. "Where are we going?"

"You'll see," he said, "and don't change the subject. You haven't answered my question."

"Which one?" Maddy realized she hadn't answered his query about why she couldn't leave Germany, but she felt uncertain how to respond. She needed to hear more from Jacob, and he hadn't said what she longed to hear.

"You know which question," he said.

He didn't pursue a response, and she didn't offer one. Instead, she followed him to the church; but rather than go inside, he steered her toward the belfry steps. She eyed him, wondering if he wanted her to climb them. The light had faded, and the shadowy staircase didn't appear inviting.

Nodding, Jacob motioned her upward, a crooked grin on his face. Having no idea what he was thinking, Maddy did as he wanted and began the lengthy and tiring climb upward to the top.

When she stepped into the open, her heart tumbled again with the lovely view she'd enjoyed another afternoon. But today the rooftops shimmered with the fiery blaze of the setting sun, while in the distance, tongues of fire licked the horizon with strands of gold and orange.

Transfixed by the beauty, Maddy marveled at the scene. Then her heart stumbled when Jacob slid his arms around her from behind and drew her against his chest.

"So beautiful," he whispered against her ear.

"It is," she said, her tone hushed and reverent.

"I mean you," Jacob said.

She stood still a moment, then gazed at him over her shoulder and saw his misted eyes filled with love. A shudder trembled through her limbs, and she clutched the belfry ledge to keep from sinking to the floor.

Jacob shifted his arm and turned her to face him. For an eternity he didn't speak; but his eyes said volumes, words she'd longed to hear forever.

"You know I love you, Maddy, but I've hesitated to say more. We come from different worlds—not Germany and the States. I mean white-collar and blue-collar, upper crust and lower class, wealth and—"

Maddy hushed him with her finger. "I've heard all this before, Jacob, but it's just not important. You are worth more to me than—"

Maddy couldn't finish her sentence. Jacob's lips had touched hers in a gentle, sweet kiss that sent her higher than the belfry tower. Embraced in his arms, her spirit soared on the fiery rooftops, and she knew that nowhere else would she find a love so complete as she'd found with Jacob.

His heart seemed to pulse beneath his knit shirt, and she rested her hand against his chest, feeling the thud in rhythm to her own. Two hearts beating as one—the way God meant it to be.

Easing his lips from hers, Jacob stayed close, and his question wrapped around her heart. "Despite it all, Maddy, will you marry me? Will you be my wife and make my life complete?"

"Whole and complete," she said. "I've waited forever to hear you ask me that wonderful question. You know I will, Jacob."

Their lips met, slowly, lingering as if delighting in a spoonful of exquisite ice cream, cherishing and savoring the moment.

As the sun pressed against the distant horizon, Jacob took Maddy's hand, and they retreated carefully down the darkened staircase to the earth.

When they reached the bottom, they stood in the church's lengthening shadow, their hands clasped.

"That wasn't a dream, was it?" Maddy asked.

"A dream come true, my love." Jacob wrapped his arm around her waist and drew her toward *Nördlinger Strasse* and Maddy's new flat.

"We have so many plans to make. So much to talk about," Maddy said, tilting her head against his shoulder as they walked.

"And we have time."

She wove her arm past his and wrapped it behind him. "I know, but then there's the castle."

He stopped and gave her a teasing frown. "The castle? I thought that wasn't what was keeping you here." A sly grin rippled across his face.

"It's not keeping me here, but since you're keeping me here, I want to be involved." She sent him a pleading look. "You don't mind, do you? I'm a history major and. . ."

She didn't need to say more. His face sparkled with mischief.

As Jacob looked into Maddy's captivating eyes, joy filled his heart. This beautiful woman had consented to be his wife, and he knew that God had been in charge. Never in his lifetime would he have considered such a miracle.

She loved him. She loved children, his German family, the castle, and his Savior. How could he not cherish her unselfish giving and her unyielding determination? All of those qualities would make a strong marriage.

He focused on her coaxing eyes and grinned. "I'd be disappointed if you weren't involved in the renovations. I think the family's counting on you."

She clapped her hands, and a bounce lightened her step. "Then that's settled," she said. "So what about the wedding? Could we be married in the chapel?"

"You mean here at St. Michael's?"

"No, at Engelturm. Please, Jacob. Can't you picture it? Your German relatives, my folks and yours. . . Have they ever been here? What do you think? Should I wear a traditional wedding dress? Or maybe I could buy a *dirndl*. Wouldn't that be great? You'd be in *lederhosen* and me in a German gown standing before that gorgeous altar, surrounded by our loved ones and God smiling down at us. Do you think the hall would be ready soon? What about. . . ?"

While Jacob's ears were barraged with Maddy's exuberant questions, his heart was engulfed with thanksgiving. As always, God had been awesome.

Epilogue

Ten Months Later

A July sun spread across the chapel floor as Maddy and her father stood waiting for a signal from Brother Karl. She felt thrilled he had agreed to come to Engelturm to perform the wedding ceremony and that Kathe and Herbert had agreed to be their witnesses.

A violinist from Engelheim had agreed to play music to accompany them, and Brother Karl had brought a few of the children from the orphanage along. Excited and fidgety, they waited near the altar to sing the hymn they'd prepared in honor of Maddy and Jacob's marriage.

Her hands trembled, clasping the spray of wildflowers from the hills surrounding the castle. The same flowers entwined a tiara in her hair. The day, the setting, and the moment were perfect.

Maddy drew her focus back to her father, noting how handsome he looked in his dark blue suit. She lightly fingered the sprigs of purple gentian and white yarrow in his lapel buttonhole, then squeezed his arm. "What do you think, Daddy? I see you eyeing your investment." She grinned, knowing her father had invested a tidy sum of money to help renovate the ancient castle.

"I'm proud of you, Maddy. Because of you, I've learned something important."

Tears glistened in his eyes, and she felt them gather on the rim of her lashes. "What have I taught you?"

"To give without a motive like you did for the orphanage. Once my initial investment is returned, I plan to give back my shares of this property to the Engels. It's theirs. They've struggled so hard to keep it."

"You're wonderful," Maddy said, her heart bursting with pride with her father's generosity.

"In the short time we've spent with these people," he continued, "they've been warm and friendly. I feel it's the right thing to do."

"Thank you," Maddy said, nestling her head for a moment against his shoulder.

"And you look lovely, my dearest daughter. Radiant and happy. I'm sad that you'll be away from us for awhile, but I know you've chosen a good husband. Not the richest, maybe, but a good one."

"He's rich, Daddy. Rich in spirit and kindness. He's the most thoughtful, dearest man I know—besides you."

His broad shoulders shook with a quiet chuckle before he leaned down and kissed Maddy's cheek. "You're a good daughter. And you'll come home eventually."

"We will. We've discussed it. After the castle is completed and we've enjoyed our time here together, then, I promise, Jacob and I will come home."

"Knowing that makes me smile, Sweetheart, and so does your work here. You've given so much of yourself, and you've done a fine job with the renovations."

"Thanks," Maddy said, joyful at hearing her father's compliment. "It has a long way to go."

"But it's been only a few months since the work began," he said, "and look, the chapel is back to its former state, I would think, and the hall is close to being finished."

"Did you see the stone building near the drawbridge?"

He nodded. "Souvenir shop, right?"

She grinned. "For the lovely wood carvings and clocks the townspeople make. God has guided me here, and He's guiding the renovation. I know it in my heart."

Strains of violin music rose softly near the altar. The sweet sounds increased and filled the room. Maddy looked ahead, beyond the guests, toward Jacob stepping through a doorway so low he had to duck his head.

Maddy's heart skipped, observing the man who would soon be her life mate, her husband, and best friend. Dressed in a gray suit and white shirt, he was handsome, yet so much more. He took her breath away. But his inner beauty stirred her far more than his broad shoulders and glinting eyes.

"Ready?"

"Ready for months, Daddy."

With a loving pat on her hand, her father moved forward, guiding her down the short aisle past the small gathering. Jacob's wonderful parents smiled at her, his mother teary-eyed, then her own mother, strong and lovely with a tender smile on her lips. When Jacob's loving gaze captured hers, Maddy knew the day would live with her forever.

Jacob held his breath as Maddy neared. Like the castle's lore, she radiated with an ethereal glow like the encamped angels who guarded the castle. Through the high arched window above the altar, the afternoon sun washed her in a heady light, streaking her white satin gown with shimmering gold.

All of his fears had evaporated like dew after he'd met her parents. Expecting them to be affected by wealth, Jacob learned he'd been wrong. They loved their daughter so completely that her love for him had become all the assurance they needed.

Reveling in the sight of his bride, Jacob captured Maddy's arm as she stepped beside him. When they turned to face Brother Karl, the violin strings silenced and a hush fell over the ancient room, except for the sound of his own breathing and the beating of his heart.

As he listened to Brother Karl's message, Maddy sent him a loving smile. "To have and to hold from this day forward. To love and cherish. . .until death. . .and even to eternity."

Drawing in a deep breath, Jacob trembled at God's abundant gift. Once strangers, he and Maddy would be together as one. Husband and wife. Best friends forever.

GAIL GAYMER MARTIN

Gail loves nothing more than to write, talk, and sing—especially if it's about her Lord. With hundreds of articles as a freelance writer and numerous church resource books, she sold her first novel to Barbour in 1998. Now, she has been blessed as an award-winning, multipublished romance author with seventeen contracted novels or novellas.

Although Gail loves fiction, her worship materials are a direct way of sharing her faith with worshiping Christians. Gail has four **Heartsong Presents** novels and five novellas published with Barbour fiction. She is also a contributing editor and columnist for *The Christian Communicator.*

Besides being active in her home church, Gail maintains her professional counselor license in the state of Michigan. She is involved in a number of writers' organizations and especially enjoys public speaking and presenting workshops to help new writers. Gail loves traveling, as well as singing with the Detroit Lutheran Singers. She lives in Lathrup Village with her husband and real-life hero, Bob Martin, who proofreads all her work. "Praise God from whom all blessings flow."

A Letter to Our Readers

Dear Readers:

In order that we might better contribute to your reading enjoyment, we would appreciate you taking a few minutes to respond to the following questions. When completed, please return to the following: Fiction Editor, Barbour Publishing, Inc., P.O. Box 719, Uhrichsville, OH 44683.

1. Did you enjoy reading *German Enchantment?*
   - ❏ Very much. I would like to see more books like this.
   - ❏ Moderately—I would have enjoyed it more if _____
   _____
   _____

2. What influenced your decision to purchase this book?
   (Check those that apply.)
   - ❏ Cover   ❏ Back cover copy   ❏ Title   ❏ Price
   - ❏ Friends   ❏ Publicity   ❏ Other

3. Which story was your favorite?
   - ❏ *Where Angels Camp*   ❏ *Dearest Enemy*
   - ❏ *The Nuremberg Angel*   ❏ *Once a Stranger*

4. Please check your age range:
   - ❏ Under 18   ❏ 18–24   ❏ 25–34
   - ❏ 35–45   ❏ 46–55   ❏ Over 55

5. How many hours per week do you read? _____

Name _____

Occupation _____

Address _____

City _____ State _____ Zip _____

RL

ＨEARTSONG ♥ PRESENTS

Love Stories
Are Rated G!

That's for godly, gratifying, and of course, great! If you love a thrilling love story but don't appreciate the sordidness of some popular paperback romances, **Heartsong Presents** is for you. In fact, **Heartsong Presents** is the only inspirational romance book club featuring love stories where Christian faith is the primary ingredient in a marriage relationship.

Sign up today to receive your first set of four never-before-published Christian romances. Send no money now; you will receive a bill with the first shipment. You may cancel at any time without obligation, and if you aren't completely satisfied with any selection, you may return the book for an immediate refund!

Imagine. . .four new romances every four weeks—two historical, two contemporary—with men and women like you who long to meet the one God has chosen as the love of their lives. . .all for the low price of $9.97 postpaid.

To join, simply complete the coupon below and mail to the address provided. **Heartsong Presents** romances are rated G for another reason: They'll arrive Godspeed!

YES!   Sign me up for Hearts♥ng!

NEW MEMBERSHIPS WILL BE SHIPPED IMMEDIATELY!
Send no money now. We'll bill you only $9.97 postpaid with your first shipment of four books. Or for faster action, call toll free 1-800-847-8270.

NAME _____

ADDRESS _____

CITY _____ STATE_____ ZIP_____

MAIL TO: HEARTSONG PRESENTS, P.O. Box 721, Uhrichsville, Ohio 44683